DO NOT REMOVE
CARDS FROM POCKET

I've travelled the world twice over,
Met the famous: saints and sinners,
Poets and artists, kings and queens,
Old stars and hopeful beginners,
I've been where no-one's been before,
Learned secrets from writers and cooks
All with one library ticket
To the wonderful world of books.

© JANICE JAMES.

DEATH STALK

The small Hebridean island of Alsaig, famous for its export of a fine malt whisky, faces a crisis. It is threatened with a takeover by an American firm which would result in many of the workers being made redundant. The owner is refusing to sell despite pressure from his family. Tension mounts as threats of sabotage are followed by an attempt on the owner's life. Then an actual murder is committed and storms lash the island, isolating it and preventing the police crossing over from the mainland.

RICHARD GRAYSON

DEATH STALK

Complete and Unabridged

ULVERSCROFT
Leicester

First Large Print Edition
published October 1989

British Library CIP Data

Grayson, Richard
  Death stalk.—Large print ed.—
  Ulverscroft large print series: mystery
  I. Title
  823′.914[F]

  ISBN 0-7089-2073-X

Published by
F. A. Thorpe (Publishing) Ltd.
Anstey, Leicestershire

Set by Rowland Phototypesetting Ltd.
Bury St. Edmunds, Suffolk
Printed and bound in Great Britain by
T. J. Press (Padstow) Ltd., Padstow, Cornwall

1

THE girl's body lay crumpled in the heather, a few feet from the road that ran along by the sea. Her dress, drenched by the rain which had fallen during the night, clung to her, showing the outlines of her prominent bones and the immaturity of her figure. It had been ripped open at the neck, leaving one of her shoulders bare and the skirt was rucked up almost to the tops of her thighs. She had been wearing nothing underneath it.

A man driving along the road had caught sight of the body and braked his battered Land-Rover to a noisy halt. Leaping from the driving seat, he ran and bent over the girl's body. Her eyes, staring in the frozen grimace of death, and the colour of her face told him at once that there was nothing he could do for her. He knelt by the body and saw the bruises on the insides of her thighs, the purplish black swelling on her lower lip and the congealed blood at one corner of her mouth.

Without knowing why, he reached out and touched her face. His fingers did not recoil from the cold, damp flesh, for he was a gamekeeper, hardened to death by long familiarity. Instead they lingered on her cheek for a few moments, an inarticulate sign not of affection but of lust now frustrated.

In the heather not far from the girl lay a bedraggled white cardigan and beside it a red plastic purse that must have fallen from one of its pockets. Opening the purse the man looked inside and found, in addition to a large key and a few coins and other odds and ends, three new ten-pound notes.

Standing up abruptly he looked along the road and the field beyond it to where the roof of a house was just visible among the trees on the lower slopes of Cnoc na Moine. Although at that hour of the morning there would be no one to hear him, he shouted above the noise of the gale that was sweeping the island.

"Matheson, you bastard, I'll kill you for this!"

When he awoke, MacDonald did not at first open his eyes. He wished also that he could shut his mind to the unwelcome sensations that were becoming depressingly familiar in the mornings: the dull ache behind reddened eyes, the parched mouth, the nausea, the self-reproach and, worse than all these, the yawning chasm in his memory. The loss of recollection which often followed an evening of heavy drinking still frightened him, even though to the best of his knowledge he had never lost control and done anything reckless or dangerously stupid during the hours of oblivion. He did not wish to think about the previous evening but, as he lay on the bed, he found himself feverishly searching the void, looking for a half-remembered image, a fragment of conversation, anything that might tell him how and with whom he had spent the missing hours.

His only reassurance was to know that he was on Alsaig. In Los Angeles there were anonymous bars and clip-joints, and faceless women and their pimps to strip

3

a man's pocketbook as thoroughly as his memory. On a tiny Hebridean island there was no stupidity he could perpetrate to cause him serious harm and always someone who would pick up the incapable drunk and take him home. On Alsaig they had sympathy for a man who had taken a dram too many.

When at last he abandoned as fruitless his attempts to recall any of the events of the previous evening, he opened his eyes and sat up, and found that he was fully clothed except for his shoes which he had kicked under the bed. Retrieving them he put them on, deciding after inspection that they would survive another day without being cleaned.

He went into the kitchen of the cottage and filled a kettle. The water ran brown from the tap as it always did after rain. When he had first arrived at the cottage and had drawn a bath, he had let the tap run for several minutes, thinking that the discolouration of the water was rust in the pipes after months of disuse. Now he knew it was colour from the peat through which every burn on the island ran. Always a pale yellow, the water turned to brown when the burns were high. After putting the kettle on the stove, he went out for air. The air was the finest thing on Alsaig, fresh and more invigorating than thrusting one's head under a cold tap.

Outside the cottage the day assaulted his senses. The wind had swung to south-easterly, driving a cold rain into his face. Alsaig, like most of the Western Isles, was never without wind, but mostly it came from the west and his cottage was sheltered by the towering height of Beinn Laimsdearg. Today there was no protection from the ferocity of the gale, which was the strongest he had known since coming to the island, and the sea beyond the rocky promontory on which the cottage stood had been whipped up into an angry, swirling mass. Low clouds, racing across the sky, hid the summit of the mountain and more than a thousand feet of its upper slopes.

Back in the living-room of the cottage, as he drank his instant coffee, he looked at the small stack of reference books, the ring-folders filled with the fruits of four years of research in American libraries, and the portable typewriter. They were the reason why he had come to Alsaig on a year's sabbatical, at the suggestion of his university, to write a book. He tried not to look at the packet of typing paper, opened but unused except for the top half-a-dozen sheets which at spasmodic intervals had followed each other crumpled into the biscuit tin that served him as a waste-paper basket, for it was an irritating reminder of his inadequacy.

He had finished his coffee and had taken the empty mug back into the kitchen when Mrs. Anderson, the woman who came in every morning to clean the cottage, arrived. He heard her knock on the front door. She always knocked, even though the door was never locked, and waited for a few moments before she came in. The door opened directly into the living-room and MacDonald supposed the knock was meant as a warning so that she should not find him in an embarrassing situation. The thought made him smile. How many bed-dable women were there on the island he wondered.

When he returned to the living-room, Mrs. Anderson had already begun to dust and tidy. As soon as she saw him she stopped work and pulled a sheet of paper from the pocket of her apron.

"There are a few things I need for cleaning, Mr. MacDonald," she said, holding the paper out towards him. "Polish, household soap and so on. Also you're running short of some groceries. See, I've made a list for you."

"That was kind of you. Thanks."

"I can get them for you if you like. I'll be away to the village to do the messages when I finish here."

"That's all right, thank-you, Mrs. Anderson. I have to go into Carrabus myself anyway."

She went into the kitchen and started working, energetically and noisily, washing the few dishes he had used since the previous day and then cleaning the sink and scrubbing the stone floor. Mrs. Anderson always worked energetically, attacking every household chore with an aggressive urgency, and when they were all done she would put on her coat and leave the cottage with an air of regret, as though she wished she could start all over again. MacDonald was sure that even if there had been a vacuum cleaner or an electric floor polisher or any other labour-saving device in the place she would have refused to use them.

Suddenly she reappeared in the living-room. "I almost forgot," she said casually, as she might tell him that a tap in the kitchen needed a new washer. "The Campbell girl's dead."

"Dead?"

MacDonald had to think for a second before he decided whom she meant by "the Campbell girl". There were at least three unrelated Campbell families on Alsaig. Then he realized from the dis-approval in Mrs. Anderson's voice that she could only be speaking of Sheena Campbell. There were few females on the island who, without stretching latitude too far, could be described as girls, for more often than not young people left Alsaig as soon as possible after they had finished their schooling to live and work on the mainland; and Sheena was probably the only one who provoked the disapproval of the normally tolerant islanders.

What puzzled him was that he could not visualize her as a corpse, a small heap of inanimate flesh. Instead he saw a different

8

picture, vague and diffuse like the recollection of a dream yet strangely haunting, of the girl's face, slightly larger than life, looking at him, laughing, mocking.

Jake Thomson stood by the window of his office on the 23rd floor of a concrete and glass prestige building that stood on Park Avenue between 51st and 52nd Streets. Beneath him he could see St. Bartholomew's Church and, a little further along, the Pan Am building. Neither the bizarre architecture of the church with its pseudo-Byzantine stonework nor the monolithic structure which stood astride the tracks and platforms of Grand Central station interested him, for he was obsessed by his own frustrations.

His desk, a massive composition in glass, rosewood and stainless steel, created specially for him by an Italian more famous for avant-garde sculpture, dominated the room in a way that Jake, short and burly, would never do. Returning to sit at it, he picked up a bound report, expensively produced by a firm of management consultants, the cover of which bore the title OPERATION INFILTRATE, with

underneath in smaller, scarlet letters TOP
SECRET.

The title was a code name of Jake's own
choice. Books about the Second World
War—the memoirs of generals who had
fought it, of politicians who had directed
it and of journalists who set out to destroy
the reputations of both—were his
favourite reading, and he was impressed
by the sense of importance and secrecy
which a code name imparted even to a
relatively minor military operation. The
name he had chosen was also misleading,
for the report was not in any sense a
plan but a comprehensive survey carried
out by the consultants of a privately
owned Scotch Whisky company, George
Matheson and Sons, Limited.

He flicked through the pages of the
report, not bothering to read them because
he knew all the facts that mattered to him.
George Matheson and Sons were the
owners of a malt whisky distillery on some
island off the west coast of Scotland. Jake
Thomson had never been to the island
and, although as a boy in Tennessee he
had earned his first dollars trafficking in
Moonshine, he did not care much for

whisky. But he had made up his mind that he was going to buy Alsaig distillery, and the reason for his irritation was that, in spite of the grossly over-generous offer Thomson Distillers had made, George Matheson and Sons were refusing to sell.

He was still flicking through the pages of the report when Bud Schweizer, the Senior Vice-President of the Thomson Distillers Corporation came into the room. Schweizer was an attorney by training and a product of Harvard who ten years previously had been working as personal assistant to a very important Senator and had been considered in Washington to be one of the smartest young men in North America. Now, after ten years as Jake's right-hand man and trouble shooter, he looked a good deal less young but was a good deal richer. This morning he also had the grey, drawn look of a man who had spent the night in a jet aeroplane crossing the Atlantic.

"How did it go?" Jake asked immediately.

"No dice." Jake swore savagely, using the crude expletives of the southern states, and Schweizer continued, "The company's fireproof and so is this guy Matheson. I spent a whole day with those Glasgow attorneys going over all the financial information they had been able to pull together and the reports of the private detectives they had hired. Those stuffed-shirt attorneys looked down their noses at me, I can tell you, but they've done a good job."

"What about the son-in-law?"

"He's in hock with the bookies but only for about sixty grand. Anyway Matheson wouldn't bail him out. It seems he doesn't like the guy and would be as pleased as hell to see his daughter's marriage collapse."

"So what do we do?"

"Fraser still thinks he can persuade Matheson to sell. He says his old man and Matheson were buddies way back. He crossed over to the island yesterday."

"Do you think he can talk Matheson into doing a deal?"

Schweizer shrugged his shoulders. "Could be. These Brits are all hung about family friendships and the old school tie and all that crap."

"Fraser's a born loser. We can't rely on the man."

"I agree. I have another plan, but there can be no harm in letting him have one more try."

"Maybe you should have told him that his job is on the line. Either we get the distillery or he gets the bullet."

"I did."

2

"WHAT did Angus Murdoch want at this hour of the morning?" Una Darroch asked her husband as she poured out his tea.

"The Campbell lass has been murdered."

"I know that."

"Who told you?"

"Dugald, when he brought the milk. The whole island must know by now."

They were alone in the dining-room, for the few guests staying in the small hotel had finished their breakfast and had left to shoot or fish on the Colville estate, or to make their business calls if they had not come to the island for pleasure. Darroch always breakfasted late, for he believed he was entitled to run his hotel in the manner of a landed proprietor living on his estate and allowing others, in his case his wife and three elderly women from the village, to do the work. He justified this laziness by saying that he was often up late

14

working in the hotel bar, which was true because he did not feel obliged to observe licensing hours as there were no police on the island to enforce them, and the bar closed only when the last customer decided he did not wish to drink any more or was too drunk to do so. Today he was even later than usual, for he had been roused from his bed when Murdoch, the distillery manager, had called to see him and they had talked for a long time.

"It's as well that the girl was not working in the hotel," Mrs. Darroch remarked as she began laying the half-dozen tables in the dining-room for lunch.

This was her way of reminding Darroch that eighteen months ago he had engaged Sheena Campbell to work in the hotel as part waitress, part chamber-maid, part kitchen help. It was an arrangement which she herself had brought to an abrupt end when she noticed Darroch's eyes following the girl around hungrily.

Darroch let her remove his empty porridge plate and replace it with one loaded with eggs and bacon and mushrooms before he spoke again. "It was Hamish who found her."

"Aye. Who else would have done?"

"What do you mean by that?"

"It can only have been Hamish who killed her."

Mrs. Darroch banged four glasses down on a table in quick succession, one for each place setting. She and Hamish Grant were distant cousins and she knew Darroch had only brought Hamish's name into the conversation to repay her for her barbed remark about Sheena. Even so she did not feel obliged to defend a man who had brought enough disgrace on her family already.

"And why should he do that?" Darroch asked, not because he believed what his wife had said but because he was interested to know how she would answer.

"Who else on the island would have killed her? Hamish has been hanging around her for this past twelvemonth, like a dog panting after a bitch on heat. And she young enough to be his grand-daughter. I suppose she teased him once too often. You'll not be forgetting how he used to beat poor Jean when they had not long been wed."

Darroch wiped his plate clean with a

16

piece of bap before he remarked: "He's disappeared."

"What do you mean, disappeared?"

"Just as I say. He took the girl's body to the doctor's house in his Land-Rover and has not been seen since. As you know Mrs. Colville has a shooting party up at Ardnahoe waiting for him, but he's not arrived."

"The police from Kilgona will be here soon enough to take him," his wife said, picking up his empty plate.

"They'll not be here this morning." Darroch pointed beyond the windows of the dining-room which were spattered with rain and driven spray from the Atlantic waves. "Angus was expecting a lorry load of casks. They telephoned him from Kilgona to say the ferry won't be sailing in this gale."

As he walked along the road in the direction of the village, MacDonald had to lean forward into the gale with almost the force that a man would need to push a broken-down car. He had put up the hood of his anorak but the rain, slanting into his face, stung his cheeks. In the seven weeks that he had spent on Alsaig he had never before experienced really bad weather. Throughout September and early October there had been fine days punctuated only occasionally by others when a light drizzle, little more than a mist, hung rather than fell over the island, and it had been warm even when the wind blew, which it did more often than not. Now, struggling against the gale, he felt something not unlike satisfaction. This was what he had been unconsciously hoping to find on a Hebridean island: a challenge from the elements and, by the standards of an American campus at least, discomfort and hardship.

He had to resist a sudden impulse to turn off the road and start climbing the slopes of Beinn Laimsdearg which stretched up into the clouds on his right. When he had decided to come to Scotland he might well have chosen one of several islands on which to live and he had been attracted to Alsaig partly by its size and remoteness, but equally by the mountain which, with its stark beauty, dominated the island, and which symbolized for him the romance and turbulence and savagery of Scotland's history.

"Laimsdearg" was a corruption of "Laimh" the Gaelic word for a hand and "Dearg" meaning blood-red or bloody and according to legend the name "Mountain of the Bloody Hand" could be traced back to the tenth century. It was at about that time that Norse invaders had landed on Alsaig. They had not conquered the island and subjugated its inhabitants, as they had some others of the Western Isles, but had settled on it as colonizers, living peaceably and intermarrying with the Gaels. Legend had it that one of the Norsemen, a prince in his own right, had fallen in love with and married the beautiful daughter of a Scottish clan chief. The marriage had been long and idyllically happy, so much so that the Norseman had been accepted as a member of the clan. When he died his wife decided that his body should be burned and its ashes scattered from the top of the mountain they had both loved. A piper, reputed to be the finest in the isles, led the sad procession up the mountain and as the ashes were thrown to the winds played a pibroch so poignant and so haunting that all who heard it were moved to tears. The widow, distraught with grief, swore that the lament the piper had played was too beautiful ever to be heard by human ears again and on her command a clansman had drawn his sword and cut off the man's hands.

Now, looking towards the mountain, MacDonald saw that the red deer had come down from the upper slopes and were standing in groups not much more than a hundred yards away from the road. They did not usually come down so far until the winter had set in, and he wondered whether some sixth sense told them that in that weather they would be safe from the stalkers' rifles. By the latest count there were over 2,000 deer on Alsaig, eight times as many as the people living on the island and far more than the lean sheep which grazed the scant grass happily side by side with them.

From his cottage to the village of Carrabus, the only village on the island, was a walk of almost exactly three miles. The road, a single track with passing places marked by black and white posts, ran for the most part close to the sea, separated from the large grey pebbles of the shore by a narrow strip of grass and rocks. At one point it cut inland to round a small cove in which the ruined buildings of a disused distillery stood, and MacDonald had just passed them when a car horn hooted behind him.

Stepping aside to let it pass, he saw it was a Volvo with a young woman at the wheel. She stopped the car and, not wishing to open her window, pointed first at MacDonald and then at the empty seat next to her, raising her eyebrows as she did so to ask him whether he wanted a lift. His first impulse was to decline her offer. Although his jeans were soaked through and clung to his legs, numbingly cold in the driving wind, he felt somehow that this was a discomfort he should endure, a penance he should inflict on himself. Then he reflected that as a stranger he was finding it difficult enough to be accepted on Alsaig without needlessly acquiring a reputation for bad manners or eccentricity. He went round the car, let himself into the front passenger seat and pulled down the hood of his anorak.

"Thanks a lot," he said to the woman

and then added, "I'm Mike MacDonald. I've rented the cottage along the road towards Gartness."

She barely smiled. "I know."

Not surprisingly she seemed to assume that she did not need to tell MacDonald who she was. On an island the size of Alsaig even a stranger would have soon learnt that she was Fiona, daughter of Alisdair Matheson, the owner of the distillery, and married to a London businessman named Stokes. She was wearing slacks, a thick sweater and an anorak, and he was struck by her exceptionally fair hair and fair skin. An unusually large number of the islanders on Alsaig, MacDonald had noticed, had dark hair, square faces and foreshortened features. This was particularly true of the younger men and adolescent girls, and he had decided that it must be the result of too close breeding. Fiona, he supposed, must be about his own age.

"Not the morning I would choose to go for a walk," she observed. Her voice had the same softness as those of all the islanders but no more than a trace of the accent. He guessed that as a girl she would have been sent away to a boarding school on the mainland, perhaps to one of those expensive academies for young ladies in Edinburgh, whose chief ambition was to change the Scottish accents of their pupils to the stilted intonations of South Kensington.

"Nor I, but I have to go to the bank," MacDonald replied. A mobile bank crossed over on the ferry to Alsaig every Tuesday from the neighbouring island of Kilgona.

"The bank won't be over today. The seas are too rough for the ferry to sail."

"What does a guy do here when he runs out of money?" he asked lightly.

The knowledge that he was short of cash had been his reason for refusing Mrs. Anderson's offer to do his shopping for him. About the only thing he could recall from the previous evening was that he had realized quite early on that he had only a few pounds left in cash and this morning he had found only one pound note and a few coins left in his pocket.

"Darroch at the hotel will always cash a cheque."

"Even for a stranger?"

"He will know you by now." Her reply made MacDonald wonder whether she had heard of his not infrequent visits to the hotel. "If you have any difficulty, tell him I said it would be all right."

They were approaching the bay on the east side of the island around which the houses of Carrabus had been built in a single row facing the sea. Most of them had been painted in bright colours, pale pink or lime green walls with red or orange woodwork, but the colour did nothing to lessen the bleakness, the sense of loneliness in a scene dominated by low clouds, a grey, heaving sea and the insistent howling of the gale. On a clear day one would have been able to see the contours of Kilgona on the horizon. Now there was nothing but spray from the waves as they dashed themselves against the rocks and the wall of the deserted harbour, cutting off the rest of the world, until it seemed that the island itself was adrift and at the mercy of the Atlantic.

"My father has been meaning to invite you up to the house for supper," Fiona said, "but the days keep slipping by."

MacDonald read the remark as an

excuse rather than an apology. "He must be busy at this time of the year, with the winter coming soon."

"Could you come tonight?"

"I guess so. If you're sure it's convenient."

They had reached the hotel which stood on a rocky mound overlooking the harbour. Apart from the Colville Hall, the schoolhouse, the doctor's surgery, MacNab's shop and the post office, it was the only building in Carrabus that was not a private dwelling. Fiona stopped the Volvo as near to the hotel as she could to let MacDonald out.

"We eat at seven-thirty," she said, almost abruptly. "Murdoch from the distillery will pick you up at your house just before seven."

Before he had time to thank her she was away, the back wheels of the car skidding slightly in a puddle and sending up a spray of muddy water to splatter his jeans. A rusty iron gate, held together with wire, swung loosely on its hinges at the entrance to the garden in front of the hotel and a path of fine, white pebbles gathered from the shore of the west of the island led to the door. The bar was on the right of the narrow hallway, opposite the dining-room. It was the largest room in the hotel, more than twice the size of the tiny residents' lounge on the first floor, which was logical, for year in year out it saw more use than any other room on Alsaig. There was no other bar on the island and, apart from the occasions when the Colville Hall was used for a ceilidh or for a meeting of the Scottish Women's Rural Institute, it was also the only place where folk could meet and talk and share a dram. In summer when holiday-makers and bird-watchers came to Alsaig, the bar was so busy that Darroch employed Dugald, the milkman, and the daughter of one of the distillery workers to help him serve in the evenings.

On that morning, however, apart from Darroch himself, who stood behind the bar counter reading a two-day-old copy of the *Stornoway Gazette and West Coast Advertiser*, the room was empty. Although it had been cleaned and the bar-counter polished by one of the village women who came to work in the hotel each day, the smell of stale beer and whisky still hung on the air from the previous night, mainly because the windows could not be opened for the wind. The smell made MacDonald realize he was glad of the excuse he had been given to visit the hotel. His mouth and throat were parched, his body still dehydrated after the previous evening's drinking and nothing would put him right more quickly than another drink.

"What will you take?" Darroch asked him directly, without even the customary morning greeting.

"A Bloody Mary, please. And have one yourself."

"It's too early for me."

"Lucky guy! I must have had a skinful last night."

"You might say that."

MacDonald watched him pouring two measures of vodka into a tumbler, filling it with tomato juice and then adding the Worcestershire sauce and ice. A Bloody Mary was his pick-me-up and at other times he would drink white wine by the glass, the new fashion in America, or late in the evening vodka on the rocks. He sensed that he would have made himself more readily accepted by the islanders if he drank the local whisky, but the malt whisky from Alsaig distillery was too strong and pungent for his taste.

"Do you think you could cash me a cheque?" he asked Darroch, adding by way of explanation, "they say the bank won't be here today."

"Yes, we can do that for you. How much would you like?"

"Could you manage fifty pounds?"

"Certainly."

As Darroch turned to the till behind him and rang open the drawer, MacDonald said as an afterthought, "Do I owe you any money from last night? If so take it out of the fifty pounds."

"No, you don't owe anything."

"Then I could not have drunk as much as I thought." MacDonald smiled. "I ought to come clean and tell you I don't recall much about last evening."

Darroch looked at him thoughtfully for a moment and then he shut the till drawer, saying, "I'll get your money from the safe so as not to leave the till short."

"Thanks a lot. Sorry to be troubling you."

"No trouble."

He had made out the cheque, except for

dating it, by the time Darroch had gone to the small office at the back of the hotel and come back with five new ten-pound notes. MacDonald was always bad about remembering dates and on Alsaig they did not seem to matter much anyway. Darroch noticed his hesitation with the pen poised.

"The sixteenth of October."

"Thanks again."

He handed over the cheque, took the ten-pound notes and then gave one back to Darroch to pay for his Bloody Mary. As he did so he glanced through the window at the side of the room which overlooked the street and saw a blue car pulling up outside the entrance. A man in a gaberdine raincoat got out, put up a yellow and red striped golf umbrella and hurried towards the hotel under its protection.

"Did you know that Sheena Campbell has been murdered?" Darroch appeared to be watching MacDonald's reaction to his question.

"Yes. Mrs. Anderson told me. Where did it happen?"

"She was found in the heather just off the road to Ballymony."

"She doesn't live in that direction does she?"

"No. She stays here in the village," Darroch paused and then added bluntly, "and some folk are wondering if you know what she was doing along there."

Before MacDonald could ask him what he meant by his question, the door opened and the man who had just arrived in the car outside came into the bar. He was about forty, slim and tall and very fair with a small blond moustache. He had left his raincoat and umbrella in the hallway of the hotel and was wearing a tweed suit and what MacDonald guessed was a regimental tie.

"You didn't see Mr. Matheson then?" Darroch remarked.

"No. He wasn't available and the distillery manager was not there either. Give me a large whisky, will you. No, a blend. I can't stand these island malts."

"This is Mr. MacDonald," Darroch said by way of an introduction. "He's from America."

The man in the tweed suit nodded at MacDonald without any noticeable enthusiasm. He took a large pull at the whisky Darroch handed him and then said, "I was shown round the distillery by the Excise Officer, if you please. Would you believe it? That could only happen on an island."

"That's true."

"I shall have to go back this afternoon. They said Mr. Matheson could see me at five."

"That's fine. Then your journey will not have been wasted, Mr. Fraser."

"As to that, we shall have to wait and see," Fraser replied gloomily. "You can fix me up with some lunch, I suppose?"

"Oh, aye, we have one or two other guests lunching."

Fraser looked down at his feet and noticed for the first time that the bottoms of his trousers were wringing wet and his suede shoes caked in mud. He swore, finished his drink in a gulp and left the bar, slamming the door as he went out in a fit of ill-temper.

"Mr. Fraser doesn't appear to like your island," MacDonald remarked.

"I would not be astonished by that."

"Before he came in you said something which seemed to imply that I should know how Sheena Campbell came to be murdered."

"Aye."

"Why is that?"

Darroch looked at him squarely in the face as he replied, "You left this bar with the girl at the back of two o'clock this morning. As far as I know no one saw her alive after that."

3

IN the police station at Port Skeir on the island of Kilgona, Sergeant Cairns was telephoning the sub-divisional headquarters of the Northern Constabulary at Stornoway. The line was poor and he had to shout to make himself heard above the gale which lashed at the roof of the station and which had already uprooted at least a score of trees, one of which was lying across the road to Lossit, the other township on the island.

"Are you saying there's been a murder?" The inspector to whom Cairns was speaking asked incredulously. "On Alsaig?"

"Aye. You will be finding it hard to believe, sir, but it's the truth."

"Who did it?"

"No one seems to know."

"Oh, come now! That's not possible, man."

Sergeant Cairns could understand the inspector's disbelief. Not a single person had been charged by the police on Alsaig for as long as anyone could remember, certainly not during the fifteen years that Cairns had been in the force. From time to time, no doubt, there had been a breach of the peace or a drunken man had assaulted his wife, but even if the police on Kilgona came to hear of it there would be no charge, for no complaint would be laid. The islesmen on Alsaig did not welcome interference from outsiders in their affairs.

"When we get over there, no doubt we will learn soon enough who killed the girl," Cairns told the inspector, "but the ferry will not be sailing today."

"Then the gale is strong out your way?"

"Too strong for that broken-down old tank-landing craft. The weather people say it's force nine and still rising with the possibility of hurricanes."

"Is there no chance of your persuading a boatman to take you over?"

"I've tried already and they only laughed at me. There are no boats of any size in Port Skeir. The fishing boats are out and even they are running for the nearest harbour. To reach Alsaig from here would mean sailing round half of Kilgona and then crossing open sea."

The inspector did not argue. He had been born on one of the outer Hebrides himself and knew from experience of the almost unbelievable strength of winds which could spring up with little warning and batter the islands: winds sweeping across more than 2,000 miles of uninterrupted ocean, strong enough sometimes to bend iron stanchions and move great blocks of masonry, strong enough to blow surf and small fish on to the top of a 600-foot cliff at Barra Head; winds that made mountainous seas in which not even a fair sized trawler could hope to survive, let alone the ancient tank-landing craft which now served as a ferry between Kilgona and Alsaig.

"You know Alsaig," he said to Cairns. "Who do you think might have killed the girl?"

"A keeper named Grant would be most people's choice. He's been chasing her for months. The girl liked to think she was a hot bit of skirt, flaunted herself, you understand, but like as not she was just a tease."

"There is a doctor on the island, is there not?"

"Yes. Doctor Shaw. He's semi-retired. Moved out there from Glasgow a few years back."

"Ask him to examine the body if he hasn't already done so and let us have his opinion on how she died and whether she had been sexually assaulted. The body has been moved to the medical centre, I suppose?"

"Aye, there's nowhere else on the island to keep it."

"As soon as the gale subsides get over to Alsaig and telephone me from there. There's no point in my flying out to Kilgona till then and anyway the flights from here to you have been cancelled for today."

"Is there nothing else we can do meantime?"

"No. There's no great call for haste. Whoever killed the girl can't get off the island and you'll have the handcuffs on him inside an hour after you arrive there."

"Poor wee lass!" Mrs. Murdoch shook her head. "What a way to die!"

36

"Some might say she got no more than she deserved." Mrs. Buchanan, the wife of the dominie, was a daughter of the manse, brought up strictly by her father, a Church of Scotland minister in Aberdeenshire.

"It's Jean Grant we should be sorry for, I'm thinking," Mrs. MacNab remarked.

The women were gathered in MacNab's store which stood halfway along the single street of Carrabus that stretched from the hotel at one end to the landing ramp of the ferry at the other. It was the only shop on Alsaig, and it had belonged to Margaret MacNab's father, and not many years previously had sold only the most basic foodstuffs and the essentials of life, candles and paraffin and rope. But Margaret was an enterprising young woman who had been sent to study on the mainland and won for herself a degree at Glasgow University and a dour, hard-working Glasgow husband. When her father had died they had taken over the shop and as post-war affluence came, belatedly, to Alsaig, stocked it with a whole range of tempting products, from non-stick pans to Calor Gas, from fishing-rods to nylon

tights. They had even installed a refriger-
ated cabinet for frozen foods and, in spite
of oppostion from Darroch and his hotel,
obtained a licence to sell wines and spirits.
Now MacNab's store, grossly over-
crowded and entered by one narrow door,
was an Aladdin's cave of indiscriminately
arranged treasures and the morning
meeting-place for the women of the island.

"Jean has a lot to put up with, poor
soul," Margaret MacNab agreed.

"Did she tell you that Hamish wanted
to go off and live with the girl in the
cottage by Gartness?"

"The American put an end to that when
he rented the cottage."

"Och, the lassie wouldna have gone with
him. She had more sense," Mrs. Buie said.
She was a kindly widow who ran the post
office which was a few yards along from
MacNab's shop and which through some
accident of history also had the only petrol
pump on the island. Running these twin
businesses did not tax Mrs. Buie unduly
and she would lock up the shop and the
pump whenever she felt so inclined.

"Maybe that's why the brute killed
Sheena."

38

While they were speaking Mrs. Darroch had come into the shop to buy potatoes. The hotel had not catered for Mr. Fraser to be having lunch. She had slipped a brown tweed coat over her apron and a plastic hood over her hair.

"So you're thinking it was Hamish Grant who killed Sheena?" she remarked to the others.

"Who else would?"

"The American MacDonald was drinking with her late last night."

"At the hotel?"

"Yes. They were in the bar together when I went to bed just before eleven, sitting and whispering on the window seat."

"She would take a drink with anyone who would offer her one," Mrs. Buchanan said censoriously.

"Aye, I know. But they left the bar together. Almost two o'clock it was."

"How do you know?"

"I heard Archie say so, not ten minutes back. MacDonald is in the bar now, drinking again."

What Una Darroch had not realized was that MacDonald had left the hotel almost immediately after her and had followed her along the street to the stores. Just as she was speaking the bell above the door to the shop gave its sharp, unmusical ring as the door was pushed open and MacDonald appeared. The women fell silent and then to cover their embarrassment, began speaking in Gaelic.

The switch in language did not disconcert MacDonald for it had happened to him before. Everyone on Alsaig spoke Gaelic as well as English except for the handful of people who had not been born on the island but were living there through choice or force of circumstances. "Incomers" they were called and on Alsaig they included MacNab and Mrs. Buchanan and Dr. Shaw. When MacDonald had first arrived on the island and went into the hotel or the stores or the post office, the other people there almost always began speaking in Gaelic. What they had not realized was that he had studied Gaelic, not as a living language, it was true, but as part of his formal academic studies and he knew enough to understand almost all of what they were saying. Listening to them, he realized that they spoke Gaelic not from any conscious wish to exclude him from their conversations, for like all the islesmen of the Western Isles they were naturally courteous, but involuntarily, to cover their own reticence. MacDonald in his turn, through shyness or modesty, had not told anyone that he understood their native tongue and having not done so at first, felt he could not do so afterwards. And so it remained a secret.

As he went round the store, mechanically collecting the items on the list which Mrs. Anderson had made for him, he was not in any case listening to what the women were saying, for his mind was still recoiling from the shock of what Darroch had told him. He knew that he had been in the hotel the previous evening and, now that the notion had been put into his head, he seemed to have a vague recollection of being with Sheena Campbell, but he could remember nothing more, certainly not leaving the place with her.

The idea that he might have killed her had at first appeared preposterous. She had meant nothing to him, except an occasional innocent diversion. In all probability they had parted in the street outside the hotel. Another man might have been waiting for her. She had given enough men on the island cause to hope, with her hot eyes, provocative little bottom and the way she would touch their arms with her fingers, caressingly, persuasively. But, even as he reassured himself, he remembered another scene, now distant in time and space, yet still frighteningly real.

He had always scoffed at violence and had never raised a fist in anger, even as a small boy, till that night when Bette-May had taunted him past endurance. It had not been the humiliation nor the cheap tricks to provoke his jealousy, but her studied contempt of everything he valued that had stretched his control past breaking point. He could still remember the black mist of rage and alcohol, see the astonishment in her pretty, spoilt face turning to horror as his hands tightened around her throat, hear the shouts of their friends as they dragged him away. If he could have done that when only half drunk, what might not have happened last night when he was stoned out of his mind.

With an effort he thrust the thought out of his mind, collected up his purchases, including a bottle of vodka, and took them to MacNab who was standing by the till at the far end of the shop. The group of women were still talking in Gaelic and now he listened to what they were saying.

"Hamish could lose his job over this," Mrs. Murdoch said, "and then what will become of Jean? He didn't arrive at Ardnahoe this morning for work and hasn't been seen since. Mrs. Colville will not be liking that."

"Her guests will not be shooting in this weather," Mrs. MacNab commented.

"Even so."

"Does nobody know where he is?" Mrs. Buie asked.

"It was he who found Sheena by the road just beyond Tigh Geal and took her body to the medical centre. That was the last anyone has seen of him."

"Aye. And he has his guns with him."

4

"TO be perfectly frank, sir," Fraser said to Matheson, "I simply can't understand why you refused our offer for Alsaig."

Matheson laughed. "And what would I do, Donald, if I sold the distillery?"

"You could retire, live wherever you fancied, do as you pleased. You'll have to stop working sooner or later."

"I've got another five years in me, I should think; perhaps ten."

"Of course but why not get out of the rat-race now?"

The two men were sitting in a room in Matheson's house which he used as an office as well as a study. The distillery was not much more than ten minutes' walk from the house and he would stroll down there most mornings for an hour or two just to look around, but he allowed Murdoch, the manager, to supervise the distilling operations. All the administration, ordering the barley, planning the filling programme, arranging for the shipment of materials inward and of filled casks outward, he did himself from his home. Cathy, the clerkess, came up from the distillery every day, to take down his letters which she would later type on an ancient manual Remington, and to do the filing. So it was not surprising that the room should look more like an office than a study. Two framed photographs hung on the wall: the first of Matheson's grandfather, George, who had built the distillery, a severe looking man with long whiskers, wearing a dark suit, stiff collar and heavy watch-chain; the second of his father, Douglas, taken in a less formal age 40 years later, in which he was pictured wearing a tweed suit and deer-stalker hat. Between these two photographs hung a third, taken in 1891 and showing the distillery workers, 22 of them, grouped in stiff, artificial poses around old George Matheson, who was sitting proudly by a huge cask of whisky.

Elsewhere there were framed certificates won by Alsaig distillery for the excellence of its whisky at a number of international exhibitions. On a table by the window an old hydrometer lay in its wooden box complete with its accompanying brass weights and alongside it was a book of conversion tables with which the readings of the hydrometer could be converted to proof strength. Neither the hydrometer nor the tables were used any longer, following the introduction of metrication and new measurements of strength in the distilling trade. The leather upholstery of the armchair in which Donald Fraser was sitting had split and the horsehair stuffing was hanging out untidily, but then the whole room was untidy with the comfort that comes of a careless but affectionate neglect.

"I want to go on working," Matheson said. "I won't pretend otherwise."

"We might be able to work out some arrangement," Fraser said, cautiously, because he did not know how far he was allowed to negotiate. "You might continue to run the distillery until you wished to retire."

"I have a responsibility to the men as well."

"How do the men come into it?"

"There are thirty men and one woman

working at Alsaig. How many of them could be sure of keeping their jobs if Thomson Distillers became the owners of the distillery?"

"I can't see why we should shed any labour."

"Labour? Who's talking of labour?" Matheson got up from behind the old, battered desk and began striding up and down the room. "These are people, Donald. Men I've known all my life. Men I grew up with. Do you know of any distillery the size of mine which has thirty-one people on its payroll?"

"No distillery except Alsaig could afford it. They have to keep costs down."

"What are you saying, laddie? Do you really believe that?" Matheson looked at Fraser sadly. Then he crossed to a cupboard underneath the bookcase, opened it and took out a bottle of Alsaig single malt whisky and held it up in front of the younger man. "The Almighty has given Scotland this; the finest drink in the world; a drink no one else can make; a drink the whole world is thirsting for. Do we really have to sell it on price? Do we really have to cut each other's throats in the market place, slashing prices, cutting costs, exporting it in metal containers, bottling it in plastic bottles, till it's worth no more than lemonade? Do you really think that is what we have to do?"

Fraser was silent. He had come to Alsaig unprepared for an argument on the economics of distilling and selling whisky. In truth he knew little about either subject. He had been appointed Managing Director of Thomson Distillers (Scotland) Ltd. five years previously when the company was being formed because Jake Thomson knew that he came of an old Scottish family which could trace its descent to nobility. Jake had assumed erroneously that Fraser's connections would help overcome those difficulties which often face a multinational company setting up a subsidiary in Britain.

Matheson sensed Fraser's discomfiture and he broke off what he was saying to smile. He was a stubborn man, fiercely independent in his views, but he was also a kind man with reserves of unexpected charm. He said, "I've no business to be lecturing you, Donald. I'm sorry. As usual I got carried away."

"No need to apologize, sir."

"What worries me is that if any of the large whisky firms bought my distillery, yours included, they would close the maltings, install stainless steel washbacks, switch to steam heating for the stills, build new racked warehouses. You know the sort of thing. It's been done by almost every distillery in Scotland."

Fraser knew it would be foolish to deny what Matheson was saying. Thomson Distillers had already bought three distilleries in Scotland and the first thing they had done was to modernize them. Every alcoholic drink that the company produced, and they made many throughout the world—Bourbon Whiskey, vodka, Cognac, rum, tequila, gin—was made more efficiently and for a few cents a gallon less than than any of their competitors.

"We would give you a guarantee as part of the deal," he told Matheson, "that there would be no redundancies. Any loss of jobs would be by natural wastage. As men retired they would not be replaced."

"You've missed the point, Donald. As I've already told you thirty-one people work in the distillery not including myself. If you include wives and children, it means that more than one hundred people of Alsaig are totally dependent on us for their livelihood; almost forty per cent of the island's population. Using your modern methods Thomson Distillers could run the place with twelve, perhaps less. Can't you see what that would mean? The island itself would no longer be viable. There would not be enough business to keep MacNab's stores going nor the hotel, not to mention MacBain and his son who do all the odd building, plumbing and decorating jobs. It would be the end of Alsaig. St. Kilda all over again. I simply cannot allow that to happen."

For the first time since Thomson Distillers had begun negotiations to buy Alsaig distillery six months previously, Fraser realized that he was fighting not a man but a principle. Privately he had always thought of Matheson as an old fool, not unlike his father, now dead, who clung tenaciously to old ideas and shut his mind to progress. That was what people in the whisky industry on the mainland also thought. Now he sensed dimly something of Matheson's love for not only his distillery but for the island. The old man was determined that Alsaig should survive, that it should never dwindle away until so few people were living on it that the government would be forced to evacuate it as they had the little island of St. Kilda fifty years ago. And feeling the strength of Matheson's conviction, Fraser was filled with a sense of helplessness and depression and fear.

"So nothing I can say will make you change your mind and sell the distillery, sir?" he asked Matheson quietly.

"No, Donald. It won't."

"Then I shall be joining the army." Fraser's laugh was forced.

"The army?"

"The army of unemployed. My job is at stake."

Matheson looked at him searchingly, wondering whether this was a subtle form of blackmail, but he decided the boy was probably telling the truth. North American companies, he knew, were ruthless in firing those who did not turn in the performance that was expected of them.

"I'm sorry," he said. "I'd like to help but the distillery is not for sale."

He looked at his watch as Fraser stood up. They had been talking for more than an hour and a half, social conversation at first, about Fraser's family and reminiscences of his childhood, before they turned to business, and it was now after six-thirty.

"You'll stay for supper, of course?" he said.

"Thank-you, sir, no." Petulantly Fraser retreated into a military stiffness. "They will be expecting me at the hotel."

"Come now, Donald. No hard feelings, please!" Matheson took Fraser's arm persuasively, knowing that his charm would be difficult to resist. "You'd be doing me a favour if you'll stay. My daughter has invited some American fellow, an academic who's here to write a book. He'll be hard work you can be sure and you're so much more accomplished in the social graces than I am."

He led Fraser from his study into the drawing-room and poured a dram for each of them. A peat fire was burning in the fireplace and its rich, smoky warmth

52

seemed somehow to soften the fierce rushing of the gale as it swept over the roof of the house and through the surrounding trees. From one window of the drawing-room one could just see the pagoda-shaped roof of the malt kiln at the distillery and beyond that the grey mass of the Atlantic. On summer days Matheson often wished his grandfather had built Tigh Geal closer to the sea with a view like the one from the distillery office, overlooking the small inlet into which the spent lees were discharged and on which, for that reason, sea-birds and even a pair of swans would swim in the fresh brightness of the early morning sun. In winter though, as now, he was glad of the protection of the small wood in which the house stood.

They had almost finished their first whisky when the front door bell rang. Almost immediately Fiona looked round the door of the drawing-room to tell her father she would answer it. Since he had not for one moment entertained the idea of answering it himself, Matheson wondered why she had taken the trouble to tell him. He also wondered why she was letting their visitor into the house when Annie, who cooked for them, would have done it.

Meanwhile MacDonald was waiting in the porch where Murdoch had left him. The distillery manager had called for him from his cottage a few minutes earlier and had scarcely spoken on the drive to Tigh Geal, except to pass the time of day. They had met more than once before and he had always found Murdoch amiable enough. Did his silence as they drove through the wind-swept island mean that he knew MacDonald had been with Sheena Campbell the previous evening? Perhaps everyone on Alsaig knew by this time.

When Fiona opened the front door of the house to him she said immediately, "There's one thing I have to ask you."

"What is it?"

"You've heard about the girl who was found dead not far from here this morning."

"Yes." MacDonald wondered whether people on the island had nothing better to talk about or whether Fiona was part of a conspiracy to make him feel guilty.

"Then please don't mention it in front of my father."

"Are you saying he hasn't heard about the murder?"

"He has, of course and it has upset him very much," Fiona replied and then as though an explanation were needed she added, "I know it's ridiculous but he feels that all the people on Alsaig are his responsibility so please be tactful."

"Right. I hear you."

As he followed her through the hallway of the house, he looked at Fiona. She had changed into a pale blue woollen dress which made her look more youthful and now that she had combed her hair out he could see the red in it. Her arms and neck were covered in freckles from exposure to the summer sun and he could see in her face traces of a fresh, natural loveliness now slipping away, spoilt by something he could not identify, weariness in her eyes perhaps or a weakness in her mouth combining to give her an expression which he found oddly familiar.

In the drawing-room after they had been introduced Matheson asked him, "You'll take a dram?"

MacDonald nodded, feeling that he deserved a drink. The bottle of vodka he had bought at MacNab's shop that morning remained unopened, for he had spent the afternoon not drowning his self-pity in alcohol, as he so often had done, but walking in the gale, following the road round the rocky shore to the north of the island and then cutting inland under the lee of Beinn Laimsdearg, continuing for three or four miles before turning for home. As he walked and afterwards, soaking in a hot bath, he had tried again to remember what he had done and might have said the previous night, trying to convince himself that he could not possibly have killed Sheena Campbell, trying to thrust back the nightmare fear that perhaps he had.

"You'll prefer your whisky on the rocks," Matheson said, reaching for the ice-bucket.

"No thanks. Just with plain water."

The old man seemed pleased as he poured an equal amount of water into the tumbler and handed it to MacDonald. Then he took Fraser's glass which was by that time empty and refilled it. He allowed his daughter to pour her own drink and MacDonald wondered whether this was a mark of his disapproval since she was drinking vodka with ice and no more than a dash of vermouth. They all sat down around the fire.

"With your name you must have Scottish blood," Matheson remarked to MacDonald.

"My grandparents on my father's side came from South Uist. They emigrated to the States in the late 1920s."

"Many folk did. Not only at that time but much earlier when the clearances began. Just think of all the good people we have lost over the years. Will we Scots never learn?"

"My grandfather was a crofter. I believe it was just the depression which drove him to look for a life abroad."

"Perhaps. Even so the islands have nearly been ruined by greed and stupidity. Thousands of crofters were evicted because the landowners realized that sheep were more profitable than agricultural rents. In the middle of the last century more than 1,500 people were forcibly evicted from their crofts on South Uist alone, put on board ships by bailiffs and press gangs and taken to Canada where, as often as not, they were left to starve. Even here on Alsaig the population was more than halved in a few years."

"But you'll agree the islands were over-populated," Fraser said. He may have thought that what Matheson was saying was meant as an attack on the motives of Thomson Distillers in trying to buy his distillery. "The crofters couldn't earn a decent living."

"I remember reading that the old Scottish families, MacLeod on Skye and MacLean on Coll, wouldn't let their people suffer."

"Yes. They ruined themselves to prevent the crofters from starving but that didn't solve anything. They went bankrupt and the people who took over their estates were lowlanders or Englishmen who cared nothing for the islands nor understood them. The name of Gordon is still hated on South Uist and Barra for what a Colonel John Gordon did after he bought the islands."

"I see you know something of our history," Fraser said patronizingly to MacDonald.

"I have always felt that a little of it was my history as well."

"Good for you!" Fiona said unexpectedly.

The three men all looked at her. The remark and the bright smile which accompanied it seemed totally out of character, as though she had suddenly decided to be flippant. Cautiously MacDonald took a sip of his whisky, wishing now that he had been bold enough to ask for a vodka instead. To his surprise it did not taste as unpleasant as he had expected. The distinctive flavour was still there, reminiscent of the strong-smelling seaweed which was to be found in rock pools along the shore of the island, but the whisky slipped down his throat smoothly, with none of the fiery burning he found and expected to find in a glass of strong vodka.

"Now the wheel has gone full circle," Matheson said. "The bottom of the market for wool has been knocked out by man-made fibres and some people are trying to reintroduce cattle to the islands. But cattle are different from sheep, they have to be folded at night, they need to be milked if they are cows, they need people."

"How was your grandfather able to afford to sail to America?" Fiona asked MacDonald.

"My grandmother was left a little money by an aunt; just enough for two steerage passages to the States. They were lucky I guess."

Fiona got up from the sofa where she was sitting and went to pour herself another drink. As she was pouring it her husband came into the room. Paul Stokes was tall and slim without seeming in any way athletic. Although his nose was too prominent for him to be described as handsome, and he had no chin to speak of, he had the complacent air of a man whom women find attractive.

"Why is it," he asked flippantly, "that whenever I come into a room my wife is refilling her glass?"

"You will not have met Mike MacDonald," Matheson said quickly.

After shaking hands with MacDonald and Fraser and pouring himself a vodka and tonic, Stokes said, "You two have chosen a bad time to come to Alsaig. What does it feel like to be a prisoner?"

"A prisoner?"

"Stormstayed they call it here. The ferry may not sail again for days."

"That isn't very likely," Matheson said.

"This is the first really bad weather I've known since I came here," MacDonald remarked.

"My dear chap, count yourself fortunate. People have been stormstayed on Alsaig for months. They say Robinson Crusoe came here to train."

"When I was a lad we were once cut off for fourteen days," Matheson said and one sensed that he found his son-in-law's flippancy irritating. "That was the longest I can recall. The seas were too rough even for the puffers."

"Were you forced to stop distilling?" Fraser made one of his rare contributions to the conversation.

"Not quite. Of course we had all the barley in store for the winter, and the peat, but we almost ran out of casks."

"How ghastly for the islanders if you stopped distilling!" There was an underlying sneer in Stokes's remark which

MacDonald could not understand. "They would all soon be suffering from withdrawal symptoms."

Matheson looked at him sharply and MacDonald wondered if he were going to make an angry retort. The old man had a reputation for a violent temper. But he said nothing. In any case at that moment a tall, grey-haired woman thrust her head round the door.

"The broth's on the table," she said. "Now don't be letting it grow cold."

After dining on lentil broth, a haunch of venison which Matheson carved at the sideboard, each person lining up to have his plate heaped high, and a sponge pudding with Drambuie sauce, they returned to the drawing-room where Annie had put out the coffee on a tray. MacDonald had supposed that he might be offered wine or at least a glass of beer with his meal but instead a decanter of whisky had been passed round and everyone had drunk it with their supper except Fiona who had refilled her glass with vodka before they went into the dining-room and taken it in with her.

"Is it true you're on Alsaig to write a book, Mr. MacDonald?" Matheson asked when they were all sitting around the fire again.

"It's really a thesis for my doctorate, but a publisher in America wants to publish it."

"On what subject?"

"The full title is *Norse Influences on Early Gaelic Culture*. I guess Harold Robbins need not worry about the competition."

"What kind of influences?"

"One can find them in almost every aspect of life in the islands and on the west coast of Scotland, in architecture, husbandry, customs and traditions. But my thesis will only deal with Norse influences in Gaelic song and verse as well as in everyday language and place names."

"Place names? Can you give us an example."

"Yes. Take your village of Carrabus. Its name is a corruption of the Norse word 'kjarr' meaning a copse or wood and 'bolstadr' a dwelling."

"Would Carbost on Skye have the same derivation?" Matheson asked.

"Sure."

In answer to further questions MacDonald explained the origins of other names on Alsaig. Smallaig on the west coast of the island took its name from "smaull" meaning sheep or cattle and "aig" the gaelicized form of the Norse word "vik", a bay or outlet, which could be found in many island place names. "Ardnahoe", the name of the estate on the south of Alsaig owned by the Colville family, came from "aird" the Gaelic for a promontory and the Norse "haugr", a cairn or burial ground. On the other hand Gartness on the opposite end of the island was pure Gaelic, "Gart an Eas" or field by the waterfall.

As MacDonald was speaking he could not avoid seeing the boredom in the faces of Fraser and Stokes. Fiona seemed scarcely to be listening, absorbed in a distant dream of her own. He told Matheson, "If the subject interests you maybe we could discuss it some other time."

"That would be grand! I might be of some help to you in your studies. Somewhere upstairs we have old notebooks of my mother in which she wrote down the words of Gaelic songs that were once sung in Alsaig and which had been passed down by word of mouth alone from generation to generation."

MacDonald imagined he could feel the lethargy which had gripped him ever since he came to Scotland slipping away. This was why he had come to Alsaig, to find original material, never published before, which would give colour and freshness to his thesis. By this time they had finished their coffee and Fraser rose to leave. Should the gale die down in the night, he explained, he would make an early start the next morning and by sailing on the first ferry to Kilgona might be able to catch a plane that would get him back in his Glasgow office by early afternoon.

Matheson saw him to the front door and when he returned Fiona remarked, "What's the matter with Donald? He scarcely spoke a word all evening."

"I had to disappoint him. His Yankee masters sent him here to make me change my mind and sell them the distillery."

MacDonald saw Fiona glance quickly at her husband. Her eyes were bright and her voice hard when she said to Matheson, "You won't give in, will you?"

"My daughter and her husband think I should sell our distillery," Matheson told MacDonald.

"Leave me out of this!" Stokes protested. "I prefer to be neutral."

"Neutral? Is that how you describe yourself?" Fiona demanded. "Now we're seeing the second face of Paul Stokes."

"Which American company wishes to buy the distillery?" MacDonald asked, hoping a question might deflect what seemed like an incipient quarrel.

"Jake Thomson's outfit. He's a hard-nosed, ambitious moonshiner."

"Someone is going to get your precious Alsaig eventually," Fiona said wearily. "Why not let them have it on your terms?"

"What you're saying is that they'll get it when I die. Don't count on that either of you. I might leave Murdoch a controlling interest instead of just a one third share. He would never sell."

MacDonald realized that the future of the distillery was a battlefield on which bitter skirmishes had been fought before.

He sensed also from the expression on the face of Paul Stokes that the Englishman was not as disinterested in the outcome as he was pretending to be. Matheson's last threat appeared to have disconcerted both Stokes and Fiona and neither of them replied.

Then as though he had decided to break the awkward silence Stokes said to MacDonald, "Earlier you were telling us the origins of place names. Do you know what the name of this house means?"

"Tigh Geal? Yes, it means white house literally speaking, but it was wrongly named."

"Why is that?"

"It is really the name of an old type of Hebridean house. There was the Tigh Dubh or black house and the Tigh Geal or white house. The black house had drystone walls and the white house cemented walls; both had thatched roofs. The Tigh Geal was superior but even so it was light years removed from your house in comfort or appearance."

"We still have the remains of some black houses on Alsaig," Matheson said, "and some that have been modernized."

Although he had drunk four large whiskies during the course of the evening, MacDonald's head was still clear and this surprised him. Recently when he had gone out to drink in the hotel, he had found that after a similar amount of alcohol he was beginning to feel that comforting sensation of incipient numbness, of being anaesthetized against loneliness and guilt and pain which were for him the first signs of drunkenness. Perhaps after all he could control his drinking still. The thought was comforting.

He was also aware that he was in danger of over-staying his welcome and so he rose to leave. Matheson appeared genuinely disappointed.

"Have you ever been round a distillery?" he asked MacDonald.

"No, never."

"Then why not come to ours tomorrow in the forenoon? I'd be glad to show you round and then we can talk some more about this book you're writing."

"I'd certainly like that, sir."

Fiona stood up as well. "I'll drive Mr. MacDonald home," she said.

"You'll do no such thing," her father

said firmly. "One of the men on night shift at the distillery will be glad to take him."

MacDonald protested that he could easily walk home, that he was accustomed to walking and enjoyed it, but the old man would not hear of it. Fiona seemed annoyed by her father's interference, but she shrugged her shoulders and let him go to his study to phone the distillery. She and her husband in the meantime saw MacDonald to the front door.

On the way through the hall, Fiona told MacDonald, "There's to be a ceilidh in the village hall tomorrow evening. I hope you'll come. It's for a good cause."

"Will you be there?"

"Yes, I have to be. I'm on the committee that's organizing it."

"She's dragging me there too, if you please," Stokes grumbled.

"Then I'll be glad to support it."

When they opened the front door of the house, they found that the gale had abated slightly. The tops of the firs and larches of the copse in which the house stood were still bowed by the force of the wind, but its fierce howling had shrunk to little more than a whine and the roar of the sea seemed muted and more distant.

"I guess the storm is over," MacDonald remarked.

"Don't you believe it," Fiona replied. "The weather here plays tricks. Often a gale will seem to die down and then in a few hours it gets up again even stronger than before. They say it's caused by the centre of pressure passing over."

Matheson was coming out of the house and heard what his daughter was saying. "Fiona's right," he commented. "By morning the gale will be back. I fancy it may be a couple of days before it blows itself out."

Fiona called back to her husband who had remained in the shelter of the porch, asking him to switch on a light which hung outside it. Now the night, by contrast, seemed even blacker. MacDonald could just make out above the tops of the trees the shadow of Cnoc na Moine, the hill beneath the shelter of which Tigh Geal had been built. They heard the sound of a car approaching, the driver revving its engine and the wheels skidding as it swung off the road on to the gravel drive that led up to the house.

"Who's driving?" Fiona asked.

Matheson did not reply. MacDonald saw his lips move but the name he was trying to say stayed locked in his throat. For the briefest moment an expression of astonishment was frozen in his features. His left shoulder jerked backwards, his body twisting until it struck the wall of the porch behind him. It was only as he was falling that they heard the rifle shot, echoing distantly on the hill.

5

A HAND tugging fiercely at his pillow woke MacDonald next morning. A woman's face which he finally recognized as that of Mrs. Anderson looked down at him. When she saw his eyes open and comprehension slowly flooding into them, she scuttled away from the bed towards the door.

"It's past ten o'clock, Mr. MacDonald," she said, indignant in her embarrassment. "I let you sleep on at first and then I couldn't rouse you, no matter how loudly I banged on the door."

Noticing her embarrassment, Mac-Donald at once concluded she had heard that he had been the last person to be seen with Sheena Campbell before the girl was found murdered. By now the whole island must know and must suspect him of having killed Sheena.

"You'll be wishing to put some clothes on," Mrs. Anderson said, averting her eyes and hurrying out of the bedroom.

Now he understood her confusion. He had been sleeping, as he always did, wearing only the bottom of his pyjamas, with one bare shoulder and one arm above the sheets. Mrs. Anderson must have assumed he had been sleeping naked and was horrified. That was why she had not shaken him by the shoulder. He dressed and went into the kitchen where she was making breakfast for him.

"Sorry about that, Mrs. Anderson," he said. "I was at Tigh Geal until early this morning."

"Aye," she replied. "I know you had supper with Mr. Alisdair last night. No doubt he kept you blethering and drinking whisky till all hours."

He smiled, knowing that the remark was not meant unkindly. Mrs. Anderson was devoted to Matheson. "I did my share of talking too," he said.

Under the unwritten rules of their relationship it would not be proper, he decided, for him to tell her about the shooting up at Tigh Geal the previous evening. Probably she knew already, but in any case she would not expect him to tell her what had happened at a dinner party in Matheson's home or to discuss it with her, however dramatic it might have been.

If she did know, she would be thinking that it had been providence which had saved Matheson's life. MacDonald himself suspected it had not been providence but the weather. The rifle bullet had entered the fleshy part of the left arm, just below the shoulder and just a few inches from his heart. It had been fired from the hill above the house at a range of at least 120 yards and even with a telescopic sight an expert shot could be forgiven for such a narrow miss at night and in a high wind.

After he had recovered from the initial shock, Matheson had not been in such pain as one might have supposed. Fiona and MacDonald had helped him into the house and, when he arrived, the distillery worker, who had come to the house to drive MacDonald home, had been sent instead to fetch Dr. Shaw from his house in Carrabus. The bullet had passed through Matheson's arm leaving a nasty wound, but it was still too early to determine whether the muscles had been permanently damaged. The doctor had patched him up until he could be taken over to Kilgona for a proper examination and x-ray at the hospital.

"Here's another day we'll be without the ferry," Mrs. Anderson said, nodding in the direction of the window and the weather outside. "The wind's as strong as it was yesterday."

"You don't think the ferry will sail?"

"Never. Now if they gave us a decent ship." She left her sentence unfinished and then added, "We'll none of us be safe with that wild, crazy Hamish Grant loose on the island with his guns."

Leaving MacDonald to eat the breakfast she had prepared for him she went away to carry on with her work in another part of the cottage. As he ate his porridge, MacDonald thought about what she had told him. He recalled Grant now; a dark, sullen man of about fifty, whose children had grown up and left the island and who lived alone with his wife in the keeper's cottage on Ardnahoe estate, taking Mrs. Colville's guests stalking on the slopes of Beinn Laimsdearg or fishing for brown trout in Loch Crois.

Grant wore his hair and sideboards long

and cut in a style that had been trendy in the States three or four years ago. One supposed that he was trying to make himself look younger than he was, for he would dress in jeans and a red and black checked shirt and cowboy boots when he came into the hotel in the evenings. MacDonald had seen him more than once, sitting on the window seat in the bar with Sheena Campbell talking in a low voice and buying her drink after drink.

If Grant had disappeared from home and had a rifle with him, it was not unreasonable to conclude that it was he who had fired the shot at Matheson. He would be expert enough with a rifle to drop a stag at much the same sort of range. Yet no one had mentioned his name the previous night at Tigh Geal in connection with the shooting. If Mrs. Anderson knew Grant was hiding somewhere on the island, with a gun, Matheson would almost certainly be aware of the fact and so in all probability would Fiona.

When the doctor had been treating Matheson in his bedroom, MacDonald had been alone with Fiona in the drawing-room. He had asked her who could possibly have wished to kill her father and had been surprised when she scarcely bothered to reply. In fact she had seemed totally unconcerned that Matheson had almost been killed, listening to what MacDonald had to say with a dreamy indifference. Stokes, startled by the noise of the shot, had come outside and it had been he who had taken control of the situation, sending for the doctor, finding towels to staunch the blood from his father-in-law's wound and pouring a stiff drink for everyone.

As he sat eating with a better appetite than he had known for weeks, MacDonald was aware that he had almost forgotten about Sheena Campbell. In the warm reassuring atmosphere of Matheson's home his fear that he might have killed the girl had, as the evening had passed, begun to seem like a grotesque and improbable nightmare and like a nightmare it had faded. Now as he thought about the shooting of Matheson, the only logical explanation it seemed was that Hamish Grant, rejected by Sheena or driven past endurance by her provocative flirting, had first killed her and then gone berserk. He resolved not to torture his memory any longer by trying to remember what had happened when he had left the hotel with the girl.

He had finished eating and was enjoying the luxury of a second cup of coffee which, to his astonishment Mrs. Anderson had managed to make entirely to his taste, when she came back into the kitchen. She was carrying his thick, white Isle of Arran sweater and held it up in front of him.

"Whatever have you been doing with your jumper, Mr. MacDonald?" she asked.

"Where did you find it?"

"Tucked in behind the suitcases on the top of your wardrobe."

"How in heaven did it get there?"

"I'll take it home and wash it for you."

MacDonald took the sweater from her and examined it. It was very damp and discoloured with streaks of mud that had not yet fully dried and reddish-brown stains which he guessed at once could only be blood.

A car's horn sounded outside the cottage as Mrs. Anderson was taking the sweater back from him. His initial surprise was replaced by something not unlike panic as he tried to think how the sweater could have come to be hidden on top of the wardrobe.

"I don't believe I've worn that sweater since I came to Alsaig. It has never been cold enough yet," he said unconvincingly.

"But it's wet through," Mrs. Anderson replied and then, not wishing him to think she was accusing him of a lie she added, "you must have forgotten, Mr. MacDonald."

"I suppose so," MacDonald said and he wondered whether she too knew that sometimes he suffered from alcoholic amnesia.

"And that will be Angus Murdoch from the distillery outside in his car."

She was right. Murdoch was sitting outside the cottage in the same car as he had used to drive MacDonald to Tigh Geal the previous evening. He had reversed and turned it in the narrow road and it was pointing towards Carrabus.

MacDonald had to shout to make himself heard above the noise of the wind. "Is anything wrong?" he asked Murdoch, wondering whether perhaps there had been some new crisis or drama at Matheson's home.

"No. It's just Mr. Alisdair is waiting for you."

"But surely he's not expecting me after last night?"

"Aye. He is."

"But is he all right?"

"Surely. It would take more than a wee gunshot wound to keep him in his bed."

After returning briefly to the cottage to fetch his anorak, MacDonald climbed into the car and they set off towards Carrabus. As on the drive to Tigh Geal the previous evening, Murdoch made no attempt at conversation, staring straight ahead as though it needed all his concentration to keep the car on the road in the buffeting wind. MacDonald wondered whether he might be resenting the fact that he was being used as a chauffeur, to drive an incomer who was also a foreigner about the island but decided that was not very likely. The islanders who had cars were, in his experience, always glad to use them as though on a tiny claustrophobic island every chance to move about was a freedom to be enjoyed. They were generous with their cars too, always stopping to give a lift to anyone who might be walking along the road, even if he were only a couple of hundred yards from his destination.

Nor was MacDonald himself in a conversational mood. The shock of seeing his blood-stained sweater and concluding that he must have deliberately hidden it had rekindled all the smouldering doubts over Sheena Campbell's death. When he had woken the morning after being with her at the hotel, he had been wearing one sweater over his shirt and jeans but recently when the evening breeze seemed chilly, he had taken to wearing two sweaters. Now he could not remember what he had been wearing when he had set out for the hotel that evening. He possessed at least half-a-dozen sweaters.

As they were approaching Carrabus, they passed the concrete ramp where the ferry came to discharge its load of lorries and cars. In the small bay the sea, protected from the worst of the gale by the island itself, was no more than very rough, but further out at sea mountainous waves could be seen breaking over Sgeir Leathan and Glas Eilean, two rocky uninhabited islands, throwing up spray that seemed to hang motionless like a grey curtain to a height of 50 feet or more.

"Will the ferry be coming today?" MacDonald asked Murdoch.

"It will not, surely, unless the wind drops and that's not likely."

"Has Hamish Grant been found yet?"

Murdoch glanced at him sideways as though wondering why he should be asking the question. "No."

Two men were unloading a Volvo estate car outside the Colville Hall and MacDonald recognized it as the car Fiona Stokes had been driving the previous day when she gave him a lift to the village. The men were struggling against the wind which kept blowing the hatch back of the car shut and which, when they struggled with their loads the few steps to the entrance of the hall, made it almost impossible to open the doors. A home-made poster, painted by the schoolmaster and advertising the ceilidh that was to be held that evening to raise funds for the school choir to attend the Mod at Oban, had been ripped away by the wind, leaving only two flapping streamers of torn yellow paper secured to the doors with drawing-pins. It had struck MacDonald that the ceilidh might have been cancelled or at least postponed following Sheena Campbell's murder, but he supposed that on Alsaig, where until quite recently fishing boats had been a staple part of the island's economy, people had become inured to violent death and it was not allowed to interrupt the routines of life.

"I suppose it was Grant who killed Sheena Campbell," MacDonald suggested, tentatively, unsure of the reply he might receive.

Murdoch did not speak for several seconds. Then he said slowly, "There will be many people thinking it was you who killed her, Mr. MacDonald."

6

A SMALL burn flowing down from Cnoc na Moine, the hill on the south of the island, was the source from which the distillery drew its water supply. The water flowed down through the peat of the hillside, unbelievably soft and more often than not light brown in colour, into a small dam that had been constructed at the back of the distillery just beyond the malt barns. Leaning against the stone wall that protected the dam, his left arm in a sling, Matheson pointed with his walking-stick towards the water.

"Our whisky is unique," he told MacDonald, "and this is the reason why. No other malt whisky distilled in Scotland has the same flavour as Alsaig."

"Because of the water you use?"

"It is water more than any other factor which determines the flavour of whisky. The peat which we use in the malt kiln is also important. You may have noticed that Alsaig whisky has a strong flavour, reminiscent of the sea?"

"Yes, I have noticed that."

"All whiskies made on islands have something of the same character; Talisker on Skye, the Islay whiskies and those distilled on the Orkneys. It's because the peat on the islands is impregnated with sea air and sea spray. And the water in this burn has flowed down through the peat."

Leaving the dam, Matheson took MacDonald round the distillery, starting at the malt barns where on the topmost of the four floors the barley brought in from the mainland of Scotland was stored. Only Scottish barley was used at Alsaig, and it was first soaked in water and then spread evenly to a depth of several inches on one of the three malting floors in the building.

They went down and watched the malt being turned by two men using flat-bladed wooden shovels or shiels. Matheson explained that this had to be done at regular intervals as the grain started to germinate and tiny roots appeared. The men were walking rhythmically as they worked, moving across the floor picking up the barley on the blades of their shiels and tossing it up so that it scattered and fell in another pile further along.

Next they went to the malt kiln where the barley from another floor, which had been germinating long enough, had been spread out over a wire mesh floor beneath which a peat fire was burning. The smoke from the fire drifting up through the green malt, as it was called, dried it and stopped the growth.

"The starch in the grain has turned into a form of sugar to feed the young plant," Matheson said, "and that's what we use to make whisky."

As they left the maltings he remarked, "You'll not find many maltings like that in Scotland any more; only three or four and they are being kept on just as a tourist attraction."

"Why is that?"

"It's just part of the mania that has seized the whisky trade; a mania to cut down costs and save a few miserable pennies. Today almost all of the malt used to make whisky is produced in huge, mechanical maltings where a handful of men can, with the help of machinery and computers, turn out thousands of tons."

The rest of the process by which whisky was made seemed simple enough to MacDonald. The malt, after being ground to grist in a mill, was mixed with hot water in a large iron vessel. This produced a hot, sugary liquid which was cooled and then filled into the wash-backs, vessels made from larch deep enough to hold as much as 8,000 gallons. Here yeast was added and fermentation began. In due course the fermented liquid, a kind of crude beer, was pumped to the stillhouse where it was distilled into spirit.

"This is the crucial stage in making whisky," Matheson said, pointing at the stills. Two of the stills were about 20 feet tall and the other two slightly less and all four were fashioned of copper in the traditional onion shape and heated by coal-fired furnaces below the concrete floor in which they were set. Once the copper had been brightly burnished but now it was tarnished to a lustreless brown. "Here the distillery owner has a choice: whether to make a decent dram or to think of his profit and run his stills to the limit and produce a whisky so adulterated with feints and foreshots that no self-respecting Scot will drink it."

He explained that the fermented liquid or "wash" that arrived at the stillhouse was distilled twice, first in one of the larger wash stills and then in a spirit still. The spirit produced at the beginning and at the end of this second distillation contained certain oils and other undesirable constituents and only the middle portion or cut of the distillation was collected. According to Matheson, it was the decision when to start and stop collecting the spirit that determined whether it would ever be a whisky worthy of the name.

They stood for a while watching the spirit from the stills as it passed through the spirit safe, a rectangular glass box, securely locked. It was the stillman who would decide from the appearance of the almost colourless spirit, and from testing its strength, which he was able to do by remote control, whether it was the right quality to be collected. Then it would be pumped into a wooden spirit receiver from which in turn it would be filled into casks.

At the end of the distillery, built along the low cliff above the sea, were the maturation warehouses, seven long, low buildings, the stone walls of which were blackened with age, and each of which had stout double doors securely locked with padlocks. Matheson and MacDonald found one warehouse which was open and into which two men were trundling hogsheads of whisky, rolling them along the ground with nonchalant ease, although each held more than 50 gallons of new spirit. Just inside the door of the warehouse a man in the dark blue uniform of Her Majesty's Customs and Excise stood watching the operation. Inside the warehouse were hundreds of filled casks, butts as well as hogsheads, row upon row of them, stacked three-high on top of each other, stretching into the dark shadows at the back of the low, gloomy building.

"We fill the new spirit into these casks," Matheson explained, "and leave it to mature. Almost all of the whisky made at Alsaig is matured in casks that formerly were used for sherry. That gives the best results."

"For how long do you keep it in here?"

"By law in order to qualify for the description of Scotch Whisky, it has to mature for a minimum of three years. In my opinion Alsaig should neither be drunk nor added to a blend until it is at least ten years old, but some of my customers send for it after seven years." Matheson grunted with contempt to show his opinion of people who would treat his whisky in such a fashion.

"And does it really improve so much in quality as it is maturing?"

"Here, I'll show you."

Matheson went to one of the casks of new spirit that had just been rolled into the warehouse and with the help of the Customs Officer withdrew the bung and using a kind of metal pipette drew out a sample of the spirit which he poured into a jar that one of the men produced.

"Take a sniff of that," he said, handing the jar to MacDonald. "It's new spirit, distilled yesterday, filled into cask today. Then take a sip of it, if you wish, but carefully. It will be well above a hundred proof."

"Didn't I read somewhere that you British had given up the old system of proof strength?"

"We have officially. That's part of the

price we paid for joining the European Community. But I'm damned if I am going to change the habits of a lifetime for a few fussy bureaucrats."

The aroma from the jar seemed to MacDonald totally unrelated to what he had expected from whisky and its taste, fiery and raw, made him wince. At the same time he could just detect the distinctive flavour he had noticed in Alsaig malt whisky before, faintly medicinal and redolent of the sea. Matheson laughed at the expression on his face.

"Come on, it's not as bad as all that, laddie! All the men who work here take a generous dram of new whisky every morning and every evening before they go home. They like it and it does them no harm. Now let's go and give you a taste of the finished product."

They left the warehouse and went into the small distillery office which was furnished more comfortably than Matheson's study up at the house. An oil painting of the distillery, viewed from across the bay and little harbour of Carrabus, which must have been painted from about the point where the ferry landed, hung on one wall. In the painting a small cargo boat was tied up at the old pier of the distillery with a row of whisky casks alongside. It seemed to MacDonald that the artist had captured the whole feeling of the island, the extraordinary clarity of the air on a fine day with distant clouds massing on the far horizon, the contrast between an almost dark blue sea edged with white and the purple heather on the slopes of Cnoc na Moine, the tranquil pace of life and the simplicity of the islanders reflected in the posture of the men who in the painting were loading the casks on to the boat.

"Now that really is something!" he exclaimed, pointing at the canvas. "It can only have been painted by someone who really loves this island."

"You'll never guess who the artist was." Matheson seemed delighted at his appreciation.

"Your daughter?"

The old man's face clouded over with what might have been sadness or discontent or irritation or a fusion of all these three. "I only wish it had been, but Fiona doesn't love Alsaig. She blames it for the mess she has made of her life."

Without adding any explanation of this remark, he went to a cupboard in one corner of the room, unlocked it and picked out three bottles containing whisky. The bottles were plain and functional and each had a white label on which had been written in ink the date when the whisky had been distilled, the number of the cask into which it had been filled and the date when the sample had been drawn.

"These are samples of three different makes of whisky, three different distillations if you like," Matheson said. "One was matured for ten years, one for fifteen and the other is a rather special whisky that you'll not be likely to taste again. It was distilled forty years ago and the sample drawn only last week."

A tray holding three tulip-shaped glasses of the type used by whisky blenders for sampling stood ready on the desk in the office together with a jug. After leaving the room briefly to fill the jug with water, Matheson poured out samples from each of the bottles and invited MacDonald to taste them.

"I'll put a little water in each glass for you first," he remarked. "That helps bring out the full aroma of the whisky."

MacDonald held the glasses up to his nose in turn and sniffed at them. Then he took a sip from each. The whisky was rich and mellow, slipping smoothly down his throat without any of the fiery burning that he felt when drinking gin or vodka. The distinctive flavour which he had noticed in the sample of new spirit was still there, but muted and in no way offensive. The 40–year-old whisky had a rich sweetness as well and was almost a dark brown colour.

"This is fantastic!" he exclaimed, holding the glass up to the light.

"You'll not taste whisky like that again."

"Why is that?"

Matheson explained that malt whisky was seldom kept maturing for more than fifteen years. After that time there was a danger that the whisky would begin to take on the flavour of wood from the cask and so become undrinkable. The sample he had given MacDonald was from a cask that had been filled during the war. At that time small quantities of Alsaig used to be distilled for private customers, mainly people who had acquired a taste for it and could afford to pay for a cask or two, and leave them to mature at the distillery until they were ready to drink.

"Our records were not very efficiently kept in those days." Matheson grinned sheepishly, like a schoolboy caught stealing apples. "And we don't know to whom the cask belongs. From time to time I make Murdoch draw a sample from it; just to make sure it's still drinkable, you understand."

He put the sample bottles and glasses back into the cupboard, took out a cut-glass decanter and two tumblers and they sat down facing each other across the desk to have a real dram, as Matheson put it. He began to talk of what was clearly his favourite subject, the whisky business and the changes that had taken place in it over the last 25 years. All changes for the worse, in his view. While he accepted that the growing popularity of Scotch throughout the world meant that more whisky had to be made to keep up with demand, and that modern methods of marketing and selling and handling were needed to deal with the huge quantities that were now involved, he would not forgive other whisky companies for allowing the quality of Scotch and particularly of malt whisky to fall.

"These people actually have the gall," he said, "the soulless chemists who are in charge of distilling the stuff today, to claim that whisky has not changed from what it used to be."

"But it has?"

"Of course. How could it not have changed when every process, the whole art of distilling has changed; and it is an art, make no mistake about that. Take malting as an example. Do you know that some distilleries use malt that has been dried over anthracite and even by oil-fired furnaces without even a whiff of peat reek. Can anyone really say that the malt made in this way in the huge mechanical maltings is no different to the malt we make on our malting floors? You might just as well say that the mass-produced cakes they sell in supermarkets are no different to the cakes that Annie bakes for us every Tuesday. And if the malt is different, the flavour of the whisky must be different."

He went on to enumerate some of the many other changes that had taken place in the whisky trade: how distillers thought only of yield, of the amount of whisky they could produce from a ton of barley and of how cheaply they could make it. Washbacks were now being made of stainless steel instead of wood simply because they could be cleaned much more easily and therefore less men need be employed. Almost every still in Scotland, except his own, was now being heated by steam or oil instead of coal.

"That alone makes a tremendous difference to the whisky," Matheson said. "When I started in the business I tasted all the great single malt whiskies, all of them, and I've tasted them today. Anyone who says they have not changed in flavour and quality over the last twenty years is either a fool or a knave."

"When did you start in the business?"

"Immediately after the war. My father put me to work, first as a labourer in the distillery and then doing all the different jobs in the malt barn, and scrubbing out the wash-backs after each fermentation with besoms made from heather. That was hard work, I can tell you."

"So you started young?"

"Not young enough really. You see my father had not intended that I should take over the distillery. I was to be trained as a lawyer in Glasgow and my elder brother Iain was to run the distillery. But Iain was killed in the war."

Once more Matheson's face clouded over. Unhappy memories and remembered sadnesses ranged back in the man's life, MacDonald decided, like milestones on a journey that was moving towards its end. There must also have been other memories less painful, moments of pleasure, the satisfaction of achievements, family celebrations, but they too were in a private past, remembered briefly from time to time but never shared.

As though to prove the point, Matheson shook off the past. "Whisky men on the mainland, the bosses of the large blending companies, will tell you that I'm old-fashioned, living in the nineteenth century and too stubborn to move with the times. They will tell you that my whisky costs fourteen pence more a gallon to make than any mainland malt whisky. So it does. Half of that is simply due to the fact that everything except the water and the peat has to be shipped in here from the mainland, the barley and the yeast and the casks and the coal for our boiler. The other seven pence is the cost of what they would call my inefficiency. But what of it? I charge twenty pence a gallon more for fillings of my whisky and they have to pay."

"Maybe that's what gets under their skins."

"No doubt. It's envy. The big companies are jealous because I've kept out of the rat-race, because I won't cut my prices and my throat, because my whisky is as good as it always was."

Glancing at his watch, MacDonald was astonished to discover that it was well after one o'clock. Finishing his whisky in one swallow, he got up to go, apologizing for keeping Matheson so late.

"Why hurry away?" Matheson asked him. "Come up to the house for luncheon. I can't say what we'll be eating but Annie always does us well."

"Thank-you, sir, but I can't impose on your family again."

"Family? The chances are I'll be eating alone as I often do."

"Why, is your daughter out?"

"She'll be in her bed still, summoning up strength to face the day," Matheson said drily. "As for my son-in-law, he shot out of the house in his car early this morning. God knows where he's gone. Muttered something about needing fresh air. Blasted fool! Fresh air on a day like this? You'd be doing me a favour if you would join me."

"It's very kind of you, but I think I should be getting back to the cottage."

"Of course. You have your work to do. It was selfish of me to press you."

"But I'd sure like to come and see you again another time." MacDonald felt a sudden sympathy for the lonely old man. "Those notebooks of your mother's might be a great help to me."

"Then come tomorrow. We'll meet here for a dram and a chat and then go up to the house for lunch."

After giving his promise and refusing an offer to have him driven home,

MacDonald left, setting off through the village and past the harbour, derelict now since the introduction of a regular ferry service. There was not a soul to be seen, for those who lived in the village were either at work in the distillery or on the Colville estate, or at home taking their dinner. Only the folk at Ardnahoe and Tigh Geal and the Manse lunched at mid-day. For everyone else it was dinner at mid-day with supper in the evening.

Seeing the deserted street, MacDonald felt that had there been hot sunshine and a dust road and a dog lying on the sidewalk scratching itself, he might easily have been in one of those small townships in the Middle West, places that had scarcely changed in a hundred years.

When he had first arrived at Alsaig, the seclusion of the island had seemed to offer only peace and tranquillity, an opportunity to allow the wounds of pride to heal, and to reassert his will and his individuality. Now it made him uneasy. He felt like a man walking precariously along a narrow path with disaster on both sides. Disaster was at his back too, like Marvell's winged chariot hurrying near, and he must make haste if he were to outstrip its pursuit. It was this sense of urgency that had made him decline Matheson's invitation to lunch at Tigh Geal. All morning the nagging fear that he might perhaps in a drunken frenzy have killed Sheena Campbell had lurked at the back of his mind. He was beginning to imagine that he could remember an argument, that he could picture the mockery in her face turning to fear, hear her strangled scream. He remembered other drunken evenings, other nightmares, other mornings of guilt and remorse. What he needed now was the courage to face up to the truth. Before anything else he must satisfy himself that he had either killed the girl or not.

7

THE Land-Rover was stuck in an ungainly posture, half on and half off the rough track that ran along the side of the peat moss on Cnoc na Moine. Its back wheels were still on the track, the offside front wheel drunkenly in the air, the nearside wheel embedded firmly in a trench from which the peat had been cut and removed. Hamish Grant, the keeper from the Colville estate, was in the driving seat, slumped forward over the steering wheel, apparently asleep or unconscious. An empty bottle that had once contained Alsaig malt whisky lay on the floor beneath the dashboard.

Another car which had been driven slowly up the track, stopped when it reached the Land-Rover, and Murdoch and Darroch got out. A sharp-eyed child returning to the schoolhouse after dinner had spotted the Land-Rover on the distant hillside and had pointed it out to the schoolmaster who had pointed it out to

Darroch. The hotelier had gone to the distillery, collected Murdoch and they had come up together to investigate.

"The man's drunk," Murdoch said, shaking Grant but getting no response. "And no wonder." He pointed at the empty whisky bottle.

"It would take more than a bottle to get Hamish fou," Darroch remarked. "Many's the time I've seen him drink more than that in my bar and still go home sober."

"I wonder where he got it."

"Who knows? But look there."

Darroch pointed towards the back of the Land-Rover, where two guns were lying on one of the bench seats. One was a double-barrelled shotgun and the other a sporting rifle fitted with a telescopic sight. A green canvas bag containing cartridges for the shotgun and bullets for the rifle lay on the seat beside them.

Murdoch shook Grant again, more roughly this time. Eventually the game-keeper groaned, opened his bloodshot eyes, stared at Murdoch and Darroch stupidly and then closed his eyes again without making any attempt to move.

"Help me to get him out of here and into the car," Murdoch said.

When they tried to move Grant from behind the steering wheel, he started to slide down towards the door on the passenger's side. With difficulty they pulled him out, got him on his feet and with one of them supporting him on each side dragged him along the track to Darroch's car.

"Shove him into the back," Murdoch said, "and I'll ride with him just in case he tries anything."

"You'll not have any trouble with him in his state," Darroch replied. He knew a thing or two about drunks.

"Maybe, but we best be sure till we've got the daft fool locked up."

After putting Grant in the back of the car, they fetched the two guns and the bag of ammunition from the Land-Rover, locked them in the boot and set out for Carrabus. They had to reverse the car for 30 yards or so to a flat piece of ground which was used for turning by the lorries that came up to fetch peats. From there they followed the track down the side of the hill to the point where it joined the road to Ballymony a short way beyond the entrance to Tigh Geal.

"Where shall we take him?" Darroch asked.

"We must keep him locked up until we can talk some sense into the man. Your cellar should be a safe place."

"I keep all my drink in there."

"So much the better. The longer he stays blind drunk the best for all of us."

"And who will be paying for what he drinks?"

"I'll replace any whisky he may take. He'll not touch anything else if there's whisky handy."

"I'd best telephone Muirhead and tell him about the Land-Rover," Darroch said. Muirhead was the factor for the Colville estate.

"Aye and I'll send the lorry up from the distillery to pull it out of the peat moss."

The island did not possess a garage because there would not have been enough business to support one. The only officially registered and taxed cars on Alsaig were those belonging to the distillery (which also had two lorries), the Colville estate, Matheson, the hotel, Dr. Shaw and

MacNab's van. At least a dozen other people ran cars but they had allowed their registrations to lapse and no longer paid the road tax. Whenever the police from Kilgona paid a visit to the island, the men who sailed the ferry would telephone from Rainich before the ferry left for Alsaig and by the time it arrived the cars had all been "laid up" in garages or in lean-to sheds. To the islanders this was in no way dishonest since no government could reasonably expect them to pay road tax when they were provided with only one road and even that was not made up for more than one third of its sixteen miles.

Mrs. Buie, who ran the post office, also had a petrol pump, and the distillery had a trained fitter on its staff whom Matheson allowed to attend to any car or tractor that needed servicing or repair. It was a pleasant, community arrangement which worked well.

"Do we have any right to lock up Hamish?" Darroch asked Murdoch. "As far as we know he's done no wrong."

"It's what he might do that worries me. No, we'll keep him locked up until he's sober and then you can talk some sense into the man."

When they reached the hotel, they pulled Grant out of the car. Still stupefied, he made no attempt to resist as they led him along the path, through the front door and along the entrance hall. A door at the end of the hall opened on to a flight of steps which led down to the cellar. Pushing him through the door they let Grant stumble down the steps and collapse on to the stone floor. Then they locked and bolted the door from the outside, leaving the key in the lock and went into the hotel office to telephone the distillery and Ardnahoe House.

Another telephone had been installed in the hallway of the hotel for the use of guests and, as they passed, Fraser was using it to call the Glasgow office of Thomson Distillers.

"Is that you Stevens?" they heard him saying. "You did get that telex off to New York didn't you? Good! Well, that bloody ferry isn't operating again today. God knows why. If you ask me it's sheer bloody idleness. Anyway it's absolutely imperative that I get off this island today.

What? No, now at once. I must get to the office before close of play today and there's only one way it can be done. You'll have to charter a chopper to fly me out. Get on to those people at Abbotsinch who run the charter service. They could get one here in a couple of hours at the most and I'd be in the office in time to phone the president before his office closes for the day. What? Of course I know a charter costs money, but there's a hell of a lot at stake, I can tell you. What do you mean, whose authority? Mine of course, you bloody fool! I must get off this island, I tell you. Tomorrow could be too late. What do you mean, I no longer have the authority? Who says so? In the telex from New York? Read it to me."

Fraser listened, presumably while a telex message was being read out to him. Then without saying another word, he put the telephone down. His face had turned deathly white.

At just about the same time as Donald Fraser was calling his office in Glasgow, Dr. Neil Shaw was telephoning Sergeant Cairns of the Kilgona police. When he retired and moved from Glasgow to Alsaig, Shaw had arranged with the Western Isles Health Board that he would continue to practise. The arrangement suited him well. Just as the number of cars on the island was not sufficient to justify a garage, so the number of inhabitants was not enough to keep a doctor fully employed, especially as much of the routine medicine required could be handled by Nurse Black. And so Shaw had a modest income to supplement his pension and ample time to indulge in his main interest, photographing birds.

The coast on the western side of Alsaig was very different to the more protected eastern shore. Lashed by the Atlantic in westerly gales for thousands of years, the coastline had been gradually worn down into long sandy beaches and wide bays. At one time crofters had lived on that side of the island, grazing their cattle on the common machair or grassland along the shore and cultivating the rich strip of soil between it and the moors. Then they had been dispossessed by landowners who had seen more profit in sheep and now, after the collapse of the market for wool, the western part of Alsaig was virtually uninhabited and Dr. Shaw, watching through his binoculars and through his camera's rangefinder could find a rich treasure of bird life for the fine photographs which won him many medals in exhibitions on the mainland.

"I examined the girl's body," he told Cairns. "As well as I was able to, that is. We're not equipped for forensic work here, you know."

"I know, sir and we're very obliged to you for what you are doing."

"I am reasonably certain that she had been sexually assaulted just before she died."

"I see. And the cause of death, sir?"

"In my opinion, and it's only an opinion, she was struck a violent blow across the throat which caused a sub-mucosa haemorrhage."

"What does that mean?"

"She would have choked to death."

"And the blow across the throat?"

"It must have been given by someone who either had medical training or a knowledge of karate."

"There is no chance that it could have been accidental?"

"None whatsoever," Shaw replied; and then because he was by nature a cautious man he added, "in my opinion at least."

Sergeant Cairns made no comment. He was wondering whether that old Dr. Shaw was letting his imagination run away with him. For a doctor on a tiny island a murder would be quite an event and he might be making the most of the important rôle which had suddenly been thrust on him. So Cairns said, "Thank-you for your trouble, Doctor. It's likely we'll be on the ferry first thing tomorrow morning, for the met. people are forecasting that the gale will be over by then."

Shaw pulled a face as he put the phone down. Contrary to what the sergeant supposed he was not getting any pleasure from the part he had been called upon to play in this regrettable affair. Although he had been living on Alsaig for almost five years and was accepted, trusted and even liked by the islanders in his professional capacity, he was always conscious that his wife and he were incomers and would remain so even if they stayed there for a lifetime. Now he felt that in their absence the police were trying to push him into a

112

position of authority from where he might be called upon to make decisions or judgements which, however correct they might be, every islander would resent.

When he went into the living-room his wife looked up from her knitting and said, "There's a young man to see you. He's waiting in the surgery."

"Has he seen Mistress Black?"

"No. He said he had to see you and it was a confidential matter. It's that American who rented the cottage up by Gartness."

When Shaw had bought his house on Alsaig, the Health Board had built an extension on to it, which had been flattered with the name of Medical Centre and there Nurse Black took care of all the islanders' minor ailments and injuries. Shaw had a small office in the centre but preferred to use his own surgery in the house. Now he found MacDonald in there, flicking over the pages of an ancient copy of *Scottish Field*. He had met the American a couple of times socially, once at a ceilidh and once when leaving the Colville Hall after one of the fortnightly film shows that were held there, but never in a professional capacity.

"What can I do for you Mr. MacDonald?" he asked.

"May I speak to you in confidence, sir?"

"Of course. I am a doctor," Shaw replied. The fellow's got a dose of clap, he was thinking, for he had served in the RAMC in the war and had a low opinion of Americans. If so the man must have brought it with him, because there was no venereal disease on Alsaig, he was sure of that.

"You know that Sheena Campbell was found dead yesterday?"

"Aye, I do."

"Would you be able to establish by medical tests whether it was I who killed her?"

Shaw looked at MacDonald searchingly, wondering whether this was some macabre practical joke or whether, like some Americans he had met, the man was a little mad. Before he had formed an opinion MacDonald continued, "I've read, in reports of criminal trials, of evidence which forensic scientists were able to produce to prove that an accused man was guilty of a violent attack on a woman; scratches on his arms, small particles of the victim's skin under his fingernails. You know the kind of thing."

"Theoretically that would be possible." Shaw had always been a cautious man.

"Then I would like to submit myself to such tests."

"They could only be done on the mainland."

"Why so?"

"We don't have the equipment here and I have no experience of forensic science. The same is true of the hospital on Kilgona."

"But it may be days before I can get to the mainland!"

Shaw did not like the way that the interview was going. MacDonald's questions, it seemed to him, were a calculated way of confessing to the murder of Sheena Campbell. He knew that after almost every murder people came forward to claim, falsely, that they had committed it and the American must be one of these unbalanced cranks. What irritated him was that the confession should be made to him. It was precisely this situation which he wished to avoid.

"Surely if you did kill the Campbell girl," he remarked to humour the madman, "you would know it and tests of the type you describe would not be necessary."

"This will sound crazy, Doctor, but I don't know."

"How is that?"

"I was drinking heavily on the night before she was found dead and I can remember nothing, but they tell me I was with Sheena in the hotel bar and that we left together in the early morning."

"I see."

From the wild drinking sprees of his medical student days, Shaw knew at first hand about alcoholic amnesia. He had encountered it often enough among patients as well when he had worked for a time at the Glasgow Royal Infirmary. The ingestion of unhealthily large quantities of alcohol at irregular intervals, usually heavy beer and cheap wine, was common in Scotland. Binge drinking the psychiatrists chose to call it. He knew too that a significantly large proportion of murders

116

and violent assaults were committed under the influence of drink.

"What do you suggest I do, Doc?"

"Tell the police what you have told me. They should be here tomorrow."

MacDonald hesitated. He had intended to tell Shaw of how Mrs. Anderson had found his blood-stained and muddy sweater, concealed apparently by himself but now, sensing that the doctor was reluctant to become involved in any discussion of Sheena's death, he decided against it. Instead he said, "I do have one good reason for believing I didn't kill Sheena."

"What's that?"

"Her death must be connected in some way with the attempt on Mr. Matheson's life last night and as you know I was with him when it happened."

"Attempt on his life?"

"Yes. That bullet must have been meant for his heart."

Shaw began almost to dislike this American who, with his blunt admissions and awkward questions was starting to open up what might be a very nasty can of worms. He said stiffly, "Mr. Matheson was shot accidentally."

"Accidentally? You must be mistaken, sir!"

"Not at all. It happened when he was cleaning his rifle."

"He told you that?"

"Certainly."

"There's no way it could have been an accident. I was standing next to him outside his house when he was shot. Whoever fired at him must have been a good distance away; on the hill above the house would be my guess."

"Mr. MacDonald, all I can say is this. Mr. Matheson is a patient of mine and a highly respected member of this community. I am perfectly satisfied that his account of how he came to be shot is a true one."

He showed MacDonald out, taking him through the house and not using the surgery door at the side, feeling it would be better if any patients who might be waiting in the medical centre should not see him leave. On the doorstep, in spite of his reluctance to take any part in the murder enquiries, he could not resist satisfying his own curiosity by asking the American another question.

"Did you ever serve in the American armed forces, Mr. MacDonald?"

"No. Why do you ask?"

"I wondered whether you ever had any training in unarmed combat."

"No, but I was a member of the karate club at university."

8

"THEID mi null gu tir mo ruin, Theid mi null thar an aiseig," sang the school choir: five boys in kilts of their family tartans and seven girls in white dresses with tartan sashes, correctly dressed, because as they all knew women do not wear the kilt. The song was the song of Alsaig, telling as so many Hebridean songs do, of an exile's longing to sail across the sea, to take the ferry to his native island. The children's soft, untrained voices were scarcely strong enough to be heard above the roar and whine of the gale that swept over the roof of the Colville Hall.

It was a wild night for a ceilidh, too wild some might have thought, but for centuries the only recreation of the islanders on stormy nights had been to gather around a peat fire in croft or cottage and sing and recite the songs and poems that had been handed down to them. The ceilidh that night was a much more formal affair, arranged to pay the expenses of sending the choir to compete in the Mod, but even so it remained true to tradition, with the entertainment being provided by the guests themselves.

MacNab from the store and Robbie Tait, one of the men from the distillery, were both pipers and they shared the piping for dancing—eightsome reels, The Gay Gordons, The Dashing White Sergeant and Strip the Willow—when virtually everyone at the ceilidh would be up and joining in. Between dances a number of people performed solo turns, singing or reciting or dancing. Tom Buchanan, the schoolmaster, who was a fine Gaelic singer and had won medals at the Mod, sang twice and so did Willy Keith, the Excise Officer, who was a creditable performer of puirt-a-beul, or mouth music. Stuart, the son of the MacNabs, performed a sword dance and his young sister danced as well. Mrs. Buchanan, who accompanied some of the singers on the piano, recited Tennyson's *Crossing the Bar* as she did at every ceilidh on the island and, because she was the wife of the dominie who was liked and respected, her recitation won more applause than it deserved. But it was the singing of the choir which was taken as the most important event of the evening, and they performed one of the songs they were rehearsing for the Mod and three others, unaccompanied and conducted by Buchanan who was himself wearing the kilt.

At one end of the main hall were the cloakrooms and at the other a small kitchen and an office. An improvised bar had been set up in the office and there whisky and soft drinks, donated by Mr. Matheson, were on sale at prices not much more than half of those charged in the hotel. Although the building had no licence, Darroch did not complain about this illegal competition as many hoteliers might have done but, recognizing inevitability, shut the hotel for the evening and came over to the hall and himself served in the bar at the ceilidh.

MacDonald had not arrived at the hall till almost nine o'clock. He had been reluctant to come to the ceilidh at all, feeling with a biblical pessimism that every man's eyes would be on him, every man's hand against him. In the end he had come, partly because he had promised Fiona that he would and partly in the slender hope that among all the people who would be there he might learn something that would convince him that he had not, as he had begun to believe, murdered Sheena Campbell.

At the back of his mind was a notion that he might ask Fiona why her father had told Dr. Shaw that he had been shot by accident. The doctor had treated Matheson alone in his bedroom and MacDonald had no idea of what might have been said. He had thought about it ever since he had left the doctor's house that afternoon and had reached the conclusion that there was only one logical explanation. Matheson had pretended the shooting had been an accident because he knew who had fired the shot and wished to protect him.

An eightsome reel was being danced when he had arrived at the hall, and the noise of the pipes and the stamping and the movement had allowed him to find an inconspicuous corner-seat among the hard wooden chairs that had been arranged along the walls of the room. He had been pleased that no one appeared to notice his arrival.

Now, as the choir was singing, he noticed that Matheson had come to the ceilidh and was sitting at the far end of the hall between Dr. Shaw and Murdoch. Surprisingly Fiona was nowhere to be seen.

The choir began another song, "Faoleag Tire-Fo-Thuinn". Listening to the lovely melody of the song about the seagulls of the islands, with its simple, classic purity of expression, MacDonald, in spite of his preoccupation with the murder of Sheena Campbell, could not help but marvel at the wealth of Gaelic songs that had been assembled in the Hebrides over the years. Based as they were on eleven different musical scales, including one of the oldest in the world, the pentatonic, they offered an extraordinary range of expression. Many of them were songs sung by folk as they worked, like the waulking songs with their strong though often irregular rhythms. More often they showed the influence of the sea which had always dominated the lives of the islesmen. There was enough material here for a book that would transcend the scholarly thesis he was supposed to be writing, a living book that could capture the spirit of the islanders and the fascination of their history. He found himself resolving that, were he to escape the net of circumstances which seemed to be tightening around him, he would begin work on that book.

While the choir was singing he noticed Fiona slip into the hall through the door that led to the kitchen. As soon as the last song was over she came across and sat in the empty seat next to him.

"I thought you had decided not to come," she remarked.

"And I thought you had done the same."

They both laughed. She said, "I was in the hall earlier but I had to go over to the hotel to fetch more bread for the sandwiches we are cutting."

"I see your father is here. Is that wise after last night?"

"Oh, he's impossible when it comes to taking care of his health! He thinks he's indestructible. But he's only making a token appearance tonight to hear the choir

125

sing. Not even he is mad enough to try dancing a reel with that shoulder."

"But your husband decided against coming?"

She seemed to hesitate fractionally before she replied, "Paul has some work to finish. He has to chair a board meeting of his company next week."

The choir had finished their performance and filed out of the hall for their reward of lemonade and cakes before they were away home to bed. MacNab, whose turn it was to pipe, went on the stage and announced that there would be one more eightsome reel before the interval.

"How adventurous are you?" Fiona asked MacDonald.

"Why do you ask?"

"I wondered whether you'd like to try your hand at one of our dances."

"Sure, why not? Out west we all come from peasant stock."

He followed her on to the floor where they joined three other couples to form a set of eight for the reel. MacDonald wondered whether he was being over-sensitive in thinking that the only reason he was accepted was because he was partnering Fiona; for Matheson, he had realized not long after arriving on Alsaig, had a special position on the island which to a casual observer might seem to be an anachronistic legacy of a feudal society but which in reality was not feudal at all. The Scots, he had soon learned, were much more democratic and had a much finer sense of equality than the English.

MacNab began to play and the ring of dancers in their set started to circle, first one way and then the other. Highland dancing was a vigorous and cheerful business on Alsaig and no one was too concerned with observing the precise and rather stilted elegance of the steps practised by country dancing societies in Edinburgh and Perth.

"You fraud!" Fiona gasped breathlessly as they whirled around. "You've danced this before!"

"I wasn't president of my university's St. Andrew's Society for nothing," MacDonald replied, grinning.

Some of the tension he had seemed to detect in Fiona's face when they had met the previous day appeared to evaporate as she danced, though she did not display the same gaiety and exuberance as most of the other dancers. She was graceful and light on her feet, but she gave the impression that the act of dancing, of performing the correct steps, required from her an intense concentration.

When the reel was over and the dancers were leaving the floor, two women came into the hall from the kitchen carrying a large urn of tea which they placed on a table that had been set up at that end of the room. Another woman, carrying a tray of cups, saucers and plates, followed them. Fiona excused herself, saying that she must go and help with the refreshments. In a short time she and the other members of the ladies' committee had filled the table with plates of sandwiches, baps filled with ham and cheese, fruit cakes and iced cakes and doughnuts. Immediately a queue began to form at the table. The refreshments offered at ceilidhs were always popular, for dancing created an appetite and most of those present had finished their tea some hours before. More importantly the refreshments, all provided by the ladies of the committee, were included in the price of the admission ticket.

MacDonald, who had cooked himself a meal before setting out for the ceilidh, did not join the queue but went instead to the bar. He had not taken a drink since the whisky Matheson had poured for him at the distillery that morning. This had not been a deliberate act of self-denial but, preoccupied with the complexities arising from Sheena Campbell's murder and the shooting of Matheson, he had forgotten to reach, as he so often did through force of habit, for the vodka bottle. He found himself wondering whether this had been what he had needed, a sense of fear, an element of menace, a challenge, to lift him from the despicable morass into which he had allowed himself to slip after the humiliation which Bette-May had inflicted on him. Then he decided that it would be an expensive cure for his personal problems if he were to finish up serving twenty years in a Scottish jail.

There were not more than half-a-dozen people in the bar. Dugald, the milkman, was serving and Murdoch was standing at the counter talking to him. Neither of their expressions changed when MacDonald came into the room and he was relieved to think that they took no interest in him. He took the whisky which Dugald poured him and went to sit in a corner of the room.

Presently all the other islanders in the bar left, trickling through into the hall to join the queue for refreshments and leaving only Murdoch and Dugald behind. Shortly after they left Darroch came into the room out of breath and plainly agitated.

"Angus, I've just been back to the hotel," he said in English and then, seeing MacDonald there, he switched to Gaelic, "Grant has gone."

"Gone? What do you mean?"

"The cellar door's open and he's no' there."

"How could that be?"

"Somebody must have opened the door and let him out. There's no other way. It was bolted on the outside."

They were speaking fast and in low voices and MacDonald had difficulty in following the conversation. What he did understand was that Darroch had looked into the cellar of the hotel shortly before seven that evening, cautiously from the top of the steps, afraid in case the keeper

130

might attack him. But Grant had been in no state to be belligerent. Still half stupefied, he could only mumble, complaining that he should not be locked up. He had done no wrong.

"He claims he drank some whisky which a camper gave him and can remember nothing more."

"There are no campers on the island just now," Murdoch pointed out.

"Well, that's what he's saying. According to him he met the man up beyond Gartness last evening. He has no idea how he came to be up on the peat moss. Swears he never drove there."

Darroch went on to explain that he had given Grant a plate of soup and some bread, together with a quarter bottle of whisky to see him through the night, and told him he would have to stay in the cellar until the police arrived the following day.

"At least he doesn't have his guns," Darroch concluded. "They're still in the boot of my car."

"He can easily get another. Did you tell him it was the American who killed the girl?"

"I did, yes."

"Then maybe it's no bad thing that he's got free."

A few minutes before midnight the ceilidh drew to a close and everyone in the hall linked arms to sing "Auld Lang Syne". It was a comparatively recent innovation at ceilidhs on Alsaig, but one which the islanders appeared to enjoy, and they sang it with a good deal more fervour than the national anthem which always followed.

During the second half of the ceilidh, MacDonald had danced three more dances with Fiona, once partnering her and Margaret MacNab in The Dashing White Sergeant, once in The Gay Gordons and once in the final dance of the evening, another eightsome reel. She also danced every other dance, each with a different partner: MacNab, Buchanan, two men whom MacDonald had only ever seen at ceilidhs and MacKenzie who owned the farm beyond Gartness.

After the national anthem, when the hall was beginning to empty, she said to him, "I've promised to drive Jessie Monro home. If you come along too, I'll drive you home afterwards."

"But she and I live at opposite ends of the island!"

"No matter." Her reply was direct and to the point and MacDonald sensed that she was not just being polite.

"Right. That will be great."

Jessie Monro had wrapped her black shawl over her head and shoulders and the three of them went out to Fiona's car. Jessie was a widow who lived on a croft between Carrabus and Ballymony. Although she admitted to eighty-two and was probably older, she still worked the croft, having refused to leave it after her husband had died. She grew oats and potatoes, but lived mainly off a handful of cows and a few sheep. In summer she would walk the cows three miles across the island to graze on common land by the western shore. She had never been known to miss a ceilidh and would dance as many dances as she could find partners for.

They drove through the village, past the distillery, towards the southern end of the island. When they came to the entrance to Tigh Geal, MacDonald realized that they would soon pass the spot by the roadside where Sheena Campbell's body had been found. He tried as he had tried so many times before, to assemble the few shadowy impressions which were all he could salvage from his memory of the night before she died. Had they walked that way together? Had he grabbed her, thrown her down in the heather when she pushed him scornfully away? Could he hear the last echo of her mocking laughter turning into a scream that ended in a choking gasp? The more he tried to picture what might have happened, such vague impressions merged with the vivid images of his imagination, until reality became inseparable from nightmare.

When they reached her home, Jessie said to Fiona, "You'll take a dram? And your man as well?"

It was not an invitation that could be refused. Jessie was living in the home she had occupied for more than 60 years, one of the Tigh Dubh or Black Houses that were once to be found all over the Hebrides, and the design of which had been evolved over the centuries to meet the primitive needs of the crofters and, at the same time, combat the weather of the outer isles. The distinctive feature of the

Tigh Dubh were double drystone walls, each four or more feet thick and a roof of thatch which was set on the inner wall, the outer wall deflecting the wind and preventing the roof from being lifted even in the strongest gales. As an added precaution the thatch was lashed down with ropes made of woven heather. At one time Jessie's house, like all the Tigh Dubh, had consisted of a single chamber some sixteen yards long and four yards wide, with a floor of hard earth which sloped from one end to the other, the crofter and his family occupying one end and the cattle the other. Traditionally they had a hearth in the centre from which the smoke of a peat fire was vented through a hole in the blackened roof. Not many years previously Jessie's house had been modernized at the expense of a benevolent government. Now it had a stone floor, a chimney and windows and had been divided into three rooms, one in which to live and one in which to sleep and a kitchen. The cows had been given a shed of their own.

Jessie led the way into the house, lit an oil lamp and then beckoned Fiona and

MacDonald in to follow her. The fire was barely smouldering and she took a peat from a stack by the hearth, threw it on and kicked the fire until a feeble spurt of flame appeared.

"A fire in October!" she exclaimed. "I must be growing old."

"And soft too," Fiona teased her.

"Aye, it's true. But when a body has no kin left she can spoil herself with a few luxuries."

MacDonald who, until he came to Alsaig, had never lived or worked in a room that was not centrally heated in winter and air-conditioned in summer, looked at the stone floor of the house, its rafters and the inner thatch of the roof blackened with smoke, its few tiny windows set well below the bottom of the roof out of the reach of the wind and sealed off from it with peat or turf in winter. He might have wondered whether Jessie was joking but he knew she was not.

The old woman fetched a bottle of Alsaig malt whisky, three glasses and a jug from a dresser that stood along one wall of the room. "I'll be away outside to get water," she said and left the room by the front door.

"Does the house not have running water?" MacDonald asked Fiona.

"No. When the government wanted to put it in Jessie refused," Fiona replied and pointed at the roof. "She said she had enough trouble keeping water out of her home without letting people pump it in."

"Where has she gone to fetch the water?" MacDonald asked suspiciously. Concern for hygiene and what he recognized as a phobia over health had been brainwashed into his thinking by the American education system.

"Better not ask," Fiona replied without smiling, and he could not be sure whether she was teasing him.

When Jessie returned, they sat around the fire and drank their whisky. When MacDonald had taken a dram up at Tigh Geal he had been pleasantly surprised at the smooth, mellow taste of what he had always considered a pungent and not very palatable whisky. Now drinking it in this humble cottage full of peat smoke out of a thick, chipped tumbler it tasted even better; almost as good as the special old whisky Matheson had given him at the distillery that morning.

"Say, this is superb!" he exclaimed. "As good as any whisky I've ever tasted."

"I told you, it's the water."

"You'll be wondering what a poor old woman like myself is doing drinking whisky, the price it is today," Jessie said. "I'll tell you. Mr. Alisdair, bless him, sends me down a bottle every month. He has never failed once, all these years since my Donald died."

"Who says we Scots are mean?" MacDonald exclaimed.

"So it's 'we Scots' now, is it?" Fiona challenged him.

"Aye," he replied, putting on a Scottish accent and holding up his glass. "I can feel my Scottish blood taking control, seeping through my veins."

"Och, the two of you waste an awful lot of time blethering," Jessie said.

Inevitably, as they drank, the conversation drifted into reminiscences of many years past and stories which gave an old woman of over eighty so much pleasure to recount. She told them of the old days when life for the people of Alsaig was little more than a struggle for survival. They were the days before and immediately after the first World War, before the growing popularity of Scotch Whisky around the world had started to bring prosperity to the island; days when the islanders lived as best they could, turning their hands to anything which might bring in a few pennies: fishing, crofting, weaving, collecting seaweed, harvesting sea birds and their eggs. But Jessie did not complain or paint a harrowing picture of the depression and poverty and the many times when she and her family had been living on the edge of starvation. Now that it was all behind her, she could look back on that life tolerantly and with good humour. What mattered to her most of all was that she still had her independence and the freedom of life on the island she loved. Fiona, who had heard all the stories before, led the old woman on, drawing the tales out one by one and adding from time to time a few words of her own.

Listening to them, MacDonald wished desperately that he could prolong not only their stay but the whole evening, that he could forget for ever the reality that awaited him tomorrow or the next day, the accusations that would be made and his own inadequate explanations. Finally it was time to go.

"We'll have to be going, Jessie," Fiona said.

At the door Jessie reached out and laid a hand on Fiona's arm. It was a gesture of affection, MacDonald realized, far more meaningful than all the polite kisses which ladies of Bearsden and Morningside placed on each other's cheeks.

"You've no call to worry over Mr. Alisdair, pet," she said and then, looking hard at MacDonald she added, "it's yourself you should be thinking of."

"I'll be all right, Jessie."

"Aye, no doubt, but you would do better with this man than the one you chose."

"That's a fine thing to say to a body," Fiona replied, smiling, "now that it's too late."

"Maybe it's too late, maybe not. We'll bide a while and see."

When they were driving away from the croft, MacDonald remarked, "Now that old lady, she's really something!"

"Don't go imagining Jessie's a sweet, sentimental old thing," Fiona warned him. "She's as tough as old boots, makes it her business to know everything, gives her opinions too freely and anywhere else but on Alsaig she would have been put behind bars long ago."

"Are you saying she's dishonest?"

"How do you suppose those mangy cows of hers produce calves year after year, even though she has never owned a bull? She takes them down at night under cover of darkness to the bulls at Ardnahoe home farm or any other farm that suits her."

"If you all know she does that, why doesn't somebody stop her?"

"We have our own ethics on Alsaig. After all, Jessie has to live."

9

AS they drove back past the distillery and through Carrabus, Fiona fell silent. MacDonald guessed that her reason for offering to drive him home was that she had something she wished to say to him and that now she was planning how and with what words she should say it.

The gale had abated slightly but was still strong enough to have made the car drift if they had been travelling on an unprotected road with a smooth surface. Ahead of them he could just make out a tiny blink of light that was the beam of a lighthouse, which stood on a small island to the north of Alsaig, flashing its warning to ships out at sea. In spite of it, more than one hundred vessels had run on to the rocks off Alsaig and been smashed to driftwood by vicious seas.

As they were approaching his cottage, Fiona suddenly asked, "Have you anything to drink in your house?"

"A bottle of vodka."

"That will do fine."

"Will you come in and have a drink then?"

"No, bring it out to the car. I'd like to drive and talk."

He did not try to dissuade her. She stopped the Volvo outside the cottage but kept the engine running as he went to fetch the bottle of vodka and two glasses. Then they drove on past the rocky point of Rubha Mor and along the coast until the road was no more than a narrow, unmade track which would finally end at MacKenzie's farm, the last habitation before the stretch of uninhabited land on the west of the island. When they were still some distance from the farm, Fiona swung the car off the road, reversed and stopped it facing the sea on a grass verge by a gap in the drystone wall that bordered the fields. Without speaking MacDonald poured two inches of vodka into each of the glasses and handed one to her. She hesitated for a moment, cradling the glass in her two hands and then swallowed a mouthful.

"Are you married, Mike?" she asked him suddenly.

"I was the last time I heard from the States."

"Does that mean your marriage is breaking up?"

"It's dead; finished. We separated months ago and my wife is getting a divorce."

"What caused the bust-up?" She asked the question brusquely, almost rudely, as though she were afraid he might resent her curiosity and refuse to answer.

"God knows. All I can say is that when things began to go wrong I blamed her, and that only made matters worse. I must have been hell to live with. Perhaps it was guilt; a belief that I had failed her."

"You felt inadequate?"

"I suppose so."

"Sexually inadequate?"

MacDonald wanted to laugh. He remembered the nights he had lain in bed with Bette-May, all the love, and later, as affection dwindled, all the lust that he had to offer her. He remembered her beautiful, athletic body, the long slim legs, the smooth, flat stomach, the inviting breasts;

a body full of promised passion. He remembered the bored, clinical way in which she had received his caresses and her obvious relief when they were done.

"No," he replied. "I wouldn't say that."

"If a man can't get sexual fulfilment at home, I suppose he has a right to look for it elsewhere."

"I doubt whether the moralists and the churchmen would agree with that thesis."

"It would be better than repressing his natural urges. Don't they say that sexual violence is usually caused by repression?"

"Possibly. I wouldn't know."

Finishing what was left of her vodka, Fiona handed him the empty glass to refill. MacDonald was starting to wonder what was the point behind her questions and what had been her motive in offering to drive him home that evening. Or perhaps there was no point, no motive. She might be just a lonely young woman, looking for company.

"I told you an untruth this evening," she remarked.

"When was that?"

"When I told you my husband had not come to the ceilidh because he had work to do. The truth is that we had a flaming row. Quarrels are hardly a novelty for us. They have decorated our marriage like sequins on a gaudy dress, but this was about the worst yet."

MacDonald could think of nothing to say except a mumbled, "I'm sorry." The break-up of his own marriage was too recent for him to be able to compose polite, meaningless platitudes about other people's marital troubles.

"Paul's company is about to go bankrupt," Fiona continued. "We're heavily in debt. The only reason he agreed to come to Alsaig was that we can live here free for a time and out of reach of debt collectors. And then I found out this morning that when he was in Glasgow a few days ago, he borrowed another £10,000 without telling me. God only knows why he needed the money—to pay off one of the many women in London who might compromise him, I suppose. Anyway when I asked him about it, he exploded."

"Most men don't like being questioned by their wives about money," MacDonald remarked.

"Paul certainly doesn't. He never did,

but he's even more sensitive now he is in financial difficulties."

"That's understandable."

Fiona turned her head to look at him. "Shall I tell you the story of our marriage?"

"If that's what you want," MacDonald replied, knowing that it was.

She had first met Paul Stokes, she told him, in the home of friends in Perthshire, not far from Loch Rannoch, to which they had both been invited to stalk deer. His brand of charm, a combination of easy informality and wit and just a hint of self-deprecation, blended with perfect manners, was one she had never encountered before and which, for that reason, she had found all the more attractive. They had met again, by arrangement this time, when she went to spend a few weeks in London, staying at the flat of an old school friend in Knightsbridge. Fiona had been impressed by Paul's apparent success in business. Had not the *Financial Times* listed him as one of the three most brilliant entrepreneurs in the City? Only after their marriage had she learnt that he owed everything to his charm and his contacts and nothing to ability. His first company, formed on a loan of several thousand pounds from an uncle and a substantial bank overdraft, had been saved from bankruptcy only when relatives and friends had joined forces to rescue it. He had formed another, and he and Fiona had lived extravagantly for a time, racing at Ascot and Goodwood, dining at the Dorchester, gambling at the Curzon House Club and dancing at whatever discotheque was the current favourite of royalty. Then quite suddenly life had turned sour. Property prices had fallen, Paul's uncle had died, friends had drifted away, no one wished to bail him out. They had moved from the flat in Eaton Square, sold the racehorses, traded in the Porsche for a second-hand Datsun.

"And since he has nothing else to blame for his failure," Fiona concluded, but without bitterness, "he blames me."

"Did he marry you because he thought that one day he'd inherit a distillery?" MacDonald could see no reason why she should have a monopoly of the intrusive questions.

"No, I don't think so. Paul's so

conceited he never even imagined that his business enterprises could fail. I suppose he just thought it might be rather smart to have a wife who owned a distillery."

"So you will inherit it?"

"Yes, when my father dies. He plans to leave a one-third share to Murdoch and the rest to me."

"And will you sell it to Thomson Distillers when the time comes?"

She answered the question obliquely. "In spite of what he said yesterday about being neutral in our family argument, Paul would certainly expect me to. That would settle his debts and give him plenty of cash to start yet another business empire."

"And you would agree to sell?" MacDonald persisted.

"What else could I do?" she asked angrily, but her anger was directed at herself. "Let Paul go to hell, stay on the island, sacrifice myself for the islanders as my father has done and drink myself into an early grave?"

"There must be other alternatives?"

He thought Fiona was going to ask him to name the alternatives but she appeared to change her mind and said, "You may as well know it was not by chance that I picked you up on the road to the village yesterday morning."

"I wondered what you might have been doing up at Gartness."

"I was waiting along the road for you to come out of your cottage."

"Why was that?"

"It was probably a rotten idea, but I thought you might be able to help me. As you can see I drink too much."

"What made you think I might be able to help?" MacDonald's immediate reaction was suspicion. Fiona's suggestion seemed so unlikely that he suspected a trap. Her drinking in the car that night seemed too contrived, as though it were a performance specially intended to convince him that she had a drink problem.

"You Americans are supposed to know about these things. Senators, film stars, baseball players, every second celebrity in the States seems to be an alcoholic these days. And didn't Alcoholics Anonymous start in America?"

"I have the impression you can control your drinking."

"God, how I wish that were true!"

The despair in her voice was not dissembled, MacDonald was sure of that. Remembering how he had noticed something oddly familiar in the expression in her eyes, he suddenly understood why. He had seen the same expression, the tense, hunted look in his own face staring back at him from a mirror every morning. Compassion and understanding replaced his doubt and suspicion.

"I'm the last person you should have come to," he said sadly.

"Why is that?"

"Since I arrived at Alsaig I haven't written a page of my thesis, I haven't finished even half a day's work. And why? Because most of the time I'm either bombed out of my mind or too hungover to care."

"Do you mean you have a drink problem?" Fiona seemed genuinely surprised.

"You'd better believe it."

"Then why have you been drinking so little this evening. And yesterday evening as well, if it comes to that? By my standards you're almost teetotal."

"That's only because something happened to frighten the shit out of me."

"What?"

"I have to stay sober if I'm to have any chance at all of proving that I didn't kill Sheena Campbell."

"Who believes you did?"

"Half the island, I guess."

He told her how he had found out from Darroch that he had been drinking with Sheena on the night before she had been murdered and that he had left the hotel with her. Then he described how Mrs. Anderson had found his blood-stained sweater hidden in the cottage. His motive for telling her about the sweater was unclear even to him. By now Mrs. Anderson had almost certainly washed the garment and, as no one else knew about it, that might well have been an end to the matter. It seemed unlikely that Fiona would be able to help him, but he wished to be completely honest with her.

When he had finished she said firmly, "You didn't kill Sheena."

"How do you know?"

"I just know, that's all."

"Does that mean you know who did kill her?"

"It's late," she replied, leaning forward to switch on the car's ignition. "I must be getting home."

MacDonald felt mildly irritated by the way she had taken refuge in what was to him a typically feminine evasion. Bette-May had been an expert in that ploy. Whenever she had felt she was losing an argument, or was in danger of having one of her many lies exposed, or did not want sex, it was too late or she was tired or she had a headache. He had expected better of Fiona.

As they drove back towards the cottage he remarked, "One thing puzzles me."

"What's that?"

"Why did your father tell Dr. Shaw that he had been shot by accident?"

"He did what?" In turning her head to stare at him she almost drove the car off the road on to the strip of grass which separated it from the rocks by the sea.

"That's what Dr. Shaw told me. If you remember, when he arrived at the house he didn't ask us how the shooting had happened, but took your father straight into his bedroom to treat the wound."

"Did Neil believe him?"

"Probably not, but if a patient told him that story he would have to accept it."

By this time they had reached the cottage and Fiona stopped the car. She kept the engine running, this time, Mac-Donald guessed, to show that she had no intention of being drawn into any further discussion on either the murder of Sheena Campbell or the shooting of her father.

"The way I figure it," he persisted, "is that your father knows who tried to kill him and is trying to protect whoever it was." Fiona only shrugged her shoulders; so he added, "Have you any idea who it might have been?"

"Hamish Grant is the only person on Alsaig who hates him."

"And why is that?"

"My father always tried to persuade Sheena not to go with Hamish." The tone of Fiona's voice made MacDonald suspect that her reply, if not actually a lie was less than the whole truth.

He stood in the wind watching the rear

lights of the Volvo, as Fiona drove away, until they disappeared around the bend in the road just before the ruins of the old distillery. They did not follow a steady course but wandered from side to side, like a drunk on the way home from a bar, and he wondered uneasily whether he should not have insisted on driving the car himself. It in no way reassured him to know that the police never took any action over car accidents on Alsaig or Kilgona unless someone was injured, and no one on the island had ever been prosecuted for driving while drunk.

The cottage, which so often had seemed lonely and uninviting when he returned to its emptiness at night, appeared to him tonight, tired and confused as he was, as a refuge, a place where he could shut himself off from the events and the people of a hostile world. All he wanted was to go inside and find oblivion in what was left in the vodka bottle and in sleep. The front door was not locked—nobody on Alsaig ever locked the door of their house—so he turned the handle and stepped into the darkness, groping for the light switch which, for some whimsical reason, had been placed not near the door but on an adjacent wall when the cottage had been modernized and electric light installed.

As the light flashed on he heard a noise behind him and turned instinctively but too late to see more than a shadowy outline of the man who had been hiding in the room waiting for him and who, before he could resist, grabbed his throat from behind with both hands. He knew the man could only be Hamish Grant.

The gamekeeper was immensely strong and he intended to kill. Even as he tried to prise open the fingers which gripped his throat, MacDonald knew he was wasting his time. He tried to conserve what air he already had in his lungs, knowing that he had only a few seconds before he became unconscious. Although in Judo and un-armed combat one was taught elaborate but effective counters to attacks from behind, there was not enough time to try one, so he took the only other counter he knew. Reaching back behind him he grabbed the man's genitals and squeezed them as hard as he could.

Grant gave a great shout of agony, released his grip on MacDonald's throat and backed away, doubling up. Mac-Donald's brain, which had begun to swirl and mist up as the grip on his windpipe had tightened, cleared and he turned to face the gamekeeper, stepping away to give himself more room in case another attack should follow.

Shaking his head and still wincing, Grant stared at him through eyes that were bloodshot with drink. His dark hair was matted and his chin unshaven, giving him the appearance of a wounded and enraged animal. Swearing obscenities, he grabbed at MacDonald again, this time from the front, reaching once more for the throat.

MacDonald was ready, balanced nicely on the balls of his feet, to execute the move he had practised so often in the gymnasium. Catching the man's right wrist and turning quickly, he threw him over his hip.

As Grant crashed to the floor, legs flying, his left shin struck the edge of the table and he shouted with pain once more. MacDonald kept a hold on his wrist and as he lay on the floor, placed his left foot firmly on his throat. Grant struggled, lashing out with his free fist, but when

MacDonald pressed down harder on his throat he stopped.

"Now hear this," MacDonald said quietly. "Whatever you may have been told, I did not kill Sheena. Do you understand that?"

Grant looked up, his stare full of stubborn hatred, but said nothing. MacDonald continued, "I shall keep you like this until you're prepared to talk about the whole matter rationally and sensibly." Again Grant made no reply so he twisted his arm until the man gasped. "Are you going to talk or do I have to bust your arm?"

This time Grant nodded, so MacDonald released him and stepped away. Slowly the gamekeeper rolled over and dragged himself to his knees, his back towards MacDonald. Then, without warning, he leapt like an animal across the room towards the fireplace, grabbed the heavy brass poker that lay there and turned, his face scarlet with exertion and rage.

"Don't be a fool man!"

"I'll kill you, you Yankee bastard!"

He came across the room, lashing out with the poker, once when he was still out of range and then again. MacDonald stepped forward inside the second blow, holding up a stiff left forearm to block Grant's arm and at the same time he kneed him in the groin. Then as Grant doubled over with pain, he struck him a chopping blow with the side of his hand across the side and back of the neck. Grant toppled sideways, fell and lay still.

Picking up a chair that had been knocked over in the fight, he sat down to regain his breath. He had not been aware of how unfit he had become after ten years of physical inactivity, but now that the shock of unexpected danger was receding, he could enjoy not only relief but self-satisfaction at the way he had survived it. Even so he was left with the problem of what he should do next. The cottage had no telephone and even if there had been one he had no idea who he could call for help.

He had thought about the problem for several minutes without finding a solution when the front door of the cottage was suddenly flung open and Murdoch came in followed by Darroch. The two of them stared at MacDonald and then at Grant as he lay stretched out on the floor and the disbelief on their faces was almost comical. An acid remark sprung to MacDonald's lips, but he realized in time that if he were to make it they would know at once that he had overheard their conversation at the ceilidh. His understanding of Gaelic had become a secret weapon which might prove very useful and he must safeguard it.

So all he said was, "He was waiting in the house, hiding, when I got home. He meant to kill me, I guess."

"The man's lost his senses," Darroch said.

"We had him locked up but he escaped."

"What's to be done with him now?"

"We will have to lock him up again," Murdoch replied promptly.

"Where?" Darroch asked.

"In one of the bonded warehouses at the distillery. He'll not get out of there."

Taking a length of cord from his pocket, Murdoch knelt down over Grant and tied his hands together securely behind his back. The keeper was beginning to regain consciousness and he moaned. With some difficulty Murdoch and Darroch pulled him to his feet, dragged him stumbling out of the cottage and pushed him into Murdoch's car which stood outside.

MacDonald watched them until they drove away and then returned to the cottage. He had some thinking to do. The timing of their arrival at the cottage not long after Fiona had left suggested that they must have been waiting along the road until she passed. Then, knowing or guessing that Grant had gone to ambush MacDonald inside the cottage, they had come to capture him, but only after they had given him enough time to carry out whatever murderous intention he had in mind. He tried to imagine what reason they could have for wanting Grant to attack him. If they were really convinced that he had killed Sheena Campbell, they had only to wait until the police arrived and arrested him. Moreover, if they had decided that Grant had not murdered Sheena, why had they locked him up? The logical explanation was that they had found out somehow that Matheson had not been shot by accident and knew that Grant had fired the bullet.

After a time he hunted in the drawer of

the kitchen table among the tools he had seen there and found a stout, wide-bladed screwdriver, a wrench and a length of wire. He was by no means certain that they would serve the purpose he had in mind, but he stuffed them into the pocket of his anorak, took the flashlight which he always kept handy for the not infrequent occasions when the island's electric power failed, went out of the cottage and set off along the road to Carrabus.

The wind was still strong but the clouds seemed higher than they had been earlier in the day, and broken in places, parting long enough from time to time to allow a shaft of moonlight to pierce the darkness briefly. Walking fast he reached the first houses of the village in not much more than 40 minutes. The one street was deserted as he expected it would be, but he trod as softly as he could, keeping in the shadow of the houses.

Before he was half way through the village, he began to get the feeling that he was being followed. Once, glancing back over his shoulder, he thought he saw a figure slipping into a gap between two houses. He stopped in the cover of a patch of shadow and waited to see if the man, if it was one, would reappear. Minutes passed and nothing happened so he dismissed the idea as a trick of his imagination and continued on his mission.

Darroch's car was standing outside the hotel, close to the wall that bordered the garden. Very gently he tried the handle of the door on the driver's side and found it was open and the ignition key was in position in the lock. It was not carelessness on Darroch's part. No one on Alsaig ever locked their car and mostly people left the ignition keys ready to switch on the engine. After all, what thief would be mad enough to steal a car when he could never get it off the island undetected? It would be recognized as he drove it on to the ferry and the police would be waiting for him by the time he reached Kilgona.

Taking the keys out, MacDonald went to the rear of the car and opened the boot. The two guns which Murdoch and Darroch had found in Grant's Land-Rover were still there, loosely covered with an old oilskin. Taking out the rifle, he saw that it was a .275 Rigby fitted with a telescopic sight. Extracting the bolt, he took the flashlight from his pocket, meaning to switch it on and wedge it pointing upright against the wheel of the car but he was saved the trouble for at that moment the clouds parted and the moon shone through. Lifting the rifle and pointing it skywards, he squinted along the barrel. There was no doubt at all in his mind now. The rifle had not been fired.

10

"YOU must have left the door open last night," Margaret MacNab told her husband.

"I'm telling you I didn't, woman. Locking the door was the last thing I did before I followed you over to the hall for the ceilidh."

"Then how could it have been opened from the outside? Look, both of the bolts are drawn back."

Mrs. MacNab pointed at the door of the shop. It had a lock with a large, old-fashioned key and two stout bolts, one at the top and one at the bottom. When MacNab had come into the shop from their living quarters at the back, to open up for business that morning, he had found the door unlocked.

"If anyone did break in, they would have taken something surely. Let's look around."

"What an idea! Who would rob the store?"

"Visitors."

"There's nobody on the island except the four staying at the hotel and a honeymoon couple from Dingwall taking bed and breakfast at the Davidson farm."

The two of them looked around the store anyway, checking each of the shelves in turn. Quite soon they learnt that MacNab was right and they had been burgled. Whoever had broken into the store had taken a bottle of whisky, a bottle of milk, a large loaf of sliced bread, a carton containing six eggs, half-a-pound of bacon, a pound of sausages, two tins of stewed steak, two tins of baked beans, six cans of beer and two packets of small cigars.

"Have you not noticed," Mrs. MacNab remarked, "that the food is all stuff that could be cooked easily over an open fire? It must have been campers."

"There are no campers on the island." MacNab enjoyed those rare occasions when he could prove his clever wife wrong. "And whoever it was who broke in without damaging the door must be an experienced thief."

"It must be Hamish Grant. He could be

living rough." It was not yet eight in the morning and the MacNabs had not heard that Hamish Grant had been recaptured after escaping from the hotel and locked up in one of the distillery warehouses.

"If it had been Hamish he'd have taken a bottle of Alsaig whisky, never a blend," MacNab replied; and then added, "I can't understand why the thief didn't go to the till. He'd have found sixty pound in cash there."

"You'll need to report it to the police when they arrive," Mrs. MacNab said.

As she was speaking, the telephone, which was fixed to the wall at one end of the shop just above the till, rang. MacNab answered it, listened to what the caller was saying and then, with not much more than a grunt of acknowledgement, put the instrument back on its hook.

"That was Gilespie from Rainich. The ferry broke from its moorings in the wind last night."

This piece of news seemed to infuriate Mrs. MacNab. "He's an incompetent fool, that Cowan. How they ever came to put him in charge of the ferry, I'll never understand! I suppose this means we'll be without a delivery for days, and us short of bread already."

"No. The vessel was beached only a short way along the shore, it seems, and no damage done. They hope to have it back in operation by this afternoon."

Buchanan was a methodical man whose life was regulated by a series of unchanging habits. As a young man at Aberdeen University he had been teased mercilessly by fellow students for the unvarying pattern of his day, the orderly neatness of his notebooks and the careful precision with which he carried out even the most trivial tasks. But when, more than 30 years previously, he had arrived in Alsaig for what was only his second teaching post, and was quite clearly destined to be his last, he had found to his surprise that the islanders neither mocked nor wished to change his way of life. Paradoxically, although they were themselves totally unable to accept the need for punctuality, or to plan any action more than a few minutes in advance, these were the qualities they admired in their schoolmaster. He was an excellent example to their children, even though their children would never profit by it, and they were proud of his reliability, his neatness in dress and appearance and his beautiful handwriting, just as they were proud of his excellent Gaelic singing.

Every morning at eight o'clock, having finished a substantial breakfast, he would walk across the small garden in front of his house to the schoolhouse which stood immediately next door. There he would begin to prepare for the day's work, setting out any books that would be needed, filling the ink-wells—for he still insisted that his charges used proper pens to write with as the only means of developing a presentable hand—placing the exercises he had corrected the evening before on the desks of the pupils and when necessary writing the lessons of the day on the blackboard. That morning he had scarcely begun these routine duties when Mike MacDonald, who knew his habits, arrived at the school.

"Tom, if it's okay by you I'd like a word with you in private," MacDonald said.

"Will it not wait?" Buchanan had a strong suspicion that he knew what

MacDonald wished to talk about. "The children will be here directly."

"If you could spare a few minutes now I'd sure appreciate it."

"Of course, Mike." Buchanan's glance at his watch was not intended to be rude but was the instinctive reaction of a man who parcelled his day out into small, economic units.

"You're the only person I can turn to for help."

What MacDonald said was true. Tom Buchanan was the only person on Alsaig with whom he had formed any relationship that resembled friendship. Their common interest in Gaelic poetry and song was the bond that had brought them together, first of all at ceilidhs in the Colville Hall. Since then MacDonald had been invited twice to the schoolmaster's home and they had stayed up long into the night talking about the legends which had inspired bards and poets hundreds of years ago. They had even drunk whisky together, for Buchanan was fond of a dram, in spite of his wife's disapproval of strong drink.

"You'll be coming to talk about Sheena

Campbell's death, I suppose," Buchanan said.

"That means you've heard people are thinking I killed her."

"Aye."

"Do you believe I did?"

"Don't be daft man! How could you kill anyone? You're a man of culture and learning, an educated man. There's no violence in you, Mike."

"As it happens, I can't prove I didn't kill Sheena. I'm not even certain in my own mind that I didn't."

"What do you mean?"

Briefly MacDonald explained that he had no recollection of what he might have done on the night Sheena Campbell had been murdered. The nagging doubts and insidious fear that he might have killed the girl had almost vanished, for he believed that Sheena must have been killed by the same person who had fired on Matheson. On an island like Alsaig it was unthinkable that there could be two unrelated violent crimes within a few hours of each other. He did not however tell Buchanan of the attempt on Matheson's life. If Matheson had decided to keep the shooting a secret, then he must have good reason for wishing to do so and MacDonald felt he should respect that wish.

"How can I help?" Buchanan asked when he had stopped speaking.

"I must find out who else on the island might have wished to kill Sheena."

"Might it not have been someone visiting Alsaig?"

"By all accounts there are only a handful of people from outside staying here at this time and none of them even seems to have known the girl."

"I still cannot see how I can help," Buchanan persisted unhappily. He was a gentle, scholarly man who had been attracted to Alsaig by the simplicity of its life and its people, and even talking of violence was repugnant to him.

"I met Sheena only two or three times and I know scarcely anything about her. You on the other hand must have seen her grow up and taught her at school. There must be something in her background or her past which would give me a clue to who might have killed the girl. People say she was having an affair with Hamish Grant."

"Affair is too strong a word. Yes, the man lost his head over her but I believe that was over. In fact I had heard he's been making a nuisance of himself with a girl from Kilgona whom Mrs. Colville has brought over to work at Ardnahoe."

"I guess there must have been other men besides Hamish."

"Oh, aye." Buchanan shook his head sadly and took his spectacles off to polish them. "Even when the lassie was still at school, there were men. It was only to be expected. Women don't keep their looks long on this island and when a man compares his ageing wife with a bonnie lass . . ." The schoolmaster spread his hands expressively.

"Has there been trouble before?"

"Nothing more serious than jealous quarrels and a few scenes. Mrs. Darroch sent her packing from the hotel, poor lass, when I doubt it was her fault."

"She did lead men on though, didn't she?"

"I suppose so. But one should not be too hard in judging the girl."

"Why not?"

"My wife would say there's bad blood

in the family but I believe we should more likely blame her unfortunate childhood. A broken home may not be so much of a handicap in Glasgow or Dundee these days, but on a small island it can cripple a child, mentally and emotionally."

"You knew her parents, then?"

"I taught them both in this school."

Sheena's mother, according to Buchanan, had been an exceptionally pretty girl, but moody and difficult, capable of great charm but also of violent tantrums. Married at an early age to a young islesman who had found work on a trawler, she had turned to drink and promiscuous sex while her husband was at sea. One day she had left her home and their six-year-old daughter without explanation and gone to live with a bookmaker in Glasgow. Less than a year later, Sheena's father had died when his ship had been lost with all hands between the Shetlands and Iceland.

"Sheena was always a strange, wee bairn," Buchanan continued. "Difficult to reach but self-possessed. I never once saw her crying."

"Was she clever?"

"No, nor stupid either, mark you. I mind the time when I once scolded her for a shoddy exercise. She looked up at me very seriously and said: 'You'll not be expecting good work from me, surely sir. After all my mother was a bastard.' To this day I've not been certain whether the wee thing knew the meaning of the word she used."

They could hear childish voices coming from the small playground in front of the schoolhouse and MacDonald, realizing that Buchanan's pupils were arriving for the day's lessons, rose to leave.

"If I were you, Mike," Buchanan said, "I'd not be too concerned by what the people here are saying."

"Why not?"

"You're a stranger, an incomer."

"So?"

"I know the people of Alsaig. They're different to the islesmen from the inner Hebrides and from islands closer to the mainland; nothing like the people of Skye where I was born. Most of the time they're kind and courteous and hospitable, but at heart they're tribal. Sheena's murder has frightened them. And when danger threatens they band together, ruthlessly, against anyone from outside. It would not surprise me if they began to accuse me of killing the lass."

Mrs. Elizabeth Colville stood looking out of the windows of the morning-room at Ardnahoe. The house, carefully placed on a hill above the rocks at the most southerly point of Alsaig and sheltered from the west winds by trees planted for that purpose, commanded a splendid view of the sea. It had been built, in an age when houses had morning-rooms as well as drawing-rooms and dining-rooms and billiard-rooms, for the father of her late husband who owned a substantial shipbuilding business on the Clyde. She had been an islander herself, born and brought up on Skye, and when her husband had taken her to honeymoon at Ardnahoe, she had been as enchanted with the house as she was with Alsaig.

The Colville family owned two-thirds of the island and almost all of the farmers and crofters were their tenants. They had purchased it long before the days when owning an island became a status symbol, and they had fulfilled their moral obligations as landowners far more conscientiously than the many English who had bought up large tracts of the Highlands at a time when Queen Victoria's liking for Balmoral made Scotland fashionable. The Colvilles had given the island a hall as a meeting place and endowed it with enough money for its upkeep. They had built a new schoolhouse, a row of six almshouses for the poor and bullied the government into installing running water, electric light and proper sanitation, and putting a surface on the one road. Almost the only enterprise they had not started or fostered was the distillery.

Bessie Colville and her husband Andrew used to holiday in Alsaig every year while he was alive, and took parties of their friends over to the island frequently throughout the year to stalk the deer and fish the loch on their estate. An invitation to a house party at Ardnahoe became highly prized in Glasgow society and even in far off London. When Andrew had died early in the 1960s Bessie had not re-married, although there was no shortage of suitors, and had moved instead to make her home on Alsaig.

She had been devoted to her husband and her way of perpetuating his memory was by continuing to invite his friends and, increasingly, the sons of his friends to be her guests at Ardnahoe. Scarcely a week passed in the shooting and fishing seasons without four or five men enjoying venison and Aberdeen Angus beef, the salmon and trout with which the loch had been stocked, the mild, but delicately flavoured cheeses, fine vintage claret and an unlimited supply of Alsaig malt whisky; only men because this was a tradition which her husband had started years before. He had never invited women to his house, not for any misogynistic reasons but as a compliment to his wife, who could thus enjoy the admiration and the flattery of all the men who came to the house without competition from any rivals.

Now as she looked out onto the water —still grey and sullen although the gale had dropped to no more than a stiff breeze —Mrs. Colville wondered how long she would be able to afford the luxury of entertaining old friends in the style to which her husband had accustomed them. The family shipyards had long since disappeared, swallowed up by larger companies struggling to survive as British ship-building dwindled inexorably away, and the income from what had once seemed gilt-edged investments made by her husband to secure her future was being eroded by inflation. Meanwhile life on Alsaig, never inexpensive since many of the necessities and all the luxuries of life had to be imported, became progressively more costly. Already she had been forced reluctantly to close up the uppermost floor of Ardnahoe as a means of economizing on fuel bills, which was why two of her guests that week had been lodged at Darroch's hotel, at her expense of course.

That morning however she had received a telephone call from Glasgow which might mean a reprieve from further economies. She might even be able to continue the hospitality which she so much enjoyed dispensing, for a few more years, perhaps even for the remainder of her lifetime. But Bessie was a good, canny Scot, brought up to mistrust unexpected good fortune, particularly when it came in the form of cash. She had decided to examine the pedigree of the apparent gift horse which was being presented to her circumspectly, and so she was not surprised to hear the sound of the door bell echoing through the hallway of the house, announcing a visitor, for this was part of her plan. Without waiting for her cook or maid to attend to it, she went to the front door and let Donald Fraser in herself.

"It's so good of you to come, Major Fraser," she greeted him.

"Delighted!"

"I would never have forgiven myself if I had allowed you to leave Alsaig without coming to Ardnahoe."

"I should have told you I was coming to the island."

"Not at all," Mrs. Colville replied as she led him into the drawing-room. "You could not be expected to remember that my late husband knew your father. It was an age ago when you were just a boy. I blame myself. I should have kept in touch. Andrew would have expected that."

What Bessie Colville was saying was to the letter true. Fraser's father had once owned a steel mill that made plates, and from time to time he had supplied the Colville shipyards. But the way in which she had greeted Fraser suggested that his father and Andrew Colville had been friends, which was by no means the truth. Colville had always treated the steelmaker with no more than a stiff courtesy, believing him to be unscrupulous and not to be trusted.

"I must confess I was surprised when you phoned me at the hotel," Fraser conceded. "It's some years since my father died and I've been away in the army of course."

"I hope you did not have to alter any of your arrangements to come and see me."

"Not at all. As a matter of fact I should have been away on the ferry this morning, but as you probably know the wretched thing isn't sailing until this afternoon."

"So I believe. That must be very annoying for you, Donald. I may call you Donald, may I not? But at least you have been able to do an old lady a kindness. There's nothing I like better than talking of old times."

They talked of the old times; of the great figures of Glasgow's commerce and industry between the wars, who were no more than names to Fraser, of the great days of Glasgow society, of the great Scottish regiments now disbanded or in decline, of shooting and fishing and sailing. It was not until Fraser stood up to leave and they were shaking hands that Bessie Colville asked him the question she had invited him there to answer.

"I'm so glad you came, Donald, and your visit has been timeous in more ways than one, for you may be able to do an old woman a service."

"How is that, Mrs. Colville?"

"I need advice. The solicitors who have been looking after my affairs have been absorbed into a larger firm and they no longer give me the personal attention they once did. I'm an old lady and I know nothing of the law, so I must have lawyers who will be patient and understanding and explain things in a way that is not too complicated."

"Yes, I can see that," Fraser said, unaware of how patronizing his remark sounded.

"So I've decided to change my lawyers. Now as a businessman you can surely advise me. You must know of a good firm of solicitors you can recommend. What firm does your company use, for instance?"

"I would never recommend them," Fraser replied. His hostility towards Thomson Distillers for the way they had treated him was spreading to include any firm or individual who had ever worked for the company in any capacity.

"But who are they?" Mrs. Colville persisted.

"Webster, Long and Henry. But if I had to appoint solicitors again I would never choose them. Why not try Stewart, Barclay and Hedley? They have served my family with tolerable efficiency for a good number of years."

Mrs. Colville waited until he had left the house and was starting his car which he had left standing outside the front door. Then she went to make a telephone call.

11

"HOW is the book coming along?" Matheson asked MacDonald.

"Slowly, I guess. Too slowly."

"You must have caught island sickness."

"What the heck's that?"

"A complaint which is supposed to infect mainlanders when they come to live in the isles."

"That's a gag isn't it?"

"Not at all. Take the whisky distilleries on the island of Islay, for example. Almost all of them are run by managers from the mainland, and the companies who own the distilleries will never send a manager over for more than three years at the very most. In that time they believe he will have been corrupted by our leisurely way of life, by our informality and lack of self-deception. So at the end of three years the man is taken back to the mainland for rehabilitation."

"If that's true," MacDonald said

laughing, "then there must be a word in Gaelic for 'Mañana'."

Matheson looked puzzled. "Mañana?"

"It's a Spanish word. Literally it means 'tomorrow', but it's used in a wider sense meaning 'why do today what you can put off till tomorrow?'"

"No." Matheson shook his head. "We'd not have any use in Alsaig for an expression of such urgency."

MacDonald realized that the old man was gently teasing him. He had come to the distillery because he had promised the old man he would, but he could not help feeling that it was a quixotic gesture and one which he might regret. Before the day was over the police would be arriving from Kilgona and he should be preparing answers for the questions they would certainly ask him. Although by this time he had convinced himself, or almost convinced himself, that he had not killed Sheena Campbell, the police would need to be convinced as well. By diligent questioning in and around the village, he might still have been able to find someone who had seen the girl after she had left him on the night before her murder, walking away from Carrabus perhaps on her way to meet another man. And now that he had discovered it had not been Hamish Grant who had fired at Matheson, he should be making some effort to establish who had.

They had strolled through the distillery together, stopping from time to time to watch some process or operation, the turning of the malt, a man checking a sample of grist from the mill to see whether it contained the right proportions of flour and husk, the stillman entering the quantity of wash that had just been charged into the still. MacDonald sensed that Matheson would walk around the plant like that every morning, not because he was checking on the way the men were doing their work, not because he wished to interfere or liked to think he was supervising it, but because he loved the place and he loved whisky and would never tire of seeing it being properly made.

"Some people say that the islanders are lazy and feckless," Matheson remarked as they were walking. "But it just isn't true. Here on Alsaig we have our own way of doing things, but when they are done they are done properly. And if it takes a little

186

more time, well, time is one of the few things which we have in abundance."

"One can't argue with a philosophy like that."

"I love the folk of Alsaig. They are proud and independent and entirely honest. And when you get to know them you'll find they have a grand sense of humour."

"But how does one get to know them?"

"Oh, it takes time, I'm aware of that. They're shy and reserved and there's nothing they like better than deflating a pompous stranger. Did I ever tell you the story of the time when we were visited by the Chancellor of the Exchequer?"

"No, tell me."

"It was years ago, when Margaret MacNab's father, old Duncan MacDowell, owned the store. The Chancellor had come over on a week's holiday and was staying at the hotel. He was a Scot named Young, one of those prissy lawyers from Edinburgh who preferred politics to hard work."

Matheson told MacDonald the story of how the Chancellor had strolled down from the hotel to the store one morning and bought a few odds and ends, some tobacco, a newspaper, a paperback novel and a packet of pipe cleaners. When they were being wrapped up for him he found he had come out of the hotel without his wallet. Explaining this to Duncan MacDowell, he had asked if he might take his purchases with him and come back later in the morning to settle the bill.

MacDowell had looked at him severely over his spectacles and then said, "Ah, Mr. Young, that may be the way you run the country, but we don't do business like that here on Alsaig."

MacDonald smiled, realizing now where Margaret MacNab had inherited her own waspish sense of humour. He followed Matheson out of the stillhouse and they crossed towards the distillery manager's office. This would be another part of the old man's daily routine: a walk round the distillery followed by a dram.

As they went into the office the telephone rang. Matheson picked up the instrument, listened to what Cathy on the switchboard in the room next door had to say and then placed one hand over the mouthpiece, saying to MacDonald, "This may take a little time, Mike."

"Would you like me to wait outside?"

"No need for that. But be a good fellow and pour us both a dram. You'll find whisky in the cupboard there." He pulled a key from his waistcoat pocket and slid it across the desk. "It's the only door in Alsaig that's ever kept locked. You can fill the water jug in the washroom next door."

Taking the key MacDonald crossed the room and opened the cupboard. The top three shelves were stacked full of sample bottles of whisky similar to those he had been shown on his previous visit to the distillery, and filled with samples drawn from different distillations and from different casks of whisky over the years. On the middle shelf stood two cut-glass decanters full of whisky, about a dozen cut-glass tumblers and several unopened bottles of Alsaig malt whisky. The bottom three shelves were piled high with an assortment of articles, no longer used but which no one had been strongminded enough to throw away: old account books dating back to the early years of the century, a set of distiller's beads used to measure the strength of spirit before the invention of the hydrometer, an old brass inkwell, an ancient flintlock pistol, a shallow silver quaich, the traditional loving-cup of the highlands and islands, a set of four battered copper jugs, graded in size.

A little whisky had been spilt on the middle shelf of the cupboard, perhaps when someone had been refilling one of the decanters. Looking around the lower shelves for something which he could use to mop it up, MacDonald saw what he thought was a pale pink duster or piece of rag, which had been thrust into a corner of the bottom shelf. Bending down to pull it out, he saw that it was neither a duster nor a rag but a pair of woman's flimsy panties.

Meanwhile Matheson was listening to what Bessie Colville had to tell him, for it was she who had phoned him. Although they met only infrequently, they were old friends, bound by the common bond of their love for Alsaig. Mrs. Colville would have liked them to see more of each other and to invite Matheson to her home, but she felt that even from a mature widow in her late fifties, such invitations might be construed as forward behaviour. Matheson for his part supposed she would be too busy entertaining her wealthy friends from Glasgow to bother much about an old-fashioned, plain-speaking distiller.

"Alisdair, is it true that young Donald Fraser came here to try and buy your distillery?" Mrs. Colville asked.

"Yes, but how did you know?"

"Dugald told one of my girls when he brought the milk."

"Good God!" Matheson exclaimed. "Is nothing secret on this island?"

Bessie laughed. "No, nor sacred either. I take it you refused his offer."

"Of course. He came on behalf of his employer, an American named Jake Thomson. Why do you ask?"

"My solicitors phoned me yesterday to find out whether I wished to sell a parcel of land on the island, most of Cnoc na Moine and part of the south slopes of Beinn Laimsdearg, taking in Loch Crois and stretching down towards the sea at Smallaig."

"Who wants to buy the land and why?"

"My solicitors had not been told the name of the would-be purchaser. It seems they have been approached by another firm of solicitors who said that their client wished to remain anonymous but that he wanted the land only for shooting and would give an undertaking not to build on it."

"What was the price offered?"

"More than generous. Just a little too high in fact. It set my nasty suspicious mind working, so I invited young Donald Fraser round to Ardnahoe this morning."

"Go on."

"I learned that the firm of lawyers who made the offer to my people, Webster, Long and Henry, also represent Thomson Distillers."

"Good God!" Matheson exclaimed. "They're after the distillery's water supply!"

"Obviously. Devious isn't it?"

Matheson swore loudly and then remembered it was a lady to whom he was speaking. "I'm sorry, Bessie, but that really is too much! Is this what business ethics have been reduced to?"

"You and I have lived too long,

Alisdair. We are both prehistoric animals stumbling about in a world that has outgrown us, helpless and at the mercy of these slick, young hustlers with their lethal weapons."

"Thank heavens you were astute enough to guess what they were up to. Bless you, Bessie." It never even occurred to Matheson to ask Mrs. Colville whether she was going to accept the offer that had been made for her land.

"There's a lesson here for both of us, Alisdair. We both know you've had the water rights on Cnoc na Moine for longer than any of us can remember, but there has never been any recognition of the fact on paper. Gentlemen's agreements are valueless when there are no gentlemen left. I could drop dead tomorrow."

"There's no fear of that, my dear. You'll outlive me and my heirs too, I shouldn't wonder."

"Maybe, but we must still look after the future. I've just spoken to my lawyers, instructed them to tell the Americans to go jump in a lake, or should it be a loch, and then to draw up papers assigning the water rights to your distillery in perpetuity."

"How much do you want for them? There will have to be a payment."

"You and I will work something out." Mrs. Colville paused. "Look, Alisdair, come round and lunch with me the day after tomorrow and we'll talk about this. Lunch will be best, for my guests will be out stalking and we'll have time for a long chat." The invitation to lunch had been an inexplicable impulse, but now that it had been made and accepted, Bessie was pleased she had given in to it.

Putting the phone down, Matheson picked up the whisky that had been placed in front of him. MacDonald had poured the dram and also found the water jug which he had filled from a tap in the small washroom next to the office. Busy with this chore, he had not been following Matheson's conversation with Mrs. Colville.

"Do you remember my saying when you were up at the house the other night that Donald Fraser's company was trying to buy the distillery?" Matheson asked him.

"Yes, and you said you had refused to sell."

"They are trying to get it another way,

using a ploy which would do credit to the dirty tricks brigade."

"What's that?"

Matheson explained that the distillery's water supply came from a burn flowing down from the hill behind it, and that the right to use the water had never been legally assigned to the company by the owners of the land. If Thomson Distillers acquired the land, and therefore the water rights, they would be in a position either to cut off the water or to tamper with it in some way. They might for example plant trees all over the hillside, which would seriously cut down the amount of water available, since trees in the first years of their growth drew a great deal of water from the land.

"By doing that they could to all intents and purposes put us out of business," Matheson concluded.

"Couldn't you find another source of supply?"

"We could use water from the island's piped supply or perhaps run some down from the other side of Beinn Laimsdearg. There's no shortage of water on Alsaig.

But that would change the nature of our whisky completely."

"Does water really make all that difference?"

"Indeed it does and I'll tell you a story to prove it."

The story was about a Glasgow firm named Jardine's which at one time had acted as agents for Alsaig distillery, selling its whisky to other companies on the mainland. Some years previously Matheson's father, dissatisfied with the performance of Jardine's had taken the agency away. To get their revenge, Jardine's had decided to build a distillery on the island which would take away much of Alsaig's business. They had built a distillery which in every respect was an exact replica of Matheson's, copying all the machinery and in particular the copper pot stills, in shape and size, to a fraction of an inch. Even so, although the new distillery used the same peat, and drew its water from a source on Beinn Laimsdearg only a few hundred yards away from Cnoc na Moine, the whisky it produced was totally different in flavour and character. It could not compete with Alsaig malt, got few orders from the big blenders and, handicapped by the costs of making whisky on an island, the distillery failed and Jardine's went into bankruptcy.

"The reason for their failure was the water," Matheson concluded. "As I told you before it's the water we use that makes our whisky unique."

"If Thomson Distillers want a distillery so badly," MacDonald remarked, "couldn't they build one elsewhere in Scotland?"

"When they began moving into the Scotch Whisky trade they bought two on Speyside and another not far from Glasgow, but they are all doing badly. The Scotch Whisky establishment has ganged together to keep them out. The big blending firms will not buy their whisky to use in their brands and Thomson does not have enough resources to make and launch a worthwhile brand of his own."

"Why are they against Thomson? There are other foreign companies in the Scotch trade, aren't there?"

"Certainly. Twenty years ago, or even ten, he would have had no difficulty in getting a foothold in the trade. A number of other foreign companies did: Canadian, North American, French, even the Spaniards. Then we Scots realized what they were doing and we closed ranks to keep any more intruders out."

"What were they doing?"

"Debasing our national drink. Some of the large foreign companies are merely pedlars of booze on an international scale. They have no real interest in distilling Scotch Whisky any more than vodka or rum or cheap brandy. It's all just liquor to them and profit is their only yardstick. They take no pride in keeping up the quality of their whisky and will do anything to cut production costs."

"And the Scottish firms are afraid Thomson will do the same?"

"Yes. So they are keeping him out. Of course if he could get hold of my distillery the whole situation would change."

Matheson explained that Alsaig malt whisky was unique. Not everyone liked its strong, peaty flavour and many people would not drink it unblended as a single malt, but it was universally recognized as supreme among the whiskies of Scotland for blending. As a result all the great brands of Scotch on sale throughout the world, the brands on which the international reputation of Scotch had been built, each contained a little Alsaig malt.

"So I don't really have to sell our whisky," Matheson said. "Year after year our order book is full, our distilling programme completed within a week or two of the season starting."

"And if Thomson gets hold of Alsaig," MacDonald remarked, "the other companies will have to do business with him."

"Exactly. In order to get hold of Alsaig malt they'll be forced to let him have some of their whisky in exchange. Almost all of the distilleries on the mainland are owned by the large blending firms and Jake will have access to all the other fine malts to produce a blend of his own. He will be a force in the trade."

"He must want that pretty badly. That business of trying to grab your water was a bit of a lowdown trick."

"Jake Thomson is used to getting what he wants. Being refused drives him mad."

"I take it he was not able to buy the land from which you draw your water?"

"No. Mrs. Colville who owns it knows that he's trying to force my hand and make me sell the distillery."

"Then don't you suppose he'll make another try to get what he wants?"

"What do you mean?"

MacDonald looked the old man squarely in the face. The people of Alsaig prided themselves on their plain speaking, so they should not take offence at plain questions. "Why did you tell Dr. Shaw that you had been shot by accident, Mr. Matheson?"

"That damned quack! He has no business to repeat what I told him!"

"It was because you believed Fraser tried to kill you, thinking that if you were dead your daughter would sell the distillery, wasn't it?"

"Something like that I suppose."

"Then if they tried to kill you once won't they try again?"

12

ALEXANDER CAMPBELL lived in a small house on the inland side of the street that ran through Carrabus, only a few doors away from Mrs. Buie's post office. The house, like several others in the village, had been built by the distillery company, for until he had retired several years previously, Campbell had worked for Matheson. Now as a pensioner he not only lived in the house for a nominal rent, but was entitled to his dram of whisky every day. Until arthritis and failing eyesight prevented him leaving the house, he would walk up to the distillery every morning with the other dozen or so pensioners where they would be given a generous measure, the best part of half a gill, of whisky. Now one of the other pensioners would collect it for him and bring it back to his house in a bottle. About twice a week would come with the bottle a present from Matheson himself, usually an ounce of tobacco.

So when he heard the front door of the house opening that morning, he assumed it was his friend with the dram, the drinking of which was his main pleasure of the forenoon. But it was a woman's voice which called out.

"May I come in, Sandy?"

"Aye, of course, Miss Fiona. Come in and sit you down."

She was still Miss Fiona to him and he recognized her voice as he would have recognized the voices of almost everyone on the island. It was an ability on which he found he was having to rely more and more as familiar faces became blurred outlines. Fiona came into the front room carrying a basket covered with a tea-cloth.

"I've brought you a few things, Sandy; a loaf which Annie just baked this morning and one or two other bits and pieces that may come in handy."

"There was no call for you to do that, Miss Fiona." Sandy knew, although she had not said so, that there would be a quarter-bottle of whisky in the basket.

"I know that, but I wanted to. There's one of Annie's black puddings, too, and you know how good they are. I'll take the basket through into the kitchen and unpack it directly." Fiona sat down in an armchair facing his old rocker and loosened the scarf which was tied over her hair. "How are you managing, Sandy?"

"Well enough, Miss, thank-you. Mrs. Reid from next door comes in every morning, and my sister Ellen, whose husband has the croft down beyond Ballymony, has promised to clean the house for me once a week."

"Will you not be moving to stay with her then?"

"No. A man is better on his own."

"We were all so upset and shocked, up at Tigh Geal, when we heard about poor Sheena."

"Aye, Miss. It was a terrible thing that happened."

Campbell had loved his grand-daughter but he could speak of her death without emotion. Fiona was not surprised. The old man had lived on Alsaig all his life, never once visiting the mainland nor even neighbouring Kilgona, and sudden death and bereavement were as much a part of life on Alsaig as solitude and privation. Sandy's father and his grandfather before him had both drowned at sea, lost when one of the small fishing boats in which they worked to secure a precarious livelihood had been swallowed without trace by the mountainous waves of a sudden Atlantic storm. He himself had been spared the necessity of going to sea by being given a job at the distillery as it expanded, but his son, too restless to work on land, had signed on as crew to a trawler and been drowned as well. Sandy, like so many of the islanders, had been conditioned to an uncomplaining acceptance of misfortune and sorrow.

"She was a good lass," he added. "We were never short for anything. I don't know how she managed, with the little money she earned and my pension, and she only eighteen, but she always found money to buy the things we needed and more besides. I mind the time when she went over to Kilgona and brought me home the wireless. It's been a great comfort to me."

Fiona looked at the radio which stood on a table close to Campbell's chair. It was a four-band set with a built in cassette player which must have cost at least £30, and she found herself wondering where Sheena could have found the money to pay for it. There was little employment for a young girl in Alsaig and Sheena had not settled in any occupation, drifting from one part-time or casual job to another, waitress at the hotel, home help to an elderly farmer and his wife, even modelling for an artist who had hired an empty cottage on the island the previous summer and had then almost drank himself to death. Matheson had promised her the job of clerkess at the distillery when in due course Cathy retired in a year or so, but now she would never live to enjoy it.

"Have you any idea who might have attacked her, Sandy?" Fiona asked. For some reason she found herself unable to talk of murder.

Campbell shook his head. "No, Miss Fiona. People seem to believe it was the American who has the cottage up by Gartness."

"Did she seem all right when you last saw her? Was anything bothering her?"

"Nothing at all. She gave me my tea and left something for my supper. Then she went to her room and prettied herself as she always did when she was going out. Oh, she was happy enough, chatting away to me from her room and humming. Just girlish things, you know."

"What time did she go out?"

"At around seven I should say. And she sounded fine when she came home again, although I never saw her."

Fiona stared at the old man, wondering whether she had misheard him and if not whether he realized what he was saying. The memory of an old man could some- times become confused.

"Then she came back home that evening?"

"Oh, aye. I had not been long in my bed."

"What time would that have been, Sandy?"

"Around midnight I should say. I'm not one for going to my bed early, Miss. Old people need little sleep."

"You're sure she came back? You could not have been mistaken?"

"Oh, no. She called out to me, said she had to be going out again but would not be long and had only come home to change. There's a fine thing for you! Changing her clothes in the middle of the night, but then she liked to dress up, our Sheena. Then before she left she called out again, 'That's me away, Grandad.' Those were the last words I heard the poor wee thing speak."

Fiona listened to what he was saying with a feeling of despair, for it seemed only to confirm the dreadful suspicion that had been haunting her ever since she had heard of Sheena's death. She said to Campbell, "Now is there anything else you need, Sandy? Anything I can bring you."

"No, Miss, thank-you. But there's one thing Sheena would have liked."

"What's that?"

"The poor bairn admired you so much, Miss Fiona; said she would like to grow up to be like you. She would have liked you to take something of hers, as a keepsake."

"I couldn't do that Sandy."

"Look in her room and see if you can find something, Miss, please. Just a wee bauble. She never had much, poor lass, but I ken well she would like you to take something. And what's to be done with her things anyway?"

To please the old man Fiona went

upstairs to the bedroom which had been Sheena's. It was a small room at the back of the house, furnished with inexpensive wooden furniture painted a bright yellow, with an orange rug on the linoleum and orange curtains. In general the room was neat and tidy except for signs showing that someone had changed there in a hurry. A pair of red slacks and a frilly pink blouse lay on the bed where they had been flung, and jars and tubes of make-up had been left on the dressing-table—lipstick, eye shadow and a bottle of perfume. Fiona had often seen Sheena wearing the slacks and blouse at ceilidhs and she wondered what had made her come home at midnight to change into something which she must have thought was smarter or more practical. The perfume was L'Air du Temps and she knew what a half ounce bottle cost; for once in Bond Street, on a quixotic impulse, Paul had rushed into a shop and bought her one.

She opened the two drawers of the dressing-table. One contained handkerchiefs and scarves, and in the other she found a flat box which had once held biscuits but which Fiona had evidently used as a jewellery box. Some of the pieces were ordinary enough; a Highland brooch in the form of a thistle with stones from the Cairngorms, glass bangles of the type which had been popular a year or two previously, two rings crudely made and set with semi-precious stones gathered from the beaches of Alsaig. Fiona remembered that two summers ago a young couple had come and lived for a time in a caravan on the island and made jewellery which they had tried to sell to the island folk, without much success. What surprised her was to find a gold bracelet, a gold watch and a string of pearls in a box which carried the name of a well-known firm of jewellers in Glasgow. She looked in the drawers of a chest in which the dead girl had kept her clothes and found among the jumpers and skirts and jeans a lambswool twin-set of jumper and cardigan still unopened in its cellophane wrapping.

There was no way that Sheena could have afforded to buy the jewellery and the twin-set from the money she earned or her grandfather's pension. What seemed even stranger was that the pearls and the bracelet and the twin-set were not the kind of things which a young girl would wish to wear, and Fiona could never recall seeing Sheena wearing them. She wondered whether they might have been presents from an older man of more conservative tastes. On the other hand it was possible that to Sheena that kind of jewellery and those clothes were symbols of fashionable life and wealth and security which she hoarded, even though she would never wear them.

She was putting the twin-set back in its place and tidying the other clothes in the drawer when she came across a packet of letters. After a moment's hesitation she opened one of the letters, reluctantly, because she had no wish to pry into a dead girl's secrets. But if there was anything to be learnt from the letters which might suggest who had killed Sheena, she felt she should know it.

The letter was written on notepaper with the name of the Alsaig Hotel printed on top and she saw at once that it was from Archie Darroch. Written in a rounded, immature hand, the letter itself was immature and childish, a mixture of sentiment and lewd suggestiveness.

"How I long to fondle your breasts," Darroch had written and again: "I can't wait to get my hands on your lovely little bottom!"

There was more in the same vein in the other letters, some of it maudlin, some of it openly obscene. Fiona was astounded to think that a middle-aged man could have been so infatuated and so indiscreet. She put the letters back where she had found them, reluctantly again, but this time because she was tempted to destroy them and save the foolish Darroch the trouble they would undoubtedly cause him when they were found by Sandy Campbell's sister or some other relative. She preferred not to imagine why Sheena had kept them. They were not the kind of letters a young girl would treasure, and she did not like to believe that Sheena had been hard enough and mercenary enough to have kept them knowing that they would give a hold over the hotel owner.

After taking one of the rings from the biscuit tin, she went downstairs and showed it to Campbell who said, "She would be glad you chose that, Miss Fiona. It was one of her favourites."

"What will you do with the rest of Sheena's things, Sandy?"

"My sister will take care of that. I suppose she will be giving them to some of the other young girls on the island."

"You should have some of them sold. She has some nice jewellery."

"I'd not like to take the money, Miss Fiona."

"I can understand that, Sandy, but why not use it to give her a nice funeral?"

"Aye, perhaps I might do that."

She left the old man thinking about her suggestion and knowing it appealed to him. Funerals were an important part of the social life of Alsaig, and by giving his grand-daughter a fine send-off, with the choir singing in the kirk and lots of food and whisky to follow, he might be able to restore some of the respect which the poor girl might have lost among the folk of the island in her short life.

After leaving his house, Fiona drove through Carrabus, past the distillery and along the road to Ballymony. She wanted time to think about the implications of what Sandy had told her and of the letters she had seen. At home there would only be

212

Paul and in all probability another bitter quarrel, for she knew her father was meeting Mike MacDonald at the distillery. MacDonald would be coming to lunch and before then she must decide how much, if anything, she would tell him of what she had learnt that morning.

Beyond the distillery and the turning which led to Tigh Geal, the road swung towards the south-west, following the curve of the coastline. She drove on past Jessie Monro's house and some other crofts, and past what had always seemed to her the rather pretentious drive to Mrs. Colville's house, Ardnahoe. After rounding the most southerly point of the island, the road veered gradually towards the north-west until it reached the flat, featureless land around the bay at Smallaig. There it stopped, petering out without warning into a track that had once led to more crofts but which was long ago abandoned and was now overgrown with tufted, spiky grass. Stopping the Volvo, she got out and began walking along the edge of the long, deserted stretch of beach.

That morning she had woken with a feeling which still persisted, that she had reached a crisis, a turning-point in her life. What precise form that crisis would take she did not know, but she knew she must prepare herself to meet it. If a decision had to be made then she was determined that it would not be another of the hasty ill-considered decisions, later to be regretted, which she could see stretching back along her life like the unsightly heaps of flotsam on the beach beside her.

It was for this reason that she had not taken the drink which usually began her day at ten in the morning or even earlier. She had wanted it and still did, needing the comforting shock of the taste on her tongue and in her throat to dispel the grotesque feeling of unreality, the feeling she experienced every morning that her mind had been separated from a body over which she no longer had control, and the trembling, illogical fear that they might never be united again. But, as she well knew, it would not have stopped at one drink; and after two or three the senses would be dulled, the judgement impaired to a point when any decision, even if she had the strength of mind to make one, would be suspect.

Not long previously she had been sent, anonymously, a pamphlet published by a caring organization on the dangers of problem drinking. Before tearing it up in a fit of indignation, she had read a paragraph or two which had included a reference to the work of Alcoholics Anonymous and its philosophy of "one day at a time". Alcoholics were advised not to think of the future but to fight the battle to stay abstinent day by day. Today, Fiona had decided, she would modify that strategy, fighting temptation one drink at a time until whatever crisis she had to face was past, whatever decisions she had to make had been made.

Ahead of her, on the machair, the strip of grassland which separated the sea from the moorland, a few cows, perhaps those belonging to Jessie Monro, were grazing. Although the islanders thought of the machair as grass, it grew not so much grass as flowering plants: clover, buttercups, daisies, speedwell, dandelions, harebells, wild thyme, small wild pansies and scores of others. With autumn coming few flowers were to be seen but Fiona remembered with a sudden pang of nostalgia the times when as a child she would drink a glass of the milk that Jessie gave her, milk from cows that had grazed on the machair in June and July and which for that reason had a sweet taste of flowers.

It was a day for nostalgic memories. Further along she came across a small herd of wild ponies. Dun coloured, with a darker stripe along their backs, they were smaller and hardier than ponies found on the mainland of Scotland. Legend had it that they were descendants of horses that had swum ashore when one of the galleons of the Spanish Armada, sailing round Scotland to escape the pursuit of the English fleet, had been wrecked on the rocks at the northern point of Alsaig.

Seeing them Fiona remembered how as a girl she would come with other children to chase the ponies, hoping to catch and to ride and to break the wild creatures, whose forefathers Phillip II had dreamed would bear conquerors in armour carrying lances and pennants proudly through the streets of London. They had never caught a single pony and would end by picking the most colourful of the wild flowers that grew in the machair, or in summer by bathing from the long, flat beaches.

Recollections of her childhood brought another memory, vague and shadowy, that had been haunting her ever since she had heard that Sheena Campbell had been found murdered. Fiona had been a tiny bairn at the time, not much more than three years old, unhappy because the mother who had given her love and comfort was no longer by her side and not yet understanding that she was dead. One night she had been woken by the noise of shouting and banging and a scream from somewhere in the house below her bedroom. Frightened she had lain in bed, trembling, and then crept out of the room and on to the landing to peep over the banisters.

Even now she could not be certain of what she had seen and not understood: a woman from the village with bruises on her cheeks and a bloody mouth, bursting from her father's study and turning to shout abuse at him; her father, leaning unsteadily against the door post, white with rage.

Now, thinking of what Sandy Campbell

had told her, and picturing Sheena coming home to change and then going out again afterwards, she shuddered as the memory was suddenly frighteningly alive.

13

"**P**EAT," Matheson said, throwing a block of it on the fire in the drawing-room, "is the greatest asset this island has. That and the people who live here of course."

"Most of the Western Isles have peat, don't they?" MacDonald asked.

"Yes. But whisky is made only on a handful of them. It is the nature of the peat as well as of the water we use, which flows down from the peat moss on the hill, that gives Alsaig whisky its unique flavour."

The two men were in the drawing-room with Paul Stokes, waiting for Fiona to return home so they could begin lunch. Stokes had said no more than a word or two of greeting when Matheson and MacDonald had arrived from the distillery and had scarcely spoken since, seeming moody and preoccupied. MacDonald wondered whether he was still brooding over his previous day's quarrel with his wife.

"Do you know that when the Japanese started trying to imitate Scotch whisky, they even imported peat from Scotland?"

"But they manage without it now?"

"Yes, because we, bloody fools that we are, allow malt whisky to be shipped to the Japanese in bulk. By blending it with the spirit they make, they are able to produce a palatable whisky which one day, no doubt, will be stealing our export markets, just as their cars have ruined our motor industry."

"Every house on Alsaig seems to burn peat," MacDonald remarked. "I've seen the quantities you cut from your peat moss for the distillery. How long will the supply last?"

"We know the answer to that too," Matheson replied, sniffing contemptuously. "Some geological nut was sent round Scotland by the Highlands and Islands Development Board to work it out. He calculated that if the population of Alsaig remains stable, and we don't increase the amount of whisky we distil, we've enough peat for 1,681 years. So it should see me out at least."

"Where on earth is Fiona?" Stokes asked suddenly.

"I have no idea."

"Going off like that and not saying when she'll be back. She should have more consideration."

"You did exactly the same thing yesterday morning, but nobody complained."

Matheson's tone was in no way accusing or provocative, but MacDonald could sense the latent hostility between the two men. This, he supposed, might well be a factor in the quarrels between Stokes and his wife.

He and Matheson talked a little longer about the peat on Alsaig and the way it had been formed over thousands of years from compressed vegetation, and presently they heard the sound of a car pulling up outside the house. When Fiona came into the room, she seemed different to him. The reason for this, he decided, must be the colour in her cheeks which were usually so pale and he wondered if she had been out walking. It also struck him, for no very good reason, that she might have been with Fraser.

"Annie will be after your hide," her father told her. "She's been complaining already that her steak pie is ruined."

"I'm sorry."

"You just have time for a quick drink and then we'll go in."

"No, I won't have a drink thanks."

Matheson looked at her with curiosity but made no comment and they went in to lunch. The first part of the meal passed off uneventfully enough, with MacDonald answering Matheson's questions about the origins of place names on Alsaig and other islands. Ballymony, he explained, was a purely Gaelic name, derived from "Baile" a town or village and "Mhonaidh" meaning moorland. Names ending in "dale", on the other hand, were mainly Norse, like Margadale on the island of Islay which came from the Norse words "Mergr" meaning narrow and "Dalr", a valley or glen. The proportion of Norse to Gaelic names was much higher in the outer Hebrides than in the islands to the south, partly because they were further from the mainland and therefore less susceptible to

222

Gaelic influence after the Norsemen had settled on them, but also because the period of Norse rule had been much shorter in islands like Islay and Mull.

As they were nearing the end of the meal Stokes said to Fiona, "By the way I shall have to go to Glasgow on business again."

"When?"

"I'm not certain yet; possibly tomorrow but more likely the day after. It will be all right if I take the Volvo, I suppose?"

"It's father's car," Fiona said briefly.

"Of course you can take it," Matheson said. "Fiona will be able to manage with the Datsun while you're away and when I drive it will have to be in the little Renault, because with my shoulder I shall only be able to manage an automatic."

"You're not going to be mad enough to drive, surely?" Fiona exclaimed.

"Only along to Ardnahoe. Bessie Colville has invited me to lunch with her the day after tomorrow."

"Then I'll drive you there."

"You'll do no such thing," her father said firmly. "You know I can't abide being driven by a man let alone by a girl. I'll be able to manage the Renault well enough."

"Are you sure?" Stokes asked.

"Of course."

"You'll be bringing back another tarpaulin, I suppose," Fiona remarked to her husband with a weary sarcasm. "That's why you need the Volvo."

"As a matter of fact, I shall be taking the one I bought on my last trip back to those crooks who sold it to me. It's a great deal smaller than the dimensions which I specified quite plainly to them, and of a very poor quality as well."

"Paul is experimenting with growing tomatoes in an old greenhouse at the bottom of the garden," Matheson explained to MacDonald.

"The greenhouse is almost a ruin," Stokes said. "The glass on one side of the roof was shattered when a tree fell on it a year ago. In the spring we will be able to bring a glazier over from Kilgona and have it repaired, but in the meantime I plan to cover the broken part with a tarpaulin."

"Who will eat all the tomatoes you grow?" MacDonald asked.

"We will be able to sell them to the

hotel and to MacNab. But we need not confine ourselves to growing tomatoes. I suggested them to start the experiment, but next year we might try peaches, tropical fruit, avocados, a whole variety of things."

The main interest of the experiment, Stokes explained, lay in how the greenhouse would be heated. At present it had a boiler fed with anthracite, but he planned to use waste heat from the distillery, pumping it up across the road and through the copse around the house. Distillers on the mainland were already using their waste heat in greenhouses and even for fish farming.

Fiona had taken no part in the discussion on her husband's experiments but had listened to it with an air of moody impatience. MacDonald guessed that she was bottling up something she wished to say but which she thought might provoke an argument or scene. Had he not been there she would have had no inhibitions.

Finally she could not restrain herself any longer and said to her father accusingly, "Why did you tell Dr. Shaw you had been shot by accident?"

"Mike has already asked me that question," Matheson replied calmly.

Fiona waited for a few seconds and as he added nothing more she said, "Does that mean you're not going to give us your reason?"

"On this occasion, my dear," her father replied gently, "I'm reserving the right to make my own decisions without explaining my motives."

"This is the first I've heard of it," Stokes said, "but I think your father's right. There's no reason to tell people. Think of the scandal it would cause."

"Scandal? Why should it cause a scandal?"

"Some might begin to wonder why anyone on the island should wish to kill him." Stokes glanced sideways at his wife as he spoke. Although his tone was bland and even, one could detect a touch of malice in the remark.

"Don't you think we should try to find out who shot at him. Shouldn't the police be told?"

"Perhaps it was an accident."

"Someone out shooting at night mistook Dad for a tiger, I suppose."

"On the other hand," Stokes suggested, "perhaps the shot was intended for Mr. MacDonald."

"That's nonsense!" Matheson exclaimed. "Why would anyone wish to harm Mike?"

"Who knows? He's a stranger and you know how the islanders hate strangers. Even after all these years people still stare at me impudently and whisper when I pass them—in Gaelic of course."

"Oh, you're paranoic about the island," Fiona said scornfully. "It's perfectly obvious that Hamish Grant fired that shot. Didn't Murdoch and Darroch find him up on the peat moss the next morning, stoned out of his mind?"

"Why on earth should Hamish wish to kill me?" Matheson demanded and one sensed that he was beginning to lose his temper. "No one on this island has ever harmed me, nor tried to."

Stokes glanced again at Fiona and immediately she looked down at her plate. MacDonald had the impression that the two of them were like children, both wishing to challenge a parent's authority or simply to be impertinent, but both afraid of the consequences.

"It's obvious to me," Stokes said slowly, "that the shooting last night, whether it was intended for you or for Mr. MacDonald must have been connected with the death of Sheena Campbell."

Matheson's face hardened in anger. "As I have already told both Fiona and you, Paul, that is a subject I will not allow to be mentioned in my house."

Fiona flushed with indignation, but managed to bite back whatever retort she was tempted to make. Instead she said, "All right. If that's the way it has to be."

"It has. And I want you both, all three of you, in fact, to promise that you'll tell no one that the shooting was not an accident."

Matheson looked at each one of the others in turn, and in turn they nodded. They finished lunch in an atmosphere of uncomfortable constraint. It was as though Matheson had put the memory of Sheena Campbell's death out of his mind and now, reminded of it, had once more to stifle whatever emotion it had aroused. Fiona made a half-hearted attempt to revive a conversation of a sort by talking of the previous evening's ceilidh and of the visit MacDonald and she had paid to Jessie Monro's croft, but Matheson did not respond. Stokes too was silent, although he seemed in no way concerned by the gaffe he had made in mentioning Sheena's death. They had finished eating and were rising from the table when Annie came into the room.

"Angus Murdoch wishes a word with you, Mr. Alisdair," she said.

Murdoch followed her into the room. He looked grim. "I'm sorry to be disturbing you at the table, Mr. Alisdair."

"What is it Angus?"

"Hamish Grant has had an accident in Number Five warehouse. He's dead."

Hamish Grant's body lay on the floor of the warehouse beside a broken cask. The whisky which had poured out of the broken staves of the cask had already disappeared through the floor of earth and clinker, leaving nothing behind except heavy fumes which still hung in the air. Hamish's clothes, which had also been soaked in the spirit, were now almost dry.

He lay at one end of a row of casks which had been stacked three-high and it had evidently been the end cask of the top row which had fallen on him, crushing his head and face. In a mass of blood and splintered bone his features were unrecognizable.

MacDonald stood beside Matheson and Murdoch staring, appalled at the devastation which a single cask had apparently wrought, and astounded that a man of Grant's strength could have been destroyed so easily. He wished now that he had stayed up at the house and been spared this grisly sight. It had been Murdoch's idea that he should come.

"I think you should come down with us, Mr. MacDonald," he had said quietly.

MacDonald knew that the suggestion and the tone in which it had been made implied Murdoch's belief that it was he who had killed Sheena Campbell. What stunned him now was the seemingly incredible coincidence that Hamish Grant was also dead, making it even more difficult to discover who had really killed the girl and to prove that he himself had in no way been involved. Once again he began to feel a sense of fatalism, that, like a character in a classic tragedy, he was being led remorselessly into a situation from which there was no escape and which was retribution for his past.

"Could the cask have rolled off the stack accidentally and fallen on him while he was sleeping on the floor?" Matheson asked Murdoch.

"No, that's not possible. The scutches would have prevented it."

"There's no chance that the men might have forgotten to put the scutches in?"

"None. Men don't make elementary mistakes like that in our distillery. Besides these casks were stacked weeks ago and haven't been moved. Why should one of them suddenly roll off?"

The casks had been stacked in the traditional method used in all old warehouses. A bottom row of sherry butts, each holding more than 100 gallons had been laid out first, and lengths of wood or "timbers" placed in two parallel strips on top of them. A second row of casks, also butts, had been balanced on these timbers. Above them once again, placed on more timbers, was a row of hogsheads, each holding about 50 gallons of whisky. The end casks of each row were secured with wooden chocks or "scutches", to prevent them rolling away and, in the case of the end casks on the two top rows, crashing to the ground.

"Perhaps he climbed up on the the stack to try and get at the whisky," Matheson suggested.

"Why should he do that? He would need to find something to break a hole in one of the staves and in that case he could just as easily have worked on one of the single casks standing there." Murdoch pointed to half-a-dozen casks which stood on their own between him and the door of the warehouse.

MacDonald looked up at the roof. There were no windows in the warehouse, but to allow some light into the gloomy building a few panes of glass had been let into the roof and one of them was positioned almost exactly above the place where the broken cask had been stacked before it fell.

"If he had been trying to get out of the warehouse, might he not have climbed up and stood on the cask. Then it might have been dislodged as he overbalanced and rolled on to him."

"Those are just sheets of glass," Murdoch replied. "They can't be opened."

"But would Grant have known that?"

"What I wish to know, Angus," Matheson said, "is how he came to be locked up in here."

"The man had taken leave of his senses. He tried to kill Mr. MacDonald last night."

"But why?"

"Who knows?"

In a few words Murdoch described how Grant had lain in wait for MacDonald in his cottage the night before. Deliberately, it seemed to MacDonald, he avoided suggesting that the attack might have been in any way connected with the murder of Sheena Campbell. It was as though he knew this was a subject which Matheson would not wish to have mentioned.

"I'm not certain you acted wisely, Angus," Matheson said. "We've no right to be locking people up and certainly not in the distillery."

"The man was off his rocker,"

MacDonald remarked. "Mentally un-balanced."

"Aye," Murdoch agreed. "We had to restrain him by force. Who knows what he would have done if we had let him free on the island."

"That's why he would have climbed up on the casks. He would stop at nothing to get away."

"Maybe," Murdoch said slowly. "Or maybe that is just what we are expected to believe."

"What do you mean?"

"If he was already dead; if he had been killed, say, with a karate blow to the throat, dropping a cask on his head would be a grand way to conceal the fact."

"Good God, man! Who on earth would have done a thing like that?" Matheson exclaimed.

"Only three people knew Hamish was locked up in the warehouse. Archie Darroch, myself and Mr. MacDonald here."

14

AT about the same time as the body of Hamish Grant was discovered in the distillery warehouse, the ferry from Kilgona arrived at Alsaig. The wind was still blowing strongly and the rough sea, coupled with the powerful tide which was always to be found off Hebridean islands, made the passage a slow and arduous one. From time to time a wave would thump against the side of the landing-craft, spilling over the side into the central well where the vehicles stood and wetting those passengers who had not taken shelter inside their vehicles, with windows firmly shut, or found a place in the small covered area at the rear of the vessel.

Only five vehicles were making the journey. A van with supplies for MacNab's shop, a lorry bound for the distillery loaded with empty casks from the blending companies on the mainland, an ambulance from the hospital at Port Skeir, an old

Ford belonging to a farmer on the island who had been to the bull sales in Perth and a small white police car. The police car and the ambulance had, by a special dispensation, been allowed to back onto the ferry last so that they would be the first to drive up on the ramp and so on to the island at Carrabus.

Sergeant Cairns and Constable Reid were in the police car and they drove immediately to the medical centre, followed by the ambulance. Doctor Shaw was waiting there for them and, while the ambulance attendants went to collect Sheena Campbell's body, he gave Cairns the report of the examination he had made.

"Whoever carries out the autopsy might like to have this," he said, "although it isn't likely to tell him anything he won't find out for himself very quickly."

"A fracture of the hyoid?" Cairns remarked after he had glanced through the report. "Tell me in layman's terms, Doctor, how she was killed."

"She would actually have died of suffocation, but the real cause of death seems to have been a blow across her throat."

"With an instrument, do you think?"

"I wouldn't say so. More likely the side of a hand."

"Would that be enough to kill?"

"Yes, surely, if it was given by anyone who had been trained in karate."

"Do you know where the body was found?"

"Yes. I made Hamish Grant take me there immediately after he brought the body in and I marked the exact spot."

"That's grand! Would you come with us and show me, please?"

Constable Reid drove them in the police car through the village and past the distillery to a point some 80 yards beyond the drive which led from the road up to Matheson's house. Shaw had marked the spot where Hamish Grant claimed to have found the body with a small pile of pebbles which he had fetched from the shore. They got out of the police car and Reid began to make a careful examination of the area around the place where the body had been lying.

"You'll not find footprints there," Shaw remarked. "Nor anything else much. It rained heavily that night and again on and off for much of the following day."

"Constable Reid will know what to look for. He was brought up on the hills and was a keeper himself before he joined the force."

The two men stood watching as Reid crouched down, examining the heather, the grass that grew around it and a clump of brownish ferns nearby. Then he moved across to the road and walked slowly along it, looking at the verge on both sides. Finally he came back to them.

"Did you say that the girl had been raped, sir?" he asked the doctor bluntly.

"Sexually assaulted? Yes, almost certainly."

"Then I believe she must have been killed at some other place and that her body was brought here afterwards. The weight of two people struggling on the ground would have left some traces, broken stems of heather, bruised grass, that not even heavy rain would have obliterated."

"That would not be surprising," Cairns said. "We should ask ourselves what the girl was doing out here late at night. Not just taking a stroll, that's for sure. It's reasonable to suppose she came out here to meet someone."

"Or with someone," Doctor Shaw suggested.

"Or, as you say, with someone. In either case it is not very likely he would have assaulted her here, out in the open. Of course if it was the keeper, Grant, who killed her, he might have taken her riding in his Land-Rover and after she was dead brought the body here and dropped it by the roadside."

"Why should he have done that?"

"To make it appear that he had not been responsible for her death." Cairns guessed that Shaw had already decided it was MacDonald who had murdered the girl, but he was not going to allow himself to be stampeded into any hasty conclusions. "If the body had been found anywhere else on the island, Grant would be immediately suspected. He's one of the few people on Alsaig who has a vehicle at his disposal."

"There are no signs of a car having been pulled up by the side of the road, Sergeant," Reid remarked.

"Then let's look at another possibility."

Cairns pointed towards the edge of the copse of trees which surrounded Tigh Geal only 50 yards or so from where they were standing. "If a man was walking with a girl along this road and wished to do a bit of kissing and cuddling, would he not take her into the woods? Go in there and take a look around, Constable Reid."

As Reid set off towards the nearest clump of trees, Cairns asked Shaw, "Did you ever have to treat this Campbell girl, Doctor?"

"Once or twice when she was a bairn, but only for childish complaints."

"Not for VD or anything like that?"

"Good Heavens, no!"

"Did she come to you for contraceptive pills?"

"No."

If the girl had been sleeping around, Cairns was thinking, she would surely have been taking precautions. It was not likely that MacNab would sell contraceptives in his store and even if he did, a single girl would never tell the island what she was up to by buying them there. Most likely she had just been a tease and a flirt, playing one man off against another for what she could get in flattering attentions and free drinks.

As he and the doctor went into the wood to help Reid in his search, Cairns remarked, "What a way to run a murder investigation! On the mainland I would have twenty men at work in these woods."

"Couldn't you get reinforcements from the mainland?"

"Aye, but think of the time it would take and the cost! Anyway I doubt they will be needed. We'll find out who killed the girl soon enough."

Surprisingly their very superficial search among the trees quickly yielded results. They found a path, leading from the disused stables and outhouses on one side of the house to the road, which at one time had probably been used as a short cut by domestic staff. A little way along the path they saw signs of what might well have been a violent struggle, and from a thorn bush a few feet away a strand of white wool was hanging.

"Might that not be from the cardigan which was found near Sheena's body?" Shaw asked.

"I'll take it," Cairns said.

"The cardigan was a very ordinary, inexpensive garment, but when she was killed Sheena was wearing a green and blue silk dress. I could not help noticing that it had the label of a well-known store in Glasgow."

"Had she been to Glasgow recently, do you know?"

"I don't believe so, but of course she might have ordered the dress by post."

"Maybe it was a present from the keeper Hamish Grant."

"He could never have afforded it on his wages."

"I think it's time I had a few words with the man."

Leaving the constable to continue searching in the trees, Cairns and Shaw walked back towards the police car which they had left standing by the road. When they came out of the trees they saw that another car, which Shaw recognized as belonging to the distillery, had been pulled up behind it. One of the distillery workers was standing by it waiting for them.

"I came looking for you, Doctor," he said and then added, "we didn't know the police were here."

"What's the matter? Has someone been taken ill?"

"Worse than that. They found Hamish Grant dead in one of the distillery warehouses."

"You will know that I'm investigating the murder of Sheena Campbell, sir," Cairns said to MacDonald.

"Yes. And the death of Hamish Grant as well, I guess."

"No, for the time being that is being treated as an accident. But I would like to ask you some questions on the other matter."

"Sure, Sergeant. Fire ahead."

It was the following morning when Cairns came to question MacDonald. There had been much to be done after he had gone to the distillery and seen Hamish Grant's body. He and Reid had carried out a thorough examination of the warehouse, marking the exact spot and position of the corpse and questioning Shaw as to the cause of death. The doctor had been unable to give them a firm opinion and only an autopsy would show whether it had actually been the falling cask that had killed Grant. A hogshead of whisky weighing more than five hundredweight and falling from a height of about six feet could as certainly kill as it could be used to destroy traces of an earlier and perhaps fatal wound.

Shortly before six o'clock, the crew of the ferry had insisted on returning to Kilgona. In the normal way the ferry would sail back within the hour, as soon as it was loaded up with whatever vehicles and passengers were making the trip, but Cairns had persuaded the crew to stay on the island far longer. Eventually, however, they had to sail so Cairns let Constable Reid accompany the ambulance and decided that he would stay on Alsaig overnight to continue his enquiries. Reid would return in the police car the following morning to collect him. Cairns had then phoned headquarters in Stornoway to report the second death and had been told that an inspector would fly out to Kilgona the following day on the scheduled flight to take charge of the investigations.

After making these arrangements, Cairns had gone to the hotel and commandeered the residents' lounge on the first floor for use as an interview room. He would have preferred to use the schoolhouse, which would have provided a more formal and impersonal setting, but Buchanan was holding a practice for his school choir that evening. Since Hamish Grant who had found Sheena Campbell's body was now dead, the first person Cairns had interviewed was Doctor Shaw. He questioned him on exactly what Grant had said when he brought the body to the medical centre and then took a statement which he attached to the doctor's report of his examination of the girl's body.

By that time it had been evening and so he had eaten a leisurely dinner at the hotel and then interviewed first Murdoch and then Darroch, who filled him in with what they knew of the girl and her relationship with Grant and her movements on the evening before her murder. There would still have been time to question MacDonald, but Cairns decided to allow the American to sweat out a night of anxiety. In his experience people who had too long a time to compose or invent answers to questions which they knew they were going to be asked by the police, very often lost their nerve and grew confused when the questions finally came.

So now, in the morning, he had driven out to Gartness in a car he had borrowed from the distillery to interview MacDonald in his cottage. To his surprise the American showed no signs of apprehension. There were people, he knew, who were calm and assured after committing a crime, even after a murder, but they were experienced, inhuman criminals. From what he had heard, MacDonald was just a weak intellectual with a drink problem and would scarcely fall into this category.

"How well did you know Sheena Campbell?" Cairns asked.

"We had met a few times; once at a ceilidh but usually in the hotel. She was often there."

"Had you ever taken her out?"

"If you mean had I dated her, the answer is no. But when we met I talked with her."

"And bought her drinks?"

"Sure. Why not?"

"What did she usually drink?"

"White rum and blackcurrant. Sometimes rum and Coke."

"Did you not consider her a bit young to be taking spirits?"

MacDonald wanted to protest that the question was unfair. Sheena had been drinking spirits long before he had met her and there was never any shortage of men to buy them for her. On an island like Alsaig, young people quickly matured to adult drinking habits. Cairns knew the question was unfair, for he himself had bought girls no older than Sheena rum or vodka or whisky in Kilgona, though only when he was off duty, naturally. But he was beginning to sense that he must needle the American, who was far too un-emotional.

As MacDonald only shrugged his shoulders, Cairns continued, "What exactly was your relationship with the girl?"

"I guess you could call them friendly, in a casual sort of way."

"Did you ever have sexual intercourse with her?"

"No."

"But you made advances?"

"I guess so."

"And how far did she allow you to go?

Kissing and hugging no doubt, but was there ever anything more?"

"Not that I can remember."

"Come now, sir, surely you would be remembering a thing like that?"

"Not necessarily. Not if I had been drinking."

"I see."

Cairns was sitting at the table in the cottage which MacDonald used as a writing-desk. A folder lay on the table in front of him and opening it he jotted down a few notes on a sheet of paper. What he wrote was of no consequence, but he wished to test the American's patience. Cairns had caught scores of brown trout and sea trout in the lochs and streams of Kilgona and he knew a bit about patience. By mentioning the subject of his drinking MacDonald had given him a perfect opening but he decided to ignore it. There would be time enough later.

"I am told you were drinking with the girl at the hotel on the evening before she was found dead. Can you recall what she was wearing?"

"No."

"It was a blue and green silk dress.

Would you know how she came to own such an expensive dress?"

"How the heck would I know?"

"You didn't buy it for her?"

"No."

"Did you give her any presents at any time?"

"No."

"Money?"

"Certainly not! I would think she'd have been as mad as hell if I had even tried to."

"Well then, sir," Cairns said patiently, "can you remember what you yourself were wearing that evening?"

The question was floated out in much the same way as a fisherman might cast a fly over the water. MacDonald was not trapped into pretending that he could not remember what he had been wearing. He realized at once that Cairns must have been told about the sweater.

"A pair of jeans and a sweater."

"Are those the jeans you have on now?"

"Yes, I think so. But I have two almost identical pairs."

"And the sweater, sir? Might I see it, please?"

"The lady who cleans for me, Mrs. Anderson, has taken it away to wash it."

"I see. Did you ask her to do that?"

"No, it was her idea." MacDonald hoped his tone would not seem defiant as he added, "The sweater was damp and muddy and covered with stains that might have been blood."

The man is a cool customer, Cairns thought admiringly, but he was still not ready to press home his advantage. He asked innocently, "Have you any idea who might have killed Sheena Campbell, sir?"

"No, I guess not."

"But you must have known she was friendly with a number of other men?" Cairns had never even heard of the French saying "Qui s'excuse, s'accuse", but he was not a stranger to the thinking behind it.

"Yes, I suppose she must have been."

It was at this time that Cairns became convinced that MacDonald was guilty of murdering Sheena Campbell, paradoxically not because the American had shown any signs of panic under interrogation, but because he had answered every question calmly and honestly. The man was not even sweating.

"The keeper, Grant, had lost his head over the girl had he not?"

"Some people seemed to think so."

"Is that why he attacked you in your house? Was it jealousy?"

"By that time it was too late for jealousy. Sheena was already dead."

"Then maybe he thought you had killed her."

"Possibly. I can't say."

"And did you kill her, Mr. Mac-Donald?"

"To be honest, I can't remember. I had been drinking heavily that night."

Cairns shut his folder of papers and put his ballpoint pen back in the pocket of his tunic. "Well at least that's an honest answer. But we can't leave it at that, Mr. MacDonald, as I'm sure you'll understand."

"What do you mean?"

"I'll need to ask you to accompany me to the police station in Kilgona."

"Does that mean I'm to be charged with murdering Sheena?"

"No sir. Not necessarily. It's simply

that an inspector is flying out from Stornoway to take charge of the investigations. He will wish to question you further and you will need to make a statement."

As soon as the beaching ramp in the bows had been winched up by the hawsers on each side, the tank landing-craft backed away from the shore. It was an ugly little vessel, looking from the front like a heavy metal box, that had been converted for service as a ferry. The tank deck could accommodate ten cars, if none of them was too large, squeezed into four rows. That morning it carried only the lorry which had brought empty casks to the distillery the previous afternoon and which was returning loaded with casks full of mature whisky, a green Rover taking two of the guests who had been staying with Mrs. Colville back to Kilgona en route for the mainland, and the police car. The ferry made two crossings each day from Kilgona to Alsaig, one in the morning and one in the middle of the afternoon and, apart from a few weeks in the summer tourist season, it was seldom full.

When Cairns and MacDonald had

reached Carrabus, Reid had been waiting for them in the police car and the ferry had been ready to sail. Once they were aboard, the vessel had backed out into the bay, swung round slowly until it was facing east and begun its journey to Kilgona, pitching and wallowing in a sea that was still too high for comfort. The low cloud that had covered the sky had broken and behind them MacDonald could see Beinn Laimsdearg, towering and black. He wondered whether he would ever tramp its slopes or even see it again. On the advice of Sergeant Cairns he had brought with him pyjamas, his toilet kit and a change of linen in a suitcase. He had accepted the advice without argument, giving way to the fatalism he had been fighting unsuccessfully for the past few days and aware only of a sense of his helplessness.

After disembarking from the ferry at Rainich, they drove the twelve miles to Port Skeir, the larger of the two townships on Kilgona and the official capital of the island. The police station was a modern building, a small concrete box situated incongruously in a back street of old weather-beaten cottages. Inside the entrance was a counter with the duty room behind it, an interview room, a small office and two cells.

Cairns and Reid led MacDonald into the interview room, gave him a cup of tea and left him alone, explaining that it would not be long before the inspector from Stornoway arrived. For the British, MacDonald reflected, a cup of tea played many rôles, comforter, tranquillizer, stimulus for mental activity, substitute for conversation, antidote to boredom. It also seemed to have a symbolic significance in the processes of justice, a last concession, like the cigarette placed between the lips of a man as he walks out to face the firing squad.

Before leaving the room, Cairns suddenly threw an unexpected question at MacDonald. "Somebody broke into MacNab's shop on Alsaig the night before last and stole provisions. You don't know anything about that I suppose?"

MacDonald looked at him calmly. "Sergeant, I have been shopping regularly at MacNab's ever since I went to Alsaig and I've always paid him cash. Why should I suddenly start stealing? As you probably know I am not short of money."

Cairns made no reply to his question, but went out to join Constable Reid in the duty room. MacDonald heard him ask Reid where the other policeman attached to the station, Constable Duncan, was and heard Reid reply that Duncan had been called out to a traffic accident. Reid was not able to say how serious the accident had been but he did know that the ambulance from the hospital had been called out as well.

"I must be away in a couple of minutes to collect the inspector," Cairns remarked. "The plane is due in twenty minutes."

The two men had been conversing in English but suddenly Reid switched to Gaelic. "Will we be charging MacDonald with murder?" he asked.

"Aye. He's guilty without any doubt."

It was the words "murder" and "guilty" which caught MacDonald's attention. They were words which he had seldom heard spoken or even read in Gaelic and he had to think for a few moments before he realized their meaning. Although what Reid and Cairns had said was not entirely unexpected, he found himself listening carefully to their conversation; carefully because they spoke quickly and his knowledge of Gaelic was fully exercised in understanding them.

"Has he admitted killing the girl?"

"No. He pretends he was too drunk to remember what happened that night."

"We've enough evidence then to make the charge stick?"

"Aye. He was seen leaving the hotel with her and his cleaning woman found a sweater caked with mud and blood stains which he had hidden in his cottage."

"Do you have the garment?"

"No. He made the woman wash it for him. But I have no doubt he will come round to a confession by and by. We've other evidence he doesn't know about as yet."

"What's that?"

"He denied giving the girl money but there were three new ten-pound notes in her purse. Darroch at the hotel can identify them. It seems they were the notes MacDonald was given when he cashed a cheque in the bar that evening when he

256

was with the girl. Darroch has the cheque to prove it."

That was the end of the conversation and a few moments later MacDonald heard Cairns leave the station, get into the police car which stood outside and drive away. At first he was not unduly concerned by what he had heard. The police's evidence seemed pretty insubstantial and would seem even more so when MacDonald was able to point out that the cheque they were talking about had been cashed only the day after Sheena's murder.

Then suddenly he remembered signing the cheque in the hotel bar, he remembered his momentary hesitation with pen poised as he wondered what the date was, he remembered Darroch prompting him. The 16th of October was the date he had written on the cheque.

When entering the police station he had noticed a calendar hanging on the wall behind the desk in the hallway. The door of the interview room had been left slightly ajar and by leaning forward he could just read it. He had cashed the cheque on Tuesday. He knew that because Tuesday was the day the mobile bank was supposed to visit Alsaig, coming over on the ferry. The calendar told him that Tuesday had been not the 16th but the 17th of October.

The discovery triggered off another recollection. He remembered Darroch being about to take £50 from the till behind the bar and then hesitating, changing his mind and, on the pretext that he did not wish to leave the till short, going into the office and returning with five brand new ten-pound notes. And there was another thing. Darroch had changed his mind about the money only after MacDonald had told him he could remember nothing of what had happened in the bar the previous night.

His mind recoiled, unwilling to take the leap to such a bizarre conclusion, for it would pose other questions that would have to be answered. How would Darroch have known of the money that had been found on the dead girl? And what about his sweater? How could that be explained?

He thought back to the time when he had woken in his cottage on the day Sheena's body had heen found. He had believed then that he had been fully dressed but it was possible he had been wearing two sweaters the previous evening and that he had taken the top one off and hidden it on top of the wardrobe. Now, suddenly, he remembered his shoes. He had looked at them that morning and seen that they were clean, clean and dry. If his sweater had been muddy and soaked with rain, how could his shoes have possibly remained dry after a three-mile walk back from Carrabus?

Now his thoughts raced unrestrained, following each other in a frantic but logical progression. The cottage door was never kept locked. He had spent most of the evening of the day on which he had cashed the cheque at Matheson's home. There would have been plenty of time for anyone so disposed to visit the cottage, find a sweater, drench it with muddy water, daub it with blood and hide it where a policeman would find it even if a cleaning woman did not. Other incidents which he had not even bothered to try and rationalize suddenly began to take on a sinister aspect.

"Good grief!" he exclaimed aloud. "I've been framed!"

15

HEARING voices outside, Mac-Donald peeped quickly through the half-open door of the interview room and saw that an old woman had come into the police station. She was complaining to Constable Reid that she had lost her handbag, which must have slipped out of her shopping basket. No, there had not been much money in the handbag, only two pound notes and a few coins, but she kept her pension book in it as well and a ring which her daughter had given her. It could only have happened when she was walking along West Street, between Bruce's stores and the post office, but she had been up and down the street three times and had not been able to find the bag. Patiently Reid began writing down what she had said and she repeated it slowly.

The interview room had two windows, one in the front overlooking the street and one on the side. MacDonald saw that the side window looked out on to a narrow lane which led from the street to a yard at the back of the station where the police cars were normally left parked. The yard was empty, for Cairns had taken one car to the airport while the other was being used by Constable Duncan.

Taking hold of the handles on the sash of the bottom half of the window at the side of the room, he slid it up noiselessly. By leaning out he was able to place his suitcase gently on the ground in the lane. All he had to do then was to slip through the open window, pick up the suitcase and walk up the lane to the street. He supposed it must be one of the simplest escapes ever made by a prisoner.

When he had been driven there from the ferry, he had noticed that the street in which the police station was situated led into what must be the main thoroughfare of the tiny town, with shops on each side, a church and two small hotels. He made his way to it, walking at a pace that would not draw attention to himself. What he must do first of all was to get as far away from the police station as he could before his disappearance was noticed. Beyond that he had no plan.

In the main street a bus was waiting while a handful of passengers boarded it. A sign on the front showed that its destination was Lossit, the other township of the island and on an impulse MacDonald climbed aboard just before it pulled away. He knew that the journey took some 30 minutes and that would give him time to think.

When the police discovered that he had left the station, they would not be able to pursue him immediately. Even if Reid were prepared to leave the station unmanned, he had no car and could not know where MacDonald had gone. That left him two alternatives. He could either try to contact Sergeant Cairns by phoning the airport or he could wait until the sergeant returned with the inspector. Knowing by now something about the mentality of the Hebrideans, MacDonald was prepared to gamble on his opting for the second choice. Reid would know that there was little chance of MacDonald getting off the island before they picked him up. Even if he were able to board one of the Loganair planes to Stornoway or Glasgow, a fugitive would be conspicuous among the dozen or so passengers. The ferry from Lossit to the mainland offered no better chance of escape. The journey took more than two hours which gave plenty of time for the Kilgona police to arrange for their counterparts on the mainland to be waiting at the gangplank as the passengers disembarked. As there was therefore no call for urgency, Constable Reid, in the leisurely manner of a true islander, would wait for his superiors to return and take matters out of his hands.

By the time the bus reached Lossit, MacDonald had formed his plan. His only chance of extracting himself from the situation into which he had been manoeuvred, to escape arrest and trial and almost certainly imprisonment, was to find out who had killed Sheena Campbell. With the evidence that had been stacked up against him no one would believe his denials and no one was likely to come forward and speak on his behalf. But the only place where he could learn the identity of the murderer and prove it was Alsaig. So he would go back to Alsaig. His plan would need luck, lots of it, good timing and no doubt improvisation but he had one factor in his favour. The police would never suppose that he would be crazy enough to return to the island, an island that was a prison in itself and where he would immediately be recognized.

As he left the bus at Lossit, he looked for a bank and found a branch of the Royal Bank of Scotland not far from the harbour. While cashing a cheque he made a point of being pleasant to the girl behind the counter and asking her at what time the ferry to the mainland would next sail. She told him there was a vessel already in the harbour which was due to sail in half-an-hour and that he could buy a ticket at the office on the pier. Sensing that his luck was in, he went and bought a passenger ticket, again engaging the man behind the window in conversation long enough to establish in his memory that he had been talking to an American.

Close to the pier was a small café in which some of the passengers for the ferry were drinking cups of tea or glasses of lemonade as they waited to go on board. Glancing through the window, MacDonald noticed a man with a camper's haversack on his back and a brightly coloured knitted cap on his head. He was sitting alone at a table by the window, so MacDonald went in, bought a cup of coffee from the counter and went to sit at the same table.

"Pardon me," he said after a few moments, "but are you planning to sail on the ferry?"

"Aye. What of it?"

"I've just arrived on the island myself."

"Oh, aye?"

The man was short and wiry, with the sharp features and aggressive expression of one who has to prove not only to the world but to himself that he is as good as anyone else and better than most. MacDonald guessed that he was a Glaswegian.

"Would you be able to tell me where I could buy a rucksack?"

"No."

"I guess you wouldn't consider selling me yours?"

The Glaswegian looked at him pityingly. "What are you on about, Jimmie? Just tell me that. What are you on about?"

"I'm just starting a walking tour of the

Western Isles. Bringing a suitcase with me wasn't a good idea. I can see that now."

"You're right there, Jimmie."

"I wondered whether, if you have finished your holiday and are going home, maybe you would sell me your rucksack."

"You can go get stuffed!"

"I'll pay £25 for it." MacDonald pulled a wad of notes from his pocket as proof of his sincerity.

Greed wrestled to overcome native Scottish caution. The rucksack, although capacious, was soiled and worn at the edges. It might be good for one, or at the most two more expeditions. Finally the Glaswegian said, "And what would I do without my rucksack? Tell me that. How would I get my stuff home?"

"Why not take my suitcase?"

The suitcase was leather and easily the most expensive piece of luggage MacDonald had ever owned. It had been bought for him by Bette-May, an extravagant present typical of his former wife, when he had gone to attend some academic conference at a university on the other coast of America. It had been the first occasion after their marriage that they had been separated and later, with hindsight, he had wondered whether it had not also been her first opportunity to be unfaithful to him.

"Tell you what I'll do, Jimmie." The Glaswegian had by this time no doubt calculated for how much he would be able to sell the suitcase when he got back home. "I'll let you have the rucksack for £35 and your case. Okay?"

"Thirty-five!"

"Take it or leave it."

"If you'll throw in your cap, it's a deal."

The man laughed loudly. "You're a character, that's what you are, Jimmie; a proper character! It's a deal."

He was ready to unpack his rucksack and transfer his belongings into the suitcase on the spot, but MacDonald persuaded him that they should make the exchange outside. A short distance from the pier they came to a small recreation ground with a couple of benches and swings for children. At that time there were no children around to be inquisitive, so they did their unpacking and repacking on one of the benches. When it was done, the Glaswegian slapped MacDonald on the back, told him once more that he was a proper character and went back to the harbour to join the passengers and vehicles that were now boarding the ferry. MacDonald did not wait to watch it sail.

Both Lossit and Port Skeir were on the eastern side of Kilgona, one at each end of a wide, curving sea loch, while Rainich, the departure point for the ferry to Alsaig was roughly equidistant from both on the west coast. The afternoon ferry for Alsaig was due to sail in just over one hour's time and MacDonald knew he could not possibly reach Rainich in that time on foot, but he set out along the road confident that as on Alsaig, he would not be walking far before he was offered a lift. His confidence was not misplaced. He had not covered much more than half-a-mile when a battered old Morris Traveller pulled up on the road beside him.

"Are you making for Rainich?" the driver called out.

"Aye."

"Then jump in man."

The owner of the Morris was wearing a heavy sweater, knickerbockers and a deerstalker hat. He blinked incessantly through his thick spectacles and drove badly, gripping the steering-wheel as though it were his last contact with life and over-compensating so that the car never held a straight course for more than a second or two. A pair of binoculars lay in the back of the car alongside a thermos flask and sandwich box, a blanket, a water-proof groundsheet, another sweater and a pair of Wellingtons.

"You'll be crossing over to Alsaig then?" he asked MacDonald.

"Aye."

"A wee bit late in the season for a camping holiday, is it not?"

"I'm meeting up with a friend there but only for a long weekend," MacDonald replied, speaking with his Scottish accent. His imitation of a Scot's accent had always been good for a laugh at parties back home and he hoped it would stand up to scrutiny now. "If the weather's rough, we'll find a bed-and-breakfast."

"You'll not be from the West coast?" the man asked.

"No. Musselburgh."

"Ah yes, near Edinburgh." The answer satisfied the man's curiosity. Everyone knew that folk from Edinburgh cultivated curious, affected accents in pursuit of what they believed was gentility. "There are some caves on the north coast of Alsaig. You could do worse than camp in them if it's too cold or windy outdoors. They're dry and clean and well above the highest watermark."

"You know the island then?"

"Aye. I've been bird-watching there more than a score of times. The bird life on Alsaig is not so rich and varied as here on Kilgona, but it makes a change."

The bird-watcher was one of those rarities, a talkative Scot. Delighted to have ensnared a captive audience, he chattered on about the bird life of Kilgona, Alsaig and the other Western Isles. Most of the birds he mentioned were no more than names to MacDonald: fulmars, puffins, guillemots, razorbills, kittiwakes. There were more than 180 species of birds to be found on Kilgona alone, and it was famous for the immense migrations of geese which came to the sandflats on its western shores: barnacle geese, grey lags, Greenland white fronts in their thousands. What pleased the man most was that the number of species to be found on Kilgona and Alsaig was increasing. Birds which had not been seen for a hundred years or more were returning and were protected by Act of Parliament.

Before legislation had been passed, sea birds, particularly the gannet, had been eaten by the islanders who made expeditions each autumn to harvest the birds on the uninhabited rocks where they bred and even salted them for export to Scottish immigrants all over the world. The great auk had been exterminated in this way and golden eagles and peregrines had been in danger of suffering the same fate.

"You'll likely meet a friend of mine on Alsaig," the bird-watcher remarked. "Name of Gibson, from the Society for the Protection of British Birds."

"Oh yes? What's he doing there?"

"The society is trying to bring the white-tailed sea-eagle back to the Isles. As an experiment they placed some young chicks on the cliffs to the north-east of Alsaig. Gibson has gone over to see how things are going."

The man was not going to Rainich

himself and he dropped MacDonald on the main road at a point where a smaller road wound down to the tiny bay with its half-a-dozen cottages clustered around the lifeboat station and the pier from which the ferry sailed. Not wishing to make himself conspicuous by waiting for the ferry on the pier, MacDonald did not walk directly to the bay but cut off the road into a field where he could sit down and watch what was happening. As the time of departure drew nearer, the vehicles that were going to make the crossing arrived. Once again it appeared as though the ferry would be carrying a meagre load: a petrol tanker on its way to fill up the storage tanks for Mrs. Buie's pump, a lorry full of anthracite, a Range Rover with two men who looked as though they might be going to Askaig for the stalking, more guests perhaps invited by Mrs. Colville to replace the two that had left only that morning, a salesman in a Ford hoping to find orders for his fertilizer from the farmers of the island.

From his vantage point MacDonald could look along the road which led in one direction back to Lossit and in the other to Port Skeir. In neither direction could he see any signs of an approaching police car. He waited until the four vehicles were being driven on to the deck of the landing craft. Then, just before the beaching ramp was raised, he climbed aboard himself. Slowly the vessel began its clumsy, laboured manoeuvres, backing away from land.

Only when they were well out at sea and one of the crew of two men had taken his money and given him a ticket for the voyage, did he decide he was now safe from immediate pursuit. Even if the police had been able by now to establish that he had not left for the mainland, it would be some time before they would know that he had returned to Alsaig.

As he watched the coast line of Kilgona melt into the horizon and the familiar contours of Alsaig, with its single, imperious peak take shape, he had the satisfaction of knowing that he had outwitted the police and escaped from the trap which was being sprung on him. Now he could set about proving his innocence. Even the knowledge that he had not the slightest notion of how and where to start did not dismay him.

16

THERE were three public telephones on Alsaig; one in the hotel, one in the post office and one just beyond the church on the road from Carrabus to Ballymony. The church itself was almost two miles from Carrabus, sited there perhaps on the principle that a good, stiff walk on Sunday mornings, particularly in inclement weather, would give the congregation time to reflect on their sins of the past week and so be better prepared for their religious observances. What tortuous piece of logic or symbolism had inspired the placing of a phone kiosk beyond the church was difficult to conceive. In any event no one had ever taken the trouble to question the arrangement.

When MacDonald had been connected to Tigh Geal by the operator and a voice which he concluded must be that of Annie, the housekeeper, answered, he did his Scottish impersonation as he asked for

Mrs. Fiona Stokes. Presently Fiona came to the phone.

"This is Mike MacDonald. Before we start talking, tell me are you alone?"

"No."

"In that case don't ask any questions or say anything which might give away who you're speaking to. Just listen to what I'm going to say, please. The police believe I killed Sheena but I've found out that the evidence against me was rigged, fabricated if you like. So I slipped out of the police station at Port Skeir before they could charge me and I'm back on Alsaig."

"I see."

"I must talk with you. You're the only person who can help me. Could you meet me?"

"Yes."

"Would it be convenient for you to come now?"

"No, not really."

"In an hour's time?"

"Yes, I could manage that."

"Then listen. Do you know the ruined broch that stands above Loch Trath?"

"Of course."

"I'll be waiting there for you in one hour's time. That will be five o'clock."

"Yes, that's fine. Good-bye."

While crossing in the ferry, MacDonald had decided that Fiona was the only person on Alsaig who might be willing and able to help him. The decision, he knew, was based almost entirely on intuition since she had given him no real reason for supposing that she might have any interest in him or sympathy for the predicament in which he found himself. Now, after leaving the phone box, he wondered whether he had been wise even to approach her. She had agreed to meet him it was true, but he had seemed to detect in her tone a hesitation, a reluctance to make any commitment. He reassured himself with the thought that she was probably not a person who ever responded to any suggestion with enthusiasm and who was by nature cautious.

On leaving the ferry, in order to avoid being seen and recognized in Carrabus, he had set out along the road to the north of the island, then cut inland and made a detour, circling the village on the lower slopes of Beinn Laimsdearg and Cnoc na

Moine on a route which took him towards the south, past the copse of trees in which Tigh Geal stood. Even so he could not be certain that he had not been noticed. One of the disadvantages of an island as barren as Alsaig was that it afforded little cover for anyone who wished to move about unseen. Such trees as were to be found grew only on the south-east. There was the copse around Tigh Geal, planted and painstakingly cultivated by Matheson's grandfather, and another, large enough to be called a wood, around Ardnahoe, which Mrs. Colville's father-in-law had imported and planted at great expense as a setting for the house he was building. Between the two estates was a sprinkling of indigenous trees, stunted in growth and sparse in foliage, little more than scrub, along the road. Further inland, higher up on Cnoc na Moine and also facing south-east was a plantation of conifers, set out in uniform and monotonous rows, a venture of the Forestry Commission begun several years previously as part of its reafforestation of Scotland.

Now, leaving the telephone kiosk, MacDonald made his way, finding what cover he could, up the slopes of Cnoc na Moine, heading for the other side of the island. Since it was not too far out of his way, he climbed over the wire fence that bordered the plantation. The trees were planted close together and he did not go very far in to find a hiding place for the rucksack, which he felt was only making him conspicuous. He placed it, together with the knitted cap, under a tree and then continued walking.

Crossing over the hill he came to the broch, a ruined fort dating back to the early Iron Age. Originally more than 40 feet high with massive double walls, it had now lost much of its stone, but one could still make out the line of the narrow galleries between the walls which were a feature of brochs. Built to give shelter against invaders, the smooth, concave walls of the round forts were impossible to scale and, with their narrow galleries which only one man at a time could penetrate, they were impregnable.

When he reached the broch it was still only twenty-five minutes to five, and he sat down with his back against the ruined wall to wait for Fiona. The wind had risen and swung to northwesterly, lowering the temperature of the day appreciably. When darkness came the cold air, sweeping south from Iceland and the polar land mass, would be bitingly cold, too cold for him to spend the night out of doors. On the other hand he could not risk going to his cottage, for if the police on Kilgona knew now that he had gone to Alsaig, they would telephone the islanders to be on the lookout for him and the cottage was the first place where they would go to look.

He could not help wondering at the way wind dominated life on Alsaig. It had already played a telling role in the consequences of Sheena Campbell's death and the attempt on Matheson's life, and were it to grow to gale force again it would give him more time to establish his innocence. It was not surprising that the people of Alsaig spoke not of the weather or rain or sunshine but of wind, so much so that one might overhear housewives tell each other that a force six wind was promised by the met. men.

As he sat waiting he noticed a man wearing a duffel coat and cloth cap and with a pair of binoculars slung over his shoulder walking up the hill towards him from the direction of the sea. His first instinct was to get up and leave, making as quickly as he could for cover. Then he realized that the man was certainly not an islander. Nobody on Alsaig would be out for a stroll at that time of day and nobody, except possibly Dr. Shaw, would be carrying binoculars. If he was a stranger, then the man would not know MacDonald and to get up and run would only arouse his suspicions.

When the man saw him, he raised his hand in a gesture of greeting and MacDonald thought he was going to walk on past. Then he seemed to change his mind and came over towards the broch to start a conversation.

"Not a bad day," he said with an unmistakably English accent.

"Not bad at all."

"It's marvellous just to be able to get out and about after that fiendish gale. It was too windy even for the birds."

"Are you a bird-watcher?"

The man laughed. "Yes and no. I'm an inspector from the Society for the Protection of British Birds."

"Then you must be Mr. Gibson."

"No. My name's Godfrey. Harold Godfrey."

"Sorry. I guess I just jumped to conclusions. It's just that I met a bird-watcher on Kilgona this morning who told me that a Mr. Gibson from your society was over here on Alsaig. Something to do with sea-eagle chicks."

Godfrey appeared disconcerted to meet someone who knew about the eagle chicks. He was a small man, elegantly dressed, with carefully manicured hands and red hair of an unnaturally bright shade. "Ah, yes. Gibson was supposed to come but he was taken ill and they sent me in his place."

"How are the chicks doing anyway?"

"Fine. Just fine."

As they were talking MacDonald heard the sound of a car's engine coming up from below the hill to their left. He looked down towards the road, assuming that it was Fiona arriving and that she would park the car at the point where the road ended and walk up the hill towards the broch. But no car appeared along the road and suddenly the noise of the engine stopped.

"Can I borrow your glasses for a moment?" he asked Godfrey.

"Of course. Why, have you seen something that interests you?"

"Not a bird."

"What then?"

"I'm not sure."

About 300 yards down the road towards the south were the last of the trees in the wood that marked the end of the Colville estate. Something in the trees, a glint of light reflected in glass perhaps, had caught his attention. Focussing the binoculars on the trees, he saw that a car, which could only be the one he had just heard approaching, had stopped on the road behind them where it was all but hidden from his view. Two men got out of it, came round the trees and began walking up the hill. They moved stealthily, keeping as close to the trees as they could, as though they hoped in that way that they would not be seen. He recognized them as Murdoch and Darroch.

"I thought I saw a stag among those

trees," MacDonald told Godfrey, "but I was mistaken."

"You would not find deer so far down the hill as that and so near human habitation. Not at this time of the year, at any rate."

Murdoch and Darroch had climbed as far as they could up the hill while still keeping to the trees. Now they would have 200 yards or so of open ground to cross before reaching the broch. If he had been standing on the other side of the wall, as he well might have been, they would probably have got to within 20 or 30 yards of him without his noticing them.

"Well so long," he said to Godfrey handing the binoculars back. "I must continue my exercise."

"Your exercise?"

"Yes, jogging. I was just resting up for a few minutes when you found me, but I must get moving again now before I start to stiffen up."

Turning away he began to run up the hill away from the broch towards the east, not hurrying but with easy rhythmic strides. He heard Murdoch or Darroch shout and saw Godfrey look in their direction, surprised, and kept going. The broch was on the upper slopes of Cnoc na Moine and only a gentle climb separated him from the summit of the hill. Murdoch and Darroch, on the other hand, if they decided to chase him would have the steepest part facing them as well as rough, uneven ground and the thickest of the heather.

Glancing over his shoulder, he saw that they were well in the open now, running as best they could and that Darroch was carrying a shotgun. Murdoch shouted at Godfrey, gesticulating, trying to tell him, perhaps, that he too should give chase, but the Englishman made no move.

Shortening and quickening his stride, MacDonald reached the summit of the hill. On the other side there was a sharp incline down at first and then a stretch of about 400 yards of gentle slope to the forestry plantation. He was running as fast as he could but the rough ground slowed him down for he knew that if his foot was to slip into one of the many ruts and holes in the heather, he would fall and might well break a leg. Before he was half-way to the plantation, his wind had gone and he groaned as he panted for air but, unfit as he was, he was at least twenty years younger than either Murdoch or Darroch. Looking over his shoulder again, he saw that they were only just reaching the top of the hill and well out of gunshot range.

Realizing that they would not be able to catch him they stopped chasing and stood silhouetted against the darkening sky, watching him escape. But MacDonald did not stop running until he was well into the plantation. There, he was confident, they would not come searching for him. The plantation, with its closely set trees, was already gloomy enough, and within a short time it would be dark. Secure in the knowledge that the police from Kilgona would be over on the morning ferry, Murdoch and Darroch could leave MacDonald to his own devices for the night. There was nowhere he could go, nothing he could do, he was a threat to no one.

Leaning against a tree to recover his breath, he began to curse. He cursed himself for his stupidity in ever coming to live on Alsaig, he cursed Murdoch and Darroch and most of all he cursed Fiona.

Now, as he remembered and began to think over the events of the past two days, he realized that there were questions he should have asked himself about Fiona before.

She had gone out of her way to invite him to dinner at Tigh Geal and it could only have been during that evening that someone had found time enough to go to the cottage, take his sweater and plant the incriminating stains of mud and blood. The following evening Fiona had left the ceilidh for a few minutes. Had she gone to free Hamish Grant from the hotel cellar? Then after the ceilidh she had driven MacDonald to Jessie Monro's house on the other side of the island. Had that been to allow Grant time to walk the three miles to the cottage and prepare his ambush?

There was one more picture which flashed on to his mind with a sudden, startling clarity. In the picture he saw Matheson and Fiona and himself standing outside the front door of Tigh Geal on the night he had dined there, waiting for the car from the distillery which was to take him home. He heard Fiona calling out to her husband in the house, telling him to switch on the lamp over the porch; the lamp which had given the unknown marksman waiting on the hill above the house the light he needed to see his target.

17

MACDONALD had been watching the house for almost 20 minutes. There was a light behind the curtained windows and from time to time he had seen the shadow of a person moving about inside the house; but he was not interested in what might be happening inside. What he wished to know was whether anyone might be on guard or on watch outside. He had circled the croft cautiously and seen no one and been down to the road and found no car. Common sense told him that no one was likely to be watching Jessie Monro's house, for no one would expect him to go there, but still he waited and watched until his lingering doubts were satisfied. Then he went and knocked gently on the door.

"The door's no' locked," Jessie shouted from inside. She had no reason to keep her doors locked for she had nothing anyone would want to steal, and no one on Alsaig would ever wish to harm her.

The atmosphere inside the converted Black House was heavy with peat smoke, for the new modern chimney that had been built worked far less efficiently than the hole in the thatched roof which had served as one for many years. Jessie had her arms full of peats which she had been bringing through from the kitchen.

"Sit you down, Mr. MacDonald," she said.

"I hope you don't think badly of me for coming uninvited."

"We're not too bothered about ceremony here on Alsaig," Jessie replied and began stacking the peats neatly on each side of the grate.

"Can I help you with that," MacDonald offered.

"It will be you that's coming to me for help I'm thinking."

"How did you guess?"

More than 80 years of life and the wind and the sun had weathered Jessie's face to the texture and colour of a dried walnut. Her small, dark eyes stared at MacDonald without smiling and he had the feeling that she knew more about life than he would ever know and more about him as well.

She said simply, "There was trouble in your face the night you came here with Miss Fiona, even though you never spoke of it."

"Yes, you're right."

"First you'll take a dram and a bite of supper and then you'll tell me about it. Folk talk better on a full stomach."

Before he had time to protest, she disappeared into the kitchen. The appetizing smell of cooking which he had noticed as soon as he entered the house had made him aware of how hungry he was, for he had eaten nothing since breakfast and precious little then. Presently Jessie came back with a tray on which she had placed a plate of what looked like stew, a knife and fork and half a tumbler of whisky. MacDonald sat down in a chair by the fire and she set the tray down on his knees.

"I won't say this isn't welcome," he said. "I haven't eaten all day. But aren't you going to eat as well?"

"I've had my supper, but I'll join you in a dram."

She went back into the kitchen and returned with another tumbler of whisky. MacDonald had the uncomfortable suspicion that it was her supper she had given him. The tray of food must have been ready in the kitchen and the stew was too hot to eat. The hospitality of the people of the Western Isles was legendary and he had heard tales of islanders going without food and drink to entertain a guest. But however guilty he might feel, it would be unthinkable to mention his suspicions or to question her.

The meat in the stew was venison, deliciously tender and cooked with wild herbs that Jessie must have picked herself. An uncharitable thought crossed his mind about how she might have got hold of such a fine piece of meat. Venison commanded handsome prices in Germany, and millions of pounds' worth were exported from Scotland each year by landowners eager to recoup the mounting costs of their estates. Then he recalled what Fiona had told him. On Alsaig the islanders had their own way of looking after Jessie Monro.

"It will be the police that you're running away from, I suppose," she remarked as he ate.

"Yes. They would like to charge me with murdering Sheena Campbell."

The noise that Jessie made expressed her contempt for the police far more eloquently than any words.

"I have to prove I didn't kill her," MacDonald added.

Jessie made no comment. From somewhere under her thick, black shawl she drew a tin containing cigarette papers and strong dark tobacco. As she rolled herself a cigarette, pinched the end and then lit it, she appeared to be thinking, wondering perhaps whether he deserved her help. Although MacDonald would never have been able to put into words his reasons for coming to Jessie, he was confident that she could help him should she choose to do so.

"I guess you knew Sheena?" he asked her.

"Aye and her mother and her mother's mother before that."

"Who on the island would have wished to kill her?"

She looked at him squarely as she replied. "No one on Alsaig surely."

"How can you be so certain?"

"There are some things a body just knows."

"I didn't kill her, Jessie."

"Aye, I believe you. You're not a man who would kill."

"Can you help me then?"

Jessie did not reply directly to the question. Instead she said, "I met the wee girl that evening before she was killed."

"Sheena? Where?"

"In the village."

"At what time?"

"It would have been at the back of six. She was on her way home from the doctor's evening surgery."

"Did you speak with her?"

"She would never pass me without stopping for a blether. Sheena and I were good friends."

MacDonald realized that Jessie was trying to tell him something and that unless he prompted her, she would tell him in her own time. That might mean in an hour or so, or the next day or next week. The only way of bringing her to the point more quickly would be by asking the right questions. He tried one at random. "How did Sheena seem when you saw her?"

"Happy. Happy and excited."

"About what?"

"She told me she had found a new boy-friend. That was the word she used. Boy-friend indeed! And she who never once went with a man less than ten years older than herself and often with men old enough to be her father."

Although he was sure the barb was not directed at him, MacDonald felt a pang of guilt. "Did she say who it was, Jessie?" he asked quickly.

Once again she did not reply but asked him a question. "Did you give the lass presents?"

"No. The police asked me the same question."

"Then did you promise her presents?"

"No." MacDonald decided it was best to be frank with this woman who, he suspected, was too old and too shrewd to be deceived by pretence or half-truths. "Jessie, you'll think I'm a louse and no doubt I am, but I never dated Sheena nor made up to her when I was sober. The only time I took any interest in her was when I had been drinking."

"Aye, I thought as much. Then you were not the boy-friend she mentioned.

'He's rich,' she told me. 'He'll buy me lovely things. I know he will.' She was just like a bairn who had been promised a new toy."

"You sure make her sound like a mercenary little bitch."

As soon as the words slipped out MacDonald knew he had blundered. Jessie's eyes grew cold, her mouth tightened in anger. She said, "Who are you to say that? Is it so sinful for a girl to want nice things? New clothes, a trinket or two, things she can keep for herself and for the day she gets married?"

"Of course not."

His answer did not placate Jessie. "I know what you're thinking. What did she do to get the things she wanted? What would she do? I can tell you one thing. She never fornicated, no matter how you and the others tried to persuade her, pouring drink into the poor, wee thing."

"Jessie, I'm not saying anything against Sheena. How can I? Everything you say is true. I'm deeply ashamed of the way I behaved."

"And well you might be!"

"All I want to do is to prove I didn't

murder her, but other people seem determined to prove that I did. They've even
lied and manufactured evidence to incriminate me."

"And who ever has done such a thing?"
Jessie asked sceptically.

"Angus Murdoch for one," MacDonald
replied, "and Archie Darroch from the
hotel. And it looks as though Fiona is part
of the conspiracy as well."

His remark about Fiona appeared to
upset Jessie, but not in the way one might
have expected. She did not become angry
or indignant, but agitated. "You must
never believe things like that about Miss
Fiona. She would never wish to harm
you."

"Well, I can tell you this. She sure
hasn't lifted a goddamn finger to help me."

"You should not be expecting her to
help you," Jessie said immediately and, it
seemed, without thinking.

"What do you mean? Why not?"

Jessie retreated into a show of impatience. "Questions, questions! A body
has better things to do than answer your
questions."

"Come on, Jessie! Tell me why she can't

help me." MacDonald sensed that this was what Jessie really wished to say but some inner constraint was holding her back. He was determined to prise it out of her.

"It's no' a thing a body can tell."

"You have my promise I won't repeat it."

She did not reply at once and he knew she was weakening. "You'll tell nobody?"

"Nobody. Not even the police."

"Surely not the police."

The old woman was silent, as though wondering how best she could begin and not wishing to be misunderstood. Finally she said, "As I've told you there's no man belonging to this island who would ever have killed Sheena, but there are more than a few who fancied her. You'll have heard of MacKenzie who has the farm beyond your cottage?"

Jessie told her story at her own pace and at first it was not much more than a catalogue of the men on Alsaig who had cast lustful eyes on Sheena Campbell. Besides the farmer at Gartness, there had been Hamish Grant and Darroch, whose wife had soon driven the girl from her job at the hotel although in Jessie's eyes she had done no wrong and Darroch had been to blame. Then there had been Jamie Gordon, a gardener at Ardnahoe and wee Fergus MacAlistair who worked part-time at the distillery as an electrician and mended the telegraph wires when the wind blew them down. According to Jessie even the Minister had fought hard and not wholly successfully to resist the temptation of Sheena's plump, pink flesh.

"You'll know Tom Buchanan, the dominie," Jessie said.

"You're having me on, Jessie. I'll never believe Tom was after the girl. He's not that type of guy."

"Maybe, maybe not. A man can have a mind for a girl and not even know it. All I can say is that in her last year at his school, he would keep her in the school-house long after the other bairns had gone, as a punishment he said. And it was often, too often."

MacDonald formed the impression that Jessie was trying to put as many men as possible in the list, as though multiplying the prevalence of a sin would dilute its sinfulness. He wondered what her motive might be.

"The lass would go up to Tigh Geal too," she said at last. "Always at night and always secretly."

"How do you know?" MacDonald asked, suppressing an urge to protest.

"I saw her once. Late at night it was. I'm often out at night. When a body gets to my age she needs little sleep. I was taking a short cut through the woods around Mr. Alisdair's house. Sheena was going up to the house along a path through the trees. I watched her go to the door at the side of the house and she knocked on it very softly. Then Mr. Alisdair opened it and let her in."

"There could be an innocent explanation for her visit."

"It was not her only visit. The next time I met Sheena I asked her. 'Oh, yes, I often go up to see him,' she told me. 'But he made me promise not to tell anybody and you're not to say a word about it either, Jessie.' She could be a proper little madam when she wished to be."

"Perhaps she was just boasting, making it all up."

"Not her. She was truthful, Sheena,

whatever anyone might say about the lass."

Now MacDonald understood what Jessie was trying to say to him. Knowing her loyalty to Matheson and her affection for his daughter, he realized too that she would not have made the suggestion lightly. It might or might not be true that Matheson had been having some secret relationship with Sheena Campbell. What was certain was that Jessie believed he had.

"So what you're saying, Jessie," he said slowly, "is that Fiona would not help me to prove I did not kill Sheena for fear that in doing so I might prove her father did."

"Aye. That's what she's affeared of."

"But you don't think he did?"

"Man, have you lost your senses?" Jessie's indignation exploded. "Mr. Alisdair never hurt a soul in his life. The wee lass was raped they say. Can you imagine himself doing such a thing?"

"Then why does Fiona think he might have killed her?"

"Because the poor thing is not thinking straight. She has troubles of her own as you may have noticed."

"With her marriage?"

She side-stepped the question as he might have expected she would. "Man, if you had known her as a girl, you would not even be recognizing her now. Such a bonnie lass! She would come with the others to my house and sit on the floor and drink milk and beg me to tell her stories. Great big eyes she had, as clear and as lovely as the sky. And as she grew older, I mind the times when I saw her with her dad. Great friends they were and she would be everywhere with him, fishing and shooting and round the distillery. He even took her stalking with him. That wee thing in a tweed skirt and jumper—Mr. Alisdair would never abide trousers on a woman—she would follow him as he crawled up the hill. By the time she was fifteen she could shoot and fish as well as any man. And she was not just bonnie and healthy and strong, but gentle and loving. Then she ups and weds and year after year when she and her man come back to the island I see the life and the love being drained from her. I see the hurt in her eyes."

Jessie stopped speaking abruptly, overcome by an emotion which she allowed

only seldom to show, much less to overcome her. If what she had suggested was
true, and MacDonald believed it was, then
he could not expect any help from Fiona.
And yet he needed help. He needed
someone who could get the answers to
questions he himself could not ask. Why
had Darroch lied to the police about the
cheque he had cashed at the hotel, for
example? Was it Murdoch who had hidden
a pair of girl's panties in the distillery
office? Who had allowed Hamish Grant
to escape from the hotel cellar? As an
incomer, a stranger to the island, he could
expect no one to volunteer those answers
even if they knew them.

Once again he felt a sense of helplessness, a feeling that time was running out
for him. He told Jessie, "I shall have to
leave now, Jessie. Thank-you for your
hospitality and thank-you for your help."

"Where will you go? If they are looking
for you the first place they'll be trying will
be your cottage."

"I don't know yet, but I have to
go."

"You could spend the night here."
Jessie's ancient face creased in a monstrous

grin, reminding MacDonald of the expressions he had seen on the faces of medieval gargoyles. "It's a year or two since I had a man beside me to warm the sheets."

"Jessie, you'll make me blush."

When she saw him to the door she laid a hand on his arm, her face serious again. "But you'll change things for Miss Fiona," she said. "You'll bring the laughter back into that face."

"I can't see how."

"Aye, you will. I knew that the first time I saw the two of you together. Jessie knows these things. Ask anybody on Alsaig. They will be telling you that Jessie knows these things."

When she opened the door of the house, he stepped out quickly and stood motionless for several seconds. As his eyes grew accustomed to the darkness he decided no one was lying in wait for him but, as a precaution, he went round to the back of the house before running for the cover of the nearest trees.

Going up the hill and circling the land on which Tigh Geal stood cut the journey along the length of the island by a good mile and a half and also enabled him to avoid Carrabus. He picked up his rucksack where he had left it and set out for Gartness, moving as swiftly as he could, still conscious that time was slipping away. In little more than twelve hours the police would be on the island, for by this time they would certainly have found out that he had returned there. As he moved northwards, with Carrabus on his right, the clouds broke briefly and a little pale moonlight filtered through. He could make out quite clearly the houses along the road and the shape of the hotel. He stopped for a moment, trying to see if Darroch's car was standing outside the hotel. It was, and so was another car which he recognized, the car belonging to Donald Fraser.

On his way to the cottage he wondered why Fraser was still on the island. He had formed the impression, from what Matheson had told him and from his own observation, that Fraser had no love for Alsaig, that he had come to the island simply to make a bid for the distillery on behalf of Thomson Distillers and that he had taken his rebuff badly. Everyone had expected him to take the first ferry that left Alsaig and get back to the mainland as fast as he could. Now, although the ferry had made the journey three times since the gale had blown itself out, Fraser apparently was still there.

When he reached Gartness, he approached the cottage with the same circumspection as he had Jessie's house. The cottage was easier to reconnoitre for it stood in the open. There were no trees on that part of the island and nowhere a person might conceal himself except behind the low drystone wall which surrounded the little piece of land belonging to the property, and the peat stack behind the kitchen door. He saw nobody behind the wall or the peat stack and no cars parked within a quarter of a mile of the place.

As an added precaution he did not switch on the light as he went into the front room of the cottage in case anyone watching from a distant vantage point might see it. Crossing the room in the dark, he tripped against a chair and, knocking his shin painfully, swore loudly and indelicately.

A woman's voice, which he recognized

immediately as Fiona's, said, "You might moderate your language when there's a lady present."

18

"HOW many men have you brought with you?" MacDonald asked her wearily.

"What are you talking about?"

"You didn't come alone to meet me at the broch, did you?"

"Now I understand. You believe it was I who told Murdoch and Darroch that you were back on Alsaig."

"Didn't you?"

"My dear Mike, you've lived on Alsaig long enough to have learnt that the telephones here have their own in-built bugging system."

The telephones were not operated by an automatic system and had no dials. A person wishing to make a call had to lift the instrument, wait until the exchange replied and ask for the number he required. The exchange was run 24 hours a day on a family shift system by Mrs. Buie and her unmarried daughter, but on occasions also by neighbours, customers calling at the post office and even by helpful children. Calls made after midnight involved a lengthy delay while Mrs. Buie or her daughter got out of bed and they had been known to rebuke the caller for his lack of consideration.

"Are you saying that Mrs. Buie listens in to calls?"

"Of course. On one celebrated occasion when Annie our cook was arguing with Margaret MacNab over an order she had placed with the store, Mrs. Buie even chipped in."

The curtains of the window in the living room were drawn apart, letting in enough light from the night sky for MacDonald to see that Fiona was sitting in one of the armchairs by the empty fireplace. He sat down in the other chair opposite her. Her manner seemed quiet and relaxed, with none of the cautious tension one would have expected in a person who might have come to betray him to the police.

"I left the house to come to the broch as soon as I could," she said. "And then, as I was driving down from our house to the road, I saw Murdoch and Darroch in their car going fast towards Ballymony. I followed them at a distance and when I saw them stop the car beyond Ardnahoe in the cover of the trees, I guessed that they knew you were back on Alsaig and were out after you. So all I could do was to hope you'd see them before they reached you."

"It was more through luck than judgement that I escaped them."

"What have you been doing since?"

"Wasting time mostly." MacDonald decided he would not tell Fiona of his conversation with Jessie Monro. Jessie's home might well prove to be the only safe house for him on the island, but that was just part of the reason.

"You still don't trust me, do you?" Fiona asked, not resentfully and not even impatiently.

"I wish I could be sure that I could."

"Would I walk half-way across the island and wait here in the dark for an hour, if I didn't wish to help you?"

"You walked?"

"Yes, across country. If Murdoch or Darroch had seen my car pass through the village they would have guessed where I was coming."

MacDonald began to get up from his chair. "Then you deserve a drink."

"Possibly, but I don't want one. Just tell me why you came back to Alsaig. Because you thought you could find out who killed Sheena?"

"No. To find out why people here have gone to such lengths to get me blamed for killing her."

He told Fiona of the conversation he had overheard between Sergeant Cairns and Constable Reid in the police station on Kilgona, of Darroch's lie about the cheque he had cashed at the hotel and of how his sweater had been stained with blood to incriminate him. She listened to him in silence and after he had finished made no immediate comment. He could just make out the outline of her face in the darkness, but could not read its expression. It may have been his imagination but she seemed unusually pale.

"If it's any help," she said at last, "Sheena didn't leave the hotel that night at two o'clock as Darroch has claimed. She was home around midnight, changed her clothes and went out again. Her grandfather told me so."

"She could still have had a date with me after she had been home. That's what the police would think I guess; that she went and changed her outfit just to please me."

"Then Archie Darroch must be made to admit to the police that he lied deliberately to incriminate you."

"And who could make him do that?"

"I think I might."

"I'd sure like to know why he picked on me as the fall guy."

When Fiona replied she spoke very slowly. MacDonald could not make up his mind whether this was because she wished to impress him with the truth of what she was about to say or because she was reluctant to tell him anything at all. "Darroch had behaved rather stupidly. He had written the girl some compromising letters."

The innuendo, MacDonald supposed, was that Darroch might himself have killed Sheena. He did not tell Fiona what Jessie had told him about Sheena's new boy-friend. It was only hearsay.

"I can't believe Darroch murdered Sheena," he remarked. "If he had, would

Murdoch help cover up for him? Murdoch seems like a pretty straight guy to me."

Fiona sighed; the sigh of one who had persevered with a task she had set herself for as long as she could, who had kept to herself a secret which she would have preferred to share, but whose will power had now been exhausted, a sigh of capitulation.

"I haven't been honest with you, Mike," she said finally.

"In what way?"

"When I picked you up on the road that morning and invited you to dinner, it was not because I hoped you could help me with my drink problem."

"No?"

"No. I too wanted to see whether I could help put the blame for Sheena's murder on to you."

MacDonald was silent. He knew now what she was going to say and he was glad that he had not broken faith with Jessie by repeating to Fiona what she had told him in her house a short time ago.

"It can only have been my father who killed Sheena; in some sort of fit of passion, I suppose. No one else would have done. And I wanted to protect him. It was wrong, but what else could I do?"

"Why on earth should he have killed the girl?"

The barriers of self-restraint crumbled and her story came flooding out. She told him how she had learnt more than a year previously that Sheena Campbell was coming to Tigh Geal to see her father, always alone and always at night. It had been Paul who had found this out. One night after she and he had gone to bed Paul, unable to sleep, had gone downstairs in search of a book to read. Hearing a female voice from Matheson's study, he had been curious enough to go and watch from an upstairs window until the visitor left. When he had told Fiona it had been Sheena, she had refused to believe him until two or three weeks later the same thing happened again, and this time he had woken her so that they could watch together. There had been more secret visits since that time, and it appeared that Sheena was going up to the house about twice a month.

"I was disgusted," Fiona said. "Disgusted and angry and ashamed. I wanted to tell him we had found out his loathsome secret, to accuse him to his face."

"But you didn't?"

"No. I asked myself who was I to be passing judgement on him. The way I have lived, the things I've done are even less excusable. I've shamed and humiliated him and he has never once even reproached me."

MacDonald had not heard her speak with such passion before. He had thought of her as reserved and introverted, an unemotional Scot. Now that she could not restrain her bitterness and self-recrimination, he suddenly wanted to comfort her but was afraid that she would reject his compassion.

"Aren't you jumping to conclusions? Even if what you say is true, it doesn't follow that your father killed Sheena. He has never struck me as a violent guy."

"He has a dreadful temper. I've seen him knock a man down."

"But would he strike a woman?"

Fiona hesitated and then she shook her head, not in answer to his question but as though to tell herself she must no longer

314

conceal what she was going to tell him. "You may as well know. After my mother died, women would come up to the house; the wives of fishermen away at sea or women he had brought over from Kilgona. Sometimes when he got drunk, there were shouts and blows and screams. Of course he adored my mother and when she died he went to pieces. Perhaps he never recovered."

"Did Sheena come up to your house on the night she was murdered?"

"How would I know? I went to bed early with the vodka bottle."

"Does anyone else on the island know about your father and Sheena?" MacDonald phrased the question carefully so that he would not inadvertently break his promise to Jessie Monro.

"I don't think so. Murdoch would be the only one, for Dad and he are closer than many brothers. But even if the islanders knew they would probably turn a blind eye. As far as they're concerned my father can do no wrong."

"So what you're implying is that Murdoch and Darroch tried to incriminate me in order to protect your father?"

315

"Something like that. At least that would be Angus's motive. Archie Darroch would like you to be blamed simply so that his little indiscretions don't come to light."

Anywhere else but on Alsaig, MacDonald would have found it impossible to believe that a man in Murdoch's position in the community would deliberately plot to implicate an innocent man in a murder, but he recalled what Buchanan had told him about the islanders. Tribal, he had called them, and when danger threatened from outside they would close ranks, lie, cheat, perjure themselves to protect one of their number. In this case they would think they were protecting their whole way of life.

"Whatever Murdoch may think," he told Fiona, "I refuse to believe your father killed Sheena. My judgement of people can't be so far out."

"There's one way to find out."

"How?"

"I shall ask him; confront him with it. He couldn't lie to me," Fiona said and then she added, "Hamish must have thought he killed her. That's why he shot at him."

"It wasn't Hamish who fired the shot that night."

"How do you know?" Fiona asked, and when MacDonald explained how he had discovered that Hamish's rifle had not been fired she said, "then if it wasn't Hamish, who did try to kill my father?"

"Why not Donald Fraser?"

"I suspected him at the time, so next morning I made some discreet enquiries at the hotel. Una Darroch assured me that Donald went straight back there after leaving Tigh Geal and started drinking in the bar. They had to put him to bed in the small hours. It seems he took to heart my father's refusal to sell the distillery."

MacDonald looked at Fiona. She seemed pale and drawn, but some of the tension he had thought he could detect in her manner when he found her in the cottage appeared to have ebbed away. He realized now that he had misjudged her and was glad he had been proved wrong. He was also aware of the effort it must have cost her to tell him something of which she was so ashamed.

"Thanks for being frank with me, Fiona," he said, wondering why he should have slipped so readily into the British habit of understatement. "It can't have been easy."

She got up to leave. "I nearly told you that night when I drove you home after the ceilidh," she said.

"So that was why you talked so much about your father."

"Yes, but I couldn't bring myself to tell you about him and Sheena."

"Well you did tonight and I'm glad."

MacDonald had stood up too and they faced each other in the darkness. Without warning she stepped forward, placed her hands on his shoulders and kissed him on the cheek.

"Now at least you know," she said softly, "that there is at least one person on Alsaig who cares what happens to you."

After Fiona had left, setting out on foot the way she had come, MacDonald changed his clothes. When he had gone with the police that morning he had been wearing a pair of light blue slacks and an old fawn corduroy jacket. Now he changed these for a pair of hard-wearing brown denims and two sweaters, the top one of a

318

heather colour. He had decided it would not be safe to sleep at the cottage that night. Murdoch and Darroch might easily come there while he was asleep and keep him prisoner at gun-point until the police arrived in the morning. So he would spend the night in one of the caves which the bird-watcher on Kilgona had mentioned. Moreover he had no intention of surrendering himself to the police in the morning, and should it prove necessary for him to hide from them on the hills, the colour of the clothes he had chosen would provide the best camouflage.

He still had the rucksack he had traded with the Glaswegian on Kilgona and he filled it with a few articles that might help to make his night of sleeping rough more comfortable: a blanket, a flask of hot coffee, what was left of the bottle of vodka, a powerful flashlight which he kept handy in the cottage for the not infrequent occasions when the electricity failed and an old pair of binoculars which he had bought in a pawn shop on his way through Glasgow on his way to Alsaig. Then he washed and shaved, cooked himself a dish of scrambled eggs and bacon and made two rounds of sandwiches with what was left of the bacon, to put into the rucksack for his breakfast the following morning.

The caves were on the most northerly point of the island, about half-an-hour's walk from the cottage. MacDonald had never visited them—no one on Alsaig ever did, for they were in no way remarkable and not easy to reach, set in cliffs above a deserted and very rocky shore. He found the spot without difficulty. There were three caves, he had been told, one reasonably large and two much smaller ones, side by side in the cliff about 25 to 30 feet above the shore.

The climb, even at night and burdened with his rucksack, was not a difficult one. He chose the cave on the right of the three, partly because it was one of the smaller ones but mainly because it was the last one that anyone coming to search for him there would try. If they did he might well hear them, as they scrambled up the cliff, and have time to escape.

The cave was not much more than eight feet wide at its entrance and ran back into the cliff for about double that distance, narrowing as it went. To MacDonald's surprise it was dry inside, which could only have been because the gales of the past few days had been from the south and south-east, hurling the sea on to the shore at the opposite end of the island. Using the flashlight, he searched the cave thoroughly and found no traces of past campers, no ashes from a fire, no empty tins, no paper.

This he felt was an encouraging sign, proving that people who came to camp in the caves, or simply to explore them, chose one of the other two in preference to the one he had selected. He drank a cup of coffee laced with vodka and then, wishing that he had brought a sleeping-bag with him, for the floor of the cave was solid rock covered only with a sprinkling of sand, he rolled himself in his blanket. For a brief moment he found himself wondering whether there had been any significance in the kiss Fiona had given him. But his body was exhausted, his nervous energy spent by the trials and tensions of the day and long before he reached a conclusion he fell into a deep sleep.

Fiona too felt exhausted when she arrived

back at Tigh Geal. For months she had not taken any exercise worthy of the name, and walking a goodish part of the length of Alsaig twice in one evening had left her muscles aching and stiff. As she approached the house Donald Fraser let himself out through the front door. For an instant an awful fear gripped her as she recalled what Mike MacDonald had said about Fraser, but the smile which Donald gave her was not the smile of a man who had just murdered an old friend of his father.

"Your old man's still up," he told her cheerfully, stepping aside and holding the door open for her. "He was wondering where you had got to."

"I've been out walking."

"As you can see so have I. I came up from the hotel on foot. Thought the exercise might do me good."

Obviously in good spirits, he strode away from the house down the drive. The dining-room was empty and Fiona guessed her father would be in his study. To turn the handle of the door required an effort of will, for she was still fighting her belief that it was in this room that Sheena

Campbell had been murdered, and imagined pictures of the scene, as the girl struggled and was then killed, flashed uninvited across her mind in loathsome detail. Her father was sitting at his desk writing a letter and he looked up and smiled as she came in but said nothing.

"What did Donald Fraser want?" she asked, sitting down to face him across the desk.

"I invited him up from the hotel to give him some good news."

"You surely haven't changed your mind and agreed to sell the distillery?" Fiona was surprised at her own indignation.

"Do I gather from your tone that you don't wish me to sell?"

"No. Not now."

"Then it's you who has changed your mind." Matheson laughed and looked pleased. "No, I simply wanted to tell Donald that I think I've found him a job."

"I thought he already had one."

Matheson explained that Fraser had been fired by Thomson Distillers, not only for failing to buy Alsaig distillery, but because Jake Thomson had decided to sell his interests in the whisky industry and pull out of Scotland altogether. Jake was like that. To accept defeat was beyond him, so instead he had made an instant decision. There was no future in Scotch; it was on the way out and he would put his money elsewhere. He had already begun negotiations to purchase a château in Bordeaux which produced an internationally known premier cru, as well as one of the smaller cognac houses.

"I felt sorry for Donald," Matheson concluded, "so I suggested he stayed over on Alsaig for a day or two while I put out a few feelers. I still have some friends in the whisky business you know."

"And you've persuaded one of them to take him on? That's a fine thing to do to a friend!"

"Don't be uncharitable! It's a selling job. Donald may know nothing about making whisky, but he might be rather good at selling it. Particularly abroad. Do you know he's quite an accomplished linguist?"

Fiona did not argue, for she knew her father had an infinite capacity for finding good in people even when precious little good existed. In any case she had no wish to waste time talking about Fraser, so she came directly to the point. "I have to ask you something Dad. It's about Sheena Campbell."

Matheson frowned. "You know I refuse to discuss that subject."

"Why? What have you got to hide?"

"What on earth do you mean?"

"It's no use." Now that at last they had reached the confrontation she had been dreading, Fiona was astonished at her own calmness. "How much longer do you suppose you can keep your sordid secret? Sheena is dead and questions are going to be asked. If no one else does, the police will want to know why she used to come up to the house at night and whether she was here on the night before she was murdered."

Matheson stared at her. The expression on his face was one Fiona had never seen before. It was as though he had started to smile, not kindly but a small, tight smile of anger and then the smile had frozen on his face leaving only a grimace on top of which amazement and dismay had been superimposed.

"God Almighty! You think I killed her!"

"Did you?"

Leaning forward, he placed his head in his hands, elbows on the desk. Fiona could see weariness and pain etched in every line of his face. When at last he spoke his voice was bitter. "You will have to ask yourself, my dear, what kind of man your father is. Is he a man who would commit adultery with an eighteen-year-old girl? Is he a man who would murder your cousin?"

Fiona closed her eyes. "Oh, my God!"

"I should have told you long ago. But it isn't quite as bad as you're probably thinking. Sheena was not my child, nor even my grandchild."

"Then whose?"

"Her mother was the illegitimate daughter of my brother Iain."

Rising from his desk, Matheson began walking up and down in front of the fire which was burning in the grate, as though the story he had to tell agitated him too much to be told sitting down. Sheena's grandmother, he told Fiona, had been a girl on Alsaig, the daughter of a crofter, who had caught his brother's eye, a girl

326

not unlike Sheena herself, who liked to be admired. No one had taken too much notice of what seemed like an innocent flirtation, and it was only after Iain had left the island to join the army and was serving in Egypt, that she had come to Iain's father and told him she was pregnant.

"My father would have made him marry her," Matheson said. "There isn't a shadow of doubt in my mind about that. He was a man of strong principles. But Iain never came back. He was killed in action not long afterwards."

"So what did happen?"

"My father persuaded one of the lads in the village, Andy Morton, to marry the girl by offering him a job in the distillery. As soon as they had been married, he sent the couple off to a distillery near Elgin belonging to one of his friends, ostensibly so that Andy could get experience of a new machine that was later to be brought into use at Alsaig. When they returned to the island a year later, they had a baby daughter."

"Sheena's mother?"

"Yes. And you know what kind of girl

she turned out to be. She married Sandy Campbell's boy and then ran off to Glasgow with another man. I sometimes wonder whether it was bad blood as the islanders would think, or whether life was loaded against her from the start."

"Does anyone else know the truth? That your brother was Sheena's grandfather, I mean."

"No. My father told no one except me. Murdoch's father, who was distillery manager in those days might have guessed. He was closer to my father than anyone, but he would have told nobody."

"Anyway you are not to blame."

"No. And by the time my father died and I took over the distillery it was too late to right the wrong he had done."

Matheson stopped pacing up and down in front of the fire and faced his daughter. In spite of the pain and embarrassment the telling had caused him, he was glad to have released the secret he had been sheltering for so long. He said, "But I felt our family had a moral responsibility for Sheena, especially after her mother had run away and her father had been drowned."

Fiona remembered the clothes and jewellery she had seen in the dead girl's room. "Have you been giving her money?"

"Yes. And the only way I could do it was to invite her up here and give her cash. I couldn't very well open a bank account for her and pay the money into it. The whole island would have known. The poor girl had a difficult enough time without that."

"I understand."

"I wanted to make sure she would not miss out on everything in life. She had been coming up here at night for a long time and I believe she enjoyed coming. She would chatter away about her ambitions and her dreams. Underneath that façade of a femme fatale which she tried so hard to cultivate, Sheena was really a nice person." Matheson paused and when he spoke again his voice was staccato with the strain of suppressed emotion. "I grew very fond of her."

All at once Fiona understood. She could picture their meetings in that room: a kind, lonely old man listening to the chatter of an eager child, seeing in her all the gaiety and optimism that had long since been eroded from his own life, finding in her company all the pleasure he should have found in a daughter.

Moved by what she saw in his face, she got up impetuously and went to him, placing a hand on his arm. More than anything she wanted to tell him how she felt, of her remorse for the selfishness which had blinded her for so long to his unhappiness and of her shame at having brought him nothing but her own self-inflicted troubles and more unhappiness, but the words would not come.

All she could say was, "Daddy, I'm so sorry."

He reached out, put his arm around her shoulders and held her close to him.

19

"I TRUST this is not going to be yet another fruitless journey, Sergeant."

"No sir. He's on the island. We can be sure of that."

"Let us hope so. I was assured he would be on this island when I arrived yesterday," Inspector Cameron said pointedly.

Cameron, who had flown out to Kilgona from Stornoway the previous day, was displeased. He had expected that he would have been able to fly back to Stornoway that afternoon, taking his prisoner with him. Instead he had been forced to spend the night on Kilgona and he knew from experience of all the domestic aggravation that this would cause. His wife, who was deeply and permanently suspicious of Cameron ever since a little incident with a woman police constable had been brought to her notice, grew furious whenever he spent a night away from home, and on his return she would take her revenge.

Cameron could now look forward to a week of sullen silences, injured looks, bitter remarks and badly cooked meals.

"What makes you so certain that the American has gone back to Alsaig?"

"He has been seen there," Sergeant Cairns told him for at least the third time. "And the crew of the ferry report that they took a man answering to his description over to Alsaig yesterday afternoon."

"I seem to recall that the crew of the ferry to the mainland said the same thing," Cameron retorted with a bitchiness which even his wife would have been hard pressed to emulate.

When Cameron and Cairns had arrived at the police station from the airport the previous day, they had learnt that MacDonald had left. "Escaped" was not a word that could be used since the American had not officially been in custody. Assuming that he would attempt to get to the mainland they had immediately driven to Lossit and, arriving after the ferry had sailed, had been told that a man carrying a brown leather suitcase had first bought a ticket for the voyage and had later been seen boarding the ship. A telephone call to the mainland had sent a police car hurrying to meet the ferry at its point of arrival, where it had picked up a belligerent little Glaswegian who was threatening to sue for false arrest and would certainly complain to his Member of Parliament. Inspector Cameron, who disliked being made to appear ridiculous, had already decided that when they caught up with the American, he would be taught that foreigners are not advised to trifle with the Scottish police.

Because he had been inconvenienced, Cameron had also taken his own small revenge on Sergeant Cairns and Constable Reid by making them report at an unnecessarily early hour at the police station that morning to prepare for the trip to Alsaig, and then by keeping them waiting for 45 minutes while he had a decent breakfast at his hotel. Cairns had spent part of the time telephoning Murdoch.

"Can we rely on this man, Murdoch?" Cameron asked.

"Aye, surely, sir. He used to be a Special until he resigned a month or two ago."

"A pity you've been so dilatory about finding another."

"It's not easy in summer. Everyone on the island is too busy with the harvest and holiday-makers and shooting parties to look after."

"If he saw the American on the island last evening," Cameron complained, "why on earth did he not grab the man and hold him until we arrived?"

"He tried to, but it seems that MacDonald saw him coming, ran off and hid in the trees."

"It sounds to me as though we'll need to mount a full-scale man hunt to find him." The Inspector was beginning to see the possibility of a second night away from home.

"I doubt it will be too difficult, sir. Apart from a few trees on the eastern side of the island, and one small forestry plantation, there's no cover at all. And there will be people about. One of the landowners has guests over for the stalking. If the American moves anywhere he'll be seen."

"The three of us can't cover much

ground," Cameron persisted. "Even on a small island."

"If you agree, sir, we can get local people to help. Murdoch said he could muster at least half-a-dozen."

"I suppose we'll have to manage as best we can. To send for more men from the force would delay things for a day at least, even if headquarters were willing to let us have some."

The three men left the station and went out to the police car which stood waiting. Sergeant Cairns was pleased to notice that the high winds of the last few days showed no signs of returning. Moreover the clouds which had persisted for the past week were breaking up and patches of blue sky could be seen to the west. When the cloud base was low, the upper slopes of Beinn Laimsdearg were shrouded in a dense mist and there a man on the run could hide indefinitely.

"Before we leave," Cameron said to Cairns as an afterthought, "call that man Murdoch and see that he warns the people on Alsaig to be on the watch for the American, especially around the outlying crofts."

"I did that this morning, sir. One might say that the man hunt has already begun."

MacDonald awoke later than he had intended. He had slept fitfully for the early part of the night, unable at first to get comfortable on the hard floor of the cave and afterwards waking from time to time, believing that he might have heard someone moving on the rocks below, conscious always of danger or startled by short, vivid dreams. Eventually, exhausted by exertion and tension, he had fallen into a deep sleep and when he woke it was already past dawn.

From where he lay, at the back of the cave, he could see a circular patch of sky towards the north. He seemed to detect a touch of frost in the air which suggested that what little wind there was had swung round to the north or east, promising a fine, sunny day. For him that would be the worst possible weather. Had the wind risen once again to gale force, the ferry, which would surely be bringing the police from Kilgona, might have been delayed, giving him a few more hours to uncover Sheena Campbell's murderer and thus prove his own innocence. Alternatively a heavy overcast sky and rain might at least have allowed him to hide more easily from the police when they began to search the island as they surely would.

Rousing himself, he sat up, ate one of his sandwiches and drank some coffee. In the night, during one of his many short uneasy bouts of sleep, he had dreamt of the events of the past few days and had woken with an idea which at the time had seemed startlingly original but which as he fell asleep once more had disappeared with all the finality of a burst bubble. It was not a new experience. In adolescence he had often woken during the night with exciting ideas for the theme of a poem or of a play he wished to write, only to find the next day that he could remember nothing more than a misshapen outline.

Now he tried to recall the idea and after several minutes of concentration, it emerged and began to take shape. As always, in the unfriendly light of morning, it appeared surprisingly banal. The idea was this: until then his thinking had been concentrated entirely on Sheena's death, mainly because it had seemed to involve himself, to threaten him. The attempt on Matheson's life had assumed in his mind a secondary rôle, and when he had recognized that in all probability the two events, murder and attempted murder, had been in some way related, he had treated it without thinking as a causal relationship, the shooting of Matheson being a consequence of the killing of Sheena. Now, the idea which had come to him in the night had suggested he should reverse the rôles and address all his powers of reasoning to why and by whom Matheson had been shot and why Matheson himself had tried to pass off the shooting as an accident.

As a starting point he went back to the moment when the shot had been fired. Matheson, Fiona and he had been standing outside the front door of Tigh Geal in a small pool of light thrown by the lamp above the porch. He remembered the roar and the whine of the gale and the restless swishing of the leaves in the trees surrounding the house. Somewhere up on the hill overlooking the house, the marksman had been standing, lining up his victim in the telescopic sight.

MacDonald tried to visualize the

assassin, a man standing out there in the darkness, equipped and ready to kill. He could picture him quite clearly; a watchful, determined man, wearing two heavy sweaters to keep out the wind, tweed trousers or perhaps shooting breeches, a deerstalker hat or a kitted cap and mittens so that his fingers would be warm enough to exert just the right, slow pull on the sensitive trigger when the time came. He would have made himself comfortable, finding something against which he could lean and steady his arm, checking the range of the shot at not much more than 100 yards. There would be no emotion in the killing, no excitement, just professionalism.

Logically the attempted shooting must have been planned in advance. No one would wait, rifle poised outside a house at night on the off-chance that the person he intended to kill would emerge and stand by the entrance in a convenient pool of light bright enough to give him a shot. No one would have gone to the trouble of getting Hamish Grant incapably drunk and taking him up on to the peat moss in his Land-Rover to be the scapegoat unless he had known or was reasonably sure of two things: that Matheson was entertaining a guest to dinner that night and that it was his habit to come out of the house to speed his guests on their way.

It was the mental picture he had formed of the man and the adjective he had used, subconsciously, to describe him which triggered off a sudden, startling idea. MacDonald remembered the stranger who was supposed to have given Hamish Grant a bottle of whisky. He recalled the shadowy figure who, he believed, had been watching and following him that night in the village when he went to check Grant's rifle. He remembered the food which had been stolen from MacNab's stores. He thought too of another factor in the problem which he had been in danger of forgetting; of why Hamish Grant had been brutally and callously killed while he was imprisoned in the warehouse.

"My God!" he exclaimed aloud. "It all fits! That's it! A professional! A hit man!"

Early that morning Paul Stokes loaded the tarpaulin he had bought a few days previously into the back of the Volvo.

Although the tarpaulin was heavy, muddy and difficult to handle, he managed to lift it unaided into the back of the estate car, pulling and pushing it until it lay in untidy folds on the floor. Then he drove down to find Robbie Tait, the fitter who looked after the machinery and equipment at the distillery and also serviced and repaired cars and tractors on the side.

"Be a good chap, Robbie," he said, "and check the tyres, the battery, the lot. The engine oil is bound to be low. My wife has been driving it and you know how women are with cars." He smiled to show that as men they could both understand and tolerate the weaknesses of women. "After you've finished, drive it to Mrs. Buie's place and have the tank filled. Tell her to put it on our account."

"Will you be wishing me to bring it back to the house afterwards, sir?" Robbie used the title instinctively, although there was no one else on Alsaig whom he or anyone else would have addressed in that way. It was a courtesy reserved for holidaymakers and incomers.

"No. Leave it in the car park by the ferry. Right at the back so it won't hamper anyone. I'm crossing to Kilgona this afternoon."

"And the keys?"

"Leave them in the car. I'll walk down when the time comes. God knows I need the exercise. Far too much good living on Alsaig." Stokes patted his stomach jovially.

As he was leaving the distillery to walk back to Tigh Geal, he met Fiona driving through the gates in the Datsun. She drew the sports car up alongside him and they looked at each other, guardedly, like two people of the same nationality meeting unexpectedly in a remote foreign country.

"What are you doing here?" Stokes asked.

"I might ask you the same question."

He told her of the arrangements he had made to have the Volvo serviced and that he would be going over to Kilgona on the afternoon ferry. Then he added, "Forgive my curiosity, but it's unusual to find you up so early in the morning."

"I'm here to see Murdoch."

"Ah, the faithful Murdoch! May one ask why?"

Fiona was tempted to tell him that he

was perfectly entitled to ask why but not entitled to assume that he would get an answer. Then, remembering how much she disliked bitchy women, she replied, "I'm worried about Daddy's safety. It's all very well for him to pretend that nobody took a shot at him the other night, but we know somebody did. And there's every reason to suppose that having failed once he will try again."

"I still think the shot was intended for your friend MacDonald."

"If it was, then Murdoch will know. I suspect he knows much more about the whole business than he has so far told us."

"You may be right." The tone of Stokes's reply was intended to show that the subject was one which he found excruciatingly boring.

After he had set off along the road, Fiona got out of the car and went to the distillery office where she found Murdoch and Darroch waiting for her. She had telephoned Murdoch twenty minutes earlier to say that she wished to speak with him and Darroch as soon as possible and she had told him in such a way that he would realize that she expected her wish to be obeyed. Informal and democratic though life on Alsaig might be, sometimes one reached a point when Matheson or his daughter would expect their orders to be obeyed without much more than a token question. As though to acknowledge this, Murdoch had left the chair behind the desk in the office, the owner's chair, unoccupied and Fiona, accepting the droit de seigneur went and sat in it.

"It was good of you to agree to see me so early in the morning," she said.

The pacifying cliché, taught on management courses and in army staff colleges at great expense, came instinctively to her, with the difference that in her case Fiona meant it. Not unexpectedly neither Murdoch nor Darroch had any cliché to offer in return but mumbled some uncomfortable reply. She continued, "What I wish to know is why the two of you have been trying to place the blame for Sheena Campbell's murder on Mike MacDonald."

The bluntness of her accusation caught the two men by surprise. More sophisticated conspirators would have had a plausible denial for reply but Darroch could only bluster. "I don't know how you can say such a thing, Miss Fiona!"

"It's you, Archie, who's mainly to blame," Fiona replied firmly. "You're the one who said that Mr. MacDonald left your hotel with Sheena on the night before she was murdered."

"And so he did."

"Maybe. But at around midnight and not at two in the morning as you claimed. Sheena's grandfather will confirm that she was back home by midnight and then went out again."

"I wouldn't know about that."

"No? You also told the police that Mike cashed a cheque for £50 on the night before Sheena was killed. You know and I know he cashed it in your bar the following morning."

"The date on the cheque is for the day before the girl was killed."

Ignoring his protest, Fiona turned on Murdoch. "And you, Angus. Was it you or Archie or both of you who took Mike's sweater from his cottage, soaked it in muddy water and a little blood and then put it back where you knew Mrs. Anderson would find it? And what about that pair of panties, Sheena's no doubt, which you secreted away in this office?"

The weaker man of the two, Darroch, was ready with more denials but Murdoch, who had known Fiona since she was a baby and who recognized the qualities she had inherited from her father, realized that pretence and evasions would be pointless. He said, "All right, Fiona, maybe we did pile up the evidence against MacDonald a wee bit. But where's the harm in that? He did kill the girl."

"What makes you so sure of that?"

"Who else can it have been?" Darroch asked.

"Any number of people, I should think," Fiona replied. "You know as well as I do that Sheena couldn't help being a troublemaker. She had caused trouble between several men on the island and their wives."

"Not serious enough for any of them to have wished to kill her."

"No? Then what about those daft letters you wrote her, Archie? What would your wife do if she saw them? And how far would you have gone to get them back?"

Darroch looked stunned and frightened.

"How did you find out about them, Miss Fiona?"

"Never mind about that. I'm not accusing you. I'm only asking why you two are so quick to blame Mike MacDonald."

"Of course he killed her," Murdoch said. "The things you're talking about might have caused family rows. A few women on the island might have wished to tear Sheena's hair out and I for one was often tempted to put her over my knee as her father would have done if the poor man had been alive, but no one on the island would have killed the lass." He spoke without conviction like a man who knows he is telling at least half a lie.

"So as Mike is the only stranger here it had to be him? Is that what you're saying?"

"Yes, Miss Fiona. And he's an American after all," Darroch chipped in.

Fiona looked at Murdoch, thinking that one could not help but admire the man's loyalty. Darroch, she knew, was only acting out of fear, terrified that he might be accused of Sheena's murder, but it was Murdoch who had conceived the plan to incriminate Mike MacDonald, who had persuaded Darroch to lie about the time MacDonald had left the hotel.

"I suppose it was you, Angus, who first found Sheena's body that morning," she remarked.

Murdoch's hesitation was only momentary. "Yes, Fiona. I was walking my dog in the trees around Tigh Geal early that morning. I picked her up and carried her as far along the road away from your house as I could. If I could have been sure nobody would see me I'd have got the car out and taken her up to Gartness by MacDonald's cottage. Later I went back to see if there was anything lying around in the trees to show where she had been murdered. I found a pair of panties near the side door to your house, brought them away and hid them in this office."

"And you did all this, tampered with evidence, manufactured false evidence, simply because you believed Mike killed Sheena?"

"Why not?" Darroch said stubbornly. "It's no' so terrible."

"It was a good try," Fiona smiled as

she shook her head, "but not a very likely story."

"What do you mean?"

"You know as well I do that you did it to protect my father, because you think it was he who killed Sheena."

"Miss Fiona!"

"You, Angus, must have known she had been going up to the house late at nights. You must have guessed he was giving her money. There can't be many secrets on Alsaig that you don't know." She paused. Murdoch's silence was the admission she had expected. "Why did you do it, Angus?"

Murdoch looked uncomfortable. A blunt and honest Scot, he disliked questions he could not answer honestly and he did not know the honest answer to the question Fiona had asked him. To have disentangled the different motives which had made him do what he had done would have needed the subtle analysis of a philosopher. Loyalty was one, tribal instinct another, but there was self-interest as well. So he chose the answer which would sound most plausible.

"If Mr. Alisdair was taken from the

island, jailed for life, that would be the end of the distillery."

"And of the island," Darroch added.

"Because you think I'd sell out to the Americans?"

"Wouldn't you, Fiona?"

Now Fiona might have been embarrassed by a question but she did not flinch from it. "Maybe at one time I might have been ready to sell, but I can tell you this now. The distillery will never be sold so long as it is in my power to prevent that."

Her statement and its decisiveness surprised Fiona, for she had not been thinking about the future of the distillery and had certainly made no conscious decision until that moment. Now suddenly she made up her mind, finally and irrevocably. She could not recall when she had last felt so positive and determined about anything, but then in the last 48 hours she had surprised herself in more ways than one.

"And I can tell you another thing. My father didn't kill Sheena nor did Mike MacDonald."

"How do you know, Fiona?"

"There's no time to explain now.

Someone tried to kill my father the other night. I suppose you've guessed that as well."

"Of course! We're not stupid. Mr. Alisdair has been handling guns all his life. How could he shoot himself accidentally and in the arm?"

"In spite of what you have thought, it wasn't Hamish who shot at him. Yes, I know you found him up on the hill the next morning but his rifle had not been fired." Fiona went on to explain how MacDonald had checked Grant's rifle.

"Then who did try to kill your father?"

"I've no idea. And we'll not find out sitting here and talking about it. What's much more important is that whoever it was is likely to try again."

"What can we do?"

"By ourselves not very much. But the police will be arriving soon. I suppose they know by now that Mike is back on the island."

"Yes. I told them so last night."

"Then when they arrive you two will have to explain that Mike didn't kill Sheena so that they can concentrate on finding out who did."

"How can we do that?" Darroch complained. "Without admitting that we tried to implicate him? That's perjury, is it not?"

"I'm sure you're clever enough to find a way," Fiona replied mercilessly. "And between us and the police we have to find a way of protecting my father as well."

"You're right," Murdoch agreed. "For a start, try and persuade him to be sensible, Fiona. The way he strolls about, from Tigh Geal down here and around the village, is just inviting someone to take a shot at him. Can you not make him stay indoors for the time being?"

"I'll try, but you know how stubborn he is, Angus."

"Aye, I do. He'll not believe that the next shot won't miss."

20

MACDONALD packed the old rucksack carefully, putting in everything he had brought with him from the cottage except the binoculars. Then he stowed it at the very back of the cave where it would not be seen by anyone who might just glance in from the entrance. In all probability the precautions he was taking were totally superfluous, for the chances of his spending another night in the cave were remote. He would be fortunate if he were ever allowed to spend another night on the island.

Climbing down from the cave he moved along the cliff and explored the cave on its left, but could find nothing to show that anyone might have been sheltering in it during the last few days. He had decided that if a man had been sent to Alsaig to kill Matheson, he would have had to find somewhere to sleep out, for only in that way would he be able to conceal his presence on the island and his identity. No house would be safe, a tent would be too conspicuous, and that left only the caves. It was true that few people from the mainland would know about the caves but a professional killer, a real hit man, would have briefed himself thoroughly, finding out everything he needed to know about Alsaig, its people and their habits.

The remaining cave, the largest of the three, also seemed at first to be empty. MacDonald could see nothing in it to show that it had ever been used as a shelter, much less traces of recent occupation. But there was a smell about the place, a faint aroma which he could not at first identify, but which might well have been the smell of food. Then suddenly he recognized what it was: the smell of fried bacon, the aftermath of breakfast cooking.

Examining the cave more carefully, he found other, tangible remnants of a meal which had escaped his notice: tiny pieces of eggshell, breadcrumbs and the metal ring opener from a can of beer. A fine grey sand of powdered rock lay on the floor of the cave and whoever had sheltered there had, before leaving, smoothed it over to hide his footmarks or any other traces of his stay. But he had done so carelessly or hastily that morning and MacDonald found one footmark near the entrance, the impact of a man's nailed boot, size eight or nine he judged.

Leaving the cave, he climbed down to the rocks and along the shore to the point where the cliffs began. There he turned inland, crossing the road and heading up the slopes of Beinn Laimsdearg. The wind had dropped to little more than a fair breeze and the broken clouds were clearing the south.

By now he was convinced that somewhere on the island was a killer, a man who had been sent to kill Matheson, a man skilled enough in his trade to have crossed over on to Alsaig unnoticed and remain undetected ever since. Having failed once in his mission, the man would be in a hurry to complete it and, now that the ferry had started sailing once more, to leave the island. He would have spent the past night in the largest of the three caves and his carelessness in removing the traces of his stay meant surely that he had no intention of using it again. If this line of reasoning were correct, Matheson was to be killed that morning and the hit man would be away on the ferry. MacDonald was almost certainly the only person on Alsaig who knew of his existence so it was he who would have to find him before he could carry out his contract.

Driven by a sense of urgency, he scrambled up the mountain. The ground was rough, pitted with holes and drained by tiny streams which trickled down the slopes, some so small that they were almost wholly hidden in the heather. Moving as quickly as he could, looking for dry footholds, MacDonald worked his way up the mountain, keeping to the eastern face and moving towards the south, for he reasoned that the hit man would also be headed in that direction, making for Tigh Geal.

At about 700 feet up he found a rocky spur which gave a vantage point from where he could look down on the central portion of the east coast of the island, stretching from the ruins of the old distillery, through the village and up to Matheson's house. All he could see of the house itself was the roof, a glimpse of white walls through the trees and the extreme end of the entrance drive where it joined the road to Ballymony.

Looking out to sea, he saw the ferry approaching from Kilgona and watched it manoeuvre, the helmsman holding its bows up against the current from the north which ran along the coast of Alsaig, so that he could bring the squat front of the landing craft squarely up to the concrete landing ramp. Two cars, the one which Murdoch usually drove and the Datsun sports belonging to Paul and Fiona came through the distillery gates and drove down through Carrabus towards the ramp. MacDonald watched them pull up on the tarmac area on the inland side of the road, where vehicles awaiting the ferry could park, and noticed that the Volvo belonging to Matheson which Fiona often drove was also waiting there, empty as far as he could tell. Two men, Murdoch and Darroch emerged from the distillery car and Fiona climbed out of the Datsun and they walked across the road to meet the police car as it came off the tank-landing craft.

Swinging the binoculars round, MacDonald began scanning the slopes that stretched down from where he was standing towards the trees around Tigh Geal. He saw nothing. There was less than a mile of open ground between him and the house and anyone moving across it should be easy to spot. The only cover to be found would be among the few scattered clumps of broom at the back of the houses of Carrabus. A cautious man, he felt, would not have gone that way but made a detour, keeping well inland, crossing the narrow valley between Beinn Laimsdearg and Cnoc na Moine, then going up the hill to the forestry plantation. From there he would be left with only a short stretch of open ground to the trees that surrounded Tigh Geal.

Looking towards the west, he saw a Land-Rover and a Range Rover standing half-way up the hill on the track which wound its way through the peat moss. The Land-Rover was the battered old vehicle in which he had often seen Hamish Grant driving around the island and the Range Rover looked like the one which had been on the ferry from Kilgona the previous afternoon. He could see nobody in or near either vehicle and realized that they must have been driven there by a party from

Mrs. Colville's house setting out to stalk deer on either Cnoc na Moine or the lower slopes of Beinn Laimsdearg. The end of the track was as far as one could drive with any comfort, and the stalkers would be further inland hidden from his view, six men in all probability, working in pairs: the underkeeper from Ardnahoe and two men recruited for the day from among local people, who would do the stalking, each followed by one of Mrs. Colville's guests armed with a rifle.

To have stalkers on the hills that morning would be a great convenience for a hit man, MacDonald realized, for anyone looking up from the village and seeing a man with a rifle on the slopes would assume he was one of the stalking party. It might also be a help to himself when the police began to search the island for him, as he was sure they would.

Still believing that the hit man would be hiding somewhere in the vicinity of Tigh Geal waiting for a chance to kill Matheson, and conscious that time was slipping away, be decided he must get closer to the house if he were to have a fair chance of spotting him. Taking a quick look at Carrabus, he saw that the police car was being driven down the road towards the Colville Hall and that Murdoch's and Fiona's cars were following. The police, he supposed would be wanting to talk to Murdoch and Darroch, perhaps to get their help in raising volunteers from the islanders to help in the search for the fugitive.

Encouraged by the thought of the delay this might mean, giving him a little more precious time, he left the rocky spur and scrambled down the side of the mountain towards the valley and Cnoc na Moine beyond. The remains of a drystone wall marking the boundary of Mrs. Colville's extensive lands, stretched across the valley, affording him a little cover. He kept as close to it as he could. Halfway across, a notice had been fixed to the wall which read:

In the interests of their own safety persons wishing to walk on the hills during the stalking season (August to February) are advised to telephone Ardnahoe House.

Knowing that he would be exposed to the

view of people in the village as he crossed the track through the peat moss, he did it on the run, dashing for the shelter of the young trees in the forestry plantation.

There he had time to regain his breath and then focus his binoculars on Matheson's home. From his new position he could see most of the house through the trees, as well as the greenhouse and the garage. The garage was some 50 yards behind the house and large enough to hold two cars. Its doors were open but from where he stood he could not see inside. He knew in any case that the Volvo and the Datsun sports were both in the village. As far as he could tell there was no movement in or around the house itself.

He had dropped the binoculars, leaving them to hang from his neck on their leather strap and was wondering what he should do next, when he heard the sharp crack of a piece of dry wood snapping followed by a rustling noise of something moving between the closely planted trees around him. The noise was so slight that he thought it had to be a deer stepping delicately as it passed through the plantation, but as a precaution he stayed where he was, motionless. Whatever it was, man or beast, passed far enough away for him not to see it or be seen by it. When the noise faded and finally stopped, he moved forward cautiously to the edge of the plantation, following it.

When he reached the open he saw it was a man who was now moving away from the trees, crossing the track on the peat moss as swiftly as he could, just as MacDonald had done. The man was short and powerful, dressed in slacks and a sweater of a colour which, at a distance, would merge into the heather on the hills and slopes of the island. He was also carrying a rifle but he held it not as though it were ready for use, loaded and safety catch off, but carelessly, letting it swing as he ran, as though it had already served its purpose.

"So you see, Inspector," Fiona said, "Mr. MacDonald did not kill Sheena Campbell."

Fiona, Murdoch and Darroch were with Cameron in the Colville Hall where he had set up his headquarters before starting a search for MacDonald. Although he wished to finish this business as soon as possible and return with a prisoner to Stornoway, the inspector was acting slowly and deliberately. A long training in police procedure, coupled with a cautious temperament and a ponderous intelligence, prevented him from ever taking any measures which were not methodically planned and thorough. Once, some years previously, when working on the mainland, he had allowed two men who had burgled an old castle of all its art treasures to slip through his fingers, when flair and a quick decision would have had them arrested. The art treasures had never been recovered and Cameron's prospects of further promotion destroyed, but even so he had never learnt the lesson.

"May I ask, Madam, what is your interest in this matter?" he asked Fiona pompously.

"Like everyone else on Alsaig, I shall feel safer when Sheena's murderer has been caught and taken away."

"No doubt. And would not the best way of achieving that be by first finding this man MacDonald and questioning him?"

The man's dour and unresponsive

attitude was beginning to irritate Fiona. She had already explained to him that, after leaving the hotel with MacDonald on the night before she had been found murdered, Sheena Campbell had returned home and then gone out again, that MacDonald himself had arrived back in his cottage without being caught in the rain that had started not long afterwards and that Darroch had remembered cashing MacDonald's cheque on the morning after the murder. She had glossed over the question of how a blood-stained sweater had come to be found in the cottage, because she did not wish to get Murdoch and Darroch into trouble with the police, although that might have to be explained in due course.

Now, she said, "Won't you at least go and speak with the girl's grandfather, Inspector, before you waste time combing the island for Mr. MacDonald?"

"I can't see the urgency. We'll have time enough to speak to the old man later," Cameron replied stubbornly.

"Except that if whoever killed Sheena was the same person who took a shot at my father, he'll likely try again."

"A shot at your father? No one has told me about this."

In a few words Fiona explained how her father had been shot and wounded. She had persuaded Matheson the previous evening that when the police arrived they would have to be told the truth about the shooting and that since Hamish Grant was now dead, there was nobody whom his silence would protect.

"It is most regrettable that your father didn't report this at the time, Madam."

"I agree, but he had his reasons for not doing so."

"Had we known we would have proceeded in a completely different manner. More officers would have been brought over to the island." Cameron almost added that had headquarters known the facts, a more senior officer would have been put in charge of the case and he might have been spared the domestic squabbles which were going to face him when he arrived home.

"Does that mean you accept that Mr. MacDonald did not kill Sheena. We know it was not he who fired at my father."

"I shall make up my mind as to that

when he has been brought in for questioning. And there is still the death of the keeper, Hamish Grant, to be explained."

"So you think he murdered Hamish?"

"According to these two gentlemen," Cameron nodded in the direction of Murdoch and Darroch, "MacDonald was the only person on the island who knew that Grant had been locked up in the distillery warehouse. Is that not so?"

"Aye, that's true enough," Darroch agreed.

"If you waste time mounting a search for Mr. MacDonald you'll only be giving the murderer time to get away."

"MacDonald escaped from us on Kilgona," Cameron said stubbornly, "and now he's out somewhere on the island hiding from us. In my experience innocent people don't run away from the police."

Realizing that she would get nowhere arguing with a stupid man who was also a stubborn man, Fiona made a small noise which only hinted at the disgust she felt and left the hall. Cameron watched her leave and then turned to Murdoch.

"What's bothering her?"

"If you ask me, she's taken a fancy to

the Yank." It was Darroch who replied. His loyalty to Matheson and his family was not as instinctive as Murdoch's.

"Stop your blethering, man!" Murdoch said sharply. "You're as bad as an old woman."

"Well, let's get to work and organize a search for him," Cameron said. "We'll need all the men you can let us have. My sergeant and the constable can lead two teams."

"Sorry, there's no one I can spare from the distillery. We're short-handed as it is."

"But on the phone you promised Sergeant Cairns at least half-a-dozen!"

"Things have changed since then. You may pick up a couple of men in the village who will help you, but no more."

Cameron could see that Murdoch was not going to be swayed. Dimly he sensed that he had antagonized the man but he could not understand how. He decided it was just perversity. These people on the smaller isles were like children, mistrustful of strangers and prone to sulk if ever they were criticized. Reluctantly he accepted that he would have to arrange a search for the American as best he could and taking the Ordnance Survey map of Alsaig which he had brought with him he spread it on a table in front of him and began asking questions of Sergeant Cairns.

Meanwhile Fiona was driving back home in a mood of frustration. Although there was nothing else she could have done to persuade Inspector Cameron to change his mind, she felt somehow that she had failed MacDonald. At the back of her mind there was also an uneasy feeling, intuitive, for she had no rational reason for it, that her father's life was now in greater danger.

She drove through Carrabus, past the distillery and up the drive to the house as quickly as she reasonably could, impelled by a growing anxiety and, as soon as she reached Tigh Geal, ran into the house heading for the study. To her relief her father was there, sitting at his desk and going through the day's mail which had arrived on the ferry. Cathy, the clerkess from the distillery, was sitting opposite him taking dictation. When Fiona walked into the room, Matheson had just finished replying to a letter from one of the whisky companies on the mainland which wished to increase its order for Alsaig whisky.

"May I have a word with you in private, please?" Fiona asked him.

"Of course. Cathy and I have just finished anyway. There was nothing much in the post. People have lost the art of writing letters and think they can do everything by phone," Matheson replied, and then added to Cathy, "if you will get those letters typed up, I'll be down to sign them later on. And take the circular from the Malt Distillers' Association and those Customs and Excise forms and give them to Angus, will you please, dear."

After the clerkess had left the room, Fiona told her father, "The police are here. They're starting a man hunt on the island for Mike."

"Bloody fools! I thought Cairns had more sense."

"He's not in charge. Some dull-witted inspector has been sent over from Stornoway. He'll not listen to reason."

"You're going to a great deal of trouble for this American, aren't you!" Matheson smiled as he teased her.

The comment brought a faint flush to

his daughter's face and, noticing it, Matheson was pleased. For too long he had been watching, sadly and helplessly, as the girl's feelings had turned inwards, entangling themselves in an obsession with her own unhappiness, becoming locked in a spiral of self-pity which ended in a numbness of despair, from which she had only found relief by drinking. Now for the first time in two years or more she was clearly concerned for this young man's safety, which could only mean that she had some sort of feelings for him. It was a good sign and what was even better, she had scarcely taken a drink, had obviously not needed a drink, for the best part of two days.

"Perhaps I should go and have a word with this inspector," he suggested.

"I don't think that's a good idea, Daddy."

"Why not?"

Before Fiona could reply, the telephone rang. Matheson answered it and then handed it to her, saying, "It's the young man himself."

Taking the phone, Fiona heard MacDonald say, "Fiona?"

"Mike are you crazy? After what I told you about telephone calls on this island!"

"I had no other choice. Listen, is your father all right?"

"Yes. I'm with him now."

"Thank God for that! I've found who tried to kill him."

"Who?"

"A professional killer. He's on the hills now."

"A professional killer? You can't be serious! Things like that don't happen in Scotland."

"Don't you believe it. He has been sleeping in the caves beyond Gartness. I guess he was hired by Thomson Distillers and sent in to do the job. A contract killing we call it."

"Where is he now?"

"He was not far from your house a short while ago, looking for a chance to shoot again, I guess. Now he has crossed the valley on to the mountain. He's carrying a rifle."

The urgency in MacDonald's voice convinced Fiona more than any detailed explanations would have done that what he

371

was saying was true. She said, "What shall we do?"

"Make sure your father doesn't go outside. He should be safe enough in the house. And tell him to keep well away from any windows."

"Right. Then what?"

"I'm going after the man."

"Mike that's madness if he has a rifle!"

"I've no choice. When the police catch up with me, they'll never believe what I've just told you and the man will be left on the island to rub out your old man in his own time."

"If you've got to go after him you must be armed. I'll bring a gun out to you."

"There isn't time, Fiona."

"Please Mike!" Fiona begged him. "I can be with you in a few minutes."

MacDonald hesitated, knowing that what she was saying made sense. "All right. But hurry."

"Where are you now?" Fiona asked and then realized immediately that if Mrs. Buie were listening to their conversation, she would already know from which telephone kiosk the call was being made. So quickly she added, "No. We had better not meet there."

"I agree."

"Then where?"

"Do you speak French?" MacDonald asked her.

"Not fluently, but I understand it."

"Right then. Rendez-vous en dix minutes au coin de la nouvelle forêt tout près de la tourbière." Although the French would never have been commended by his old professor, MacDonald hoped it would at least tell Fiona where he wished to meet her. He added in English, "Did you get that?"

"Yes. I'll be there."

Fiona set the phone down, aware that her father was looking at her, expecting that she would spell out MacDonald's message and instructions, but she had already decided there was no time for explanations. So all she said was, "Daddy, I want you to promise me you'll stay in the house till I return." Matheson started to protest but she cut him short. "Please, Daddy, I haven't time to explain now. Just promise me what I ask."

"Oh, all right," her father agreed,

reluctantly because agreement seemed to imply an admission that he needed protection. "I was not planning to go out anyway. Not until I drive round to lunch with Bessie Colville, that is."

Impulsively Fiona kissed him on the cheek and then hurried out of the room. Her father's guns, Paul's, and the rifle she used to use in the days when she went stalking, were all kept locked in a cupboard built into the wall just outside the dining-room. First she had to fetch the key to the cupboard which was kept, for some historic family reason now forgotten, in a china urn in the drawing-room. Looking at the guns and rifles, she hesitated momentarily and then chose her own which, since it was lighter, an inexperienced shot as she guessed Mike was, would find easier to handle. It was not until she reached the front door of the house that she remembered bullets and went back to fetch a box of 20.

The Datsun was standing in front of the house. She climbed in, standing the rifle against the passenger seat next to her, started the engine and began driving away from the house. It was only when she had almost reached the road that a sudden thought struck her and she brought the car to a halt. MacDonald must surely have called her from the public telephone on the road to Ballymony. If Mrs. Buie or her daughter had listened into their conversation, they would almost certainly have told the police who would at once make for the telephone kiosk. In that case they would have to drive past the entrance to Tigh Geal and if Fiona drove out into the road in front of them, they would guess where she was going and would follow her instead. So, as a precaution, she decided to wait where she was and give them time to pass. For five long minutes she waited but no car drove past on the road to Ballymony. Then, losing patience, she drove out into the road, turned right towards Ballymony and then turned again up the track that led to the peat moss.

What Fiona did not know was that Mrs. Buie had in fact recognized MacDonald's voice, listened in to their conversation and then told not the police but Murdoch of the call. Murdoch, who by this time was almost as irritated by Inspector Cameron as Fiona had been, had not passed the information on to the police. As a result Sergeant Cairns and Constable Reid had set out in the police car with two volunteers from the village, to start their search at MacDonald's cottage, after which they intended to see whether he was hiding in the caves, before beginning to look for him on the hills. Inspector Cameron, in the meantime, was phoning his home in Stornoway to see if he could make peace with his wife.

Meanwhile back at Tigh Geal, Stokes, who had been writing letters in his bedroom, had looked out of his window and seen Fiona driving away in the Datsun. Going downstairs he had found Matheson in the study.

"Was that Fiona driving off?" he asked.

Matheson resisted an urge to point out that it could scarcely have been anyone else. "Yes," he replied.

"She seemed in a hurry. What's the trouble?"

"Mike MacDonald phoned. From what I heard of their conversation I gather he believes there's a professional assassin loose on Alsaig trying to kill me. What do the Americans call that kind of thing? A contract killing? Anyway he's going after the man and Fiona has taken him a gun. After that I suppose she'll go and tell the police."

"A contract killing!" Stokes laughed. "What an idea! Our friend MacDonald has allowed his imagination to be carried away by all those Gaelic legends he's been studying." He crossed to the window of the study, looked out and said casually, "It's a bore that Fiona has gone off in the Datsun, though. The Volvo is down at the distillery being serviced and I rather wanted to go down to the village and pick up a few things at MacNab's place."

"Then take the Renault. It's in the garage."

"Are you sure that's all right?"

"Of course. I shan't be needing it until lunch-time."

21

WHEN MacDonald reached the forestry plantation, he stopped to regain his breath. He had run all the way to the telephone kiosk by the kirk and run back too, as best he could uphill and through the heather. Now, retrieving the binoculars which he had left hidden among the trees so that they should not impede him as he ran, he started scanning the terrain opposite him.

Nothing moved on the lower slopes of Beinn Laimsdearg nor in the valley which separated the mountain from the hill on which MacDonald was standing. He began to regret the impulse which had made him leave the plantation to go and phone Fiona. His objective had been to warn Matheson, but if while he had been away the unknown killer had managed to go into hiding, the gesture would have been counter-productive. The man would have ample time to finish his mission after MacDonald had been caught by the police and taken off the island. Matheson could not stay sheltering in his house for ever.

He swept the mountain opposite him once more with the glasses. To his left and a few hundred feet up he could see a herd of red deer, the hinds feeding quietly around a fine stag. No doubt the stalkers would already be wriggling their way up the slopes through the heather towards them. Their target would be the stag, not for his antlers, splendid trophy though some might think them, but because each year the herd had to be culled and an agreed number of stags, usually selected from among the oldest beasts, would be shot to prevent the deer multiplying to such an extent that the island would not be able to support them and many would starve to death.

MacDonald supposed that the hired killer would know that stalkers would be out that day and would keep as far away from them as he could, not through fear of being accidentally shot, but in case he might be seen and later identified. Swinging the glasses slowly towards the right, he scoured the slopes carefully once again. Still he could see no sign of any human being.

Letting the glasses drop to swing round his neck, he cursed himself for not having followed the hit man long enough at least to have seen where he was going before he went to call Fiona. It was only then that his naked eye suddenly caught a brief glint of reflected light from the mountain opposite him. Quickly he trained the glasses on the place from where the flash of light had come. Then he understood why he had seen nothing there before. The man was lying down, stretched at full length on the same rocky spur which MacDonald himself had used as a vantage point before crossing the valley and like MacDonald he was scanning the terrain around him using the sight which he had detached from his rifle as a telescope. It was the reflection of the sunlight in the lens of the sight that had caught MacDonald's attention.

He watched as the telescopic sight swept the hills and slopes. It appeared to pause in its track as it was pointed in his direction and he stepped quickly back into the shelter of the trees, but the hesitation was only momentary. A few seconds later the man, apparently satisfied with what he had seen or not seen, rose to his feet, fixed the sight back on his rifle, climbed down from the rock and began moving down the slope in the direction of Carrabus.

MacDonald watched him. He seemed assured and relaxed, walking upright and not troubling to look for cover. When he was not much more than 300 yards or so from the houses on the edge of the village, he stopped, bent down and picked a bulky object from out of the heather. MacDonald saw it was a rucksack, not unlike the one he had acquired on Kilgona. The man appeared to be packing or repacking the rucksack and presently he put it back in its hiding-place and began walking back up the slopes of Beinn Laimsdearg once again. He was no longer carrying the rifle.

Looking back along the track in the direction from which Fiona would come, MacDonald could see no sign of her. He could not understand what could possibly have delayed her. By now, he felt sure, the police would have heard that he had been using the public telephone on the road to Ballymony and would have driven there.

When they arrived and found the kiosk deserted, they would surely move inland on foot, using it as a starting point in their search for him. Even if they walked slowly it would not be many minutes before they reached the plantation.

The man on the slopes opposite him had changed course, still heading up the mountain but veering north, as though he intended to round it well below the summit. Were he to continue in that direction, he would eventually come to the wild, uninhabited western side of Alsaig. Alternatively, once on the other flank of Beinn Laimsdearg, he could drop down to the shore on the north of the island where he would easily be able to find a hiding-place among the rocks. In either case, he would soon be out of MacDonald's view and to find him again would be a long and perhaps impossible operation.

Impatiently MacDonald looked back again along the track and as Fiona was still not in sight, took an impulsive decision. He would leave the plantation, crossing the valley alongside the drystone wall, cut down from there towards Carrabus and take a look at the rucksack which the hit man had hidden in the heather. There at least he might find some clue to the man's identity and proof that he had been sent to kill Matheson, which he could show to the police. If Fiona arrived in the meantime, he would still be close enough to call out to her or beckon her to join him.

Leaving the plantation, he ran across the track, ducked below the wall and crossed the valley as rapidly as he could. While he ran he heard a rifle shot. Although it must have been fired by one of the stalking party, and they would be at least half-a-mile away, its report rang out sharp and clear, echoing only seconds later. At the end of the wall he stopped to look back but Fiona had still not arrived.

He found the rucksack without difficulty for it had not been concealed as efficiently as one might have expected. Could this be a sign that the man was growing over-confident, MacDonald wondered? Opening it he quickly turned over its contents; a change of clothing, a pair of training shoes for moving swiftly on the roads where nailed boots would betray one, a knife with a broad, extremely sharp blade, a spoon, fork and mug, a small camping stove and a blanket. He could find no name tags on the clothes and even the makers' labels had been removed. The knife and the camping equipment were of a type that one might buy at almost any hardware store.

After he had repacked the rucksack and was thrusting it back into the heather, he saw the rifle lying alongside. The telescopic sight had been refixed on its mounting. Picking up the rifle he sniffed at the barrel. If it was the gun that had been used to fire at Matheson, then it had since been cleaned. MacDonald was not surprised. He had already formed the impression that the hit man was thorough and efficient in his trade.

Scanning the slopes above him through the binoculars, he considered the situation. Fiona's car had still not appeared on the track. It was possible that she had seen the police and their helpers moving up Cnoc na Moine from the direction of the kirk and, not wishing to lead them to him, had stopped the car in the shelter of the trees back where the track began. Ahead of him, well up the side of Beinn Laimsdearg, he could see the hired killer, moving at a leisurely pace but always further away. He was already far enough away to be almost out of sight and would have been difficult to spot had he not, for some reason, put on a green and orange knitted cap not unlike the one MacDonald had acquired from the little Glaswegian on Kilgona.

MacDonald decided he would follow him. It was a calculated decision based, he believed, on all the relevant factors as a good decision should be. The most important consideration was that the hired killer no longer had his rifle. Although powerfully built he was not a large man and MacDonald was confident that if it came to a physical confrontation, his knowledge of karate was sufficient to cope with any assault. In any event his plan was merely to trail the man, keeping him under observation until he saw where he went into hiding. The ferry had already begun its return trip to Kilgona—less than ten minutes earlier he had noticed it backing away from the landing ramp and turning out at sea until it was headed for the neighbouring island. That meant that the hit man could not leave Alsaig until

the afternoon at the very earliest and h•
had still not executed his contract.

Moving quickly, for he wished to clos•
the gap between them, he began climbin•
up the slope, keeping the green and orang•
cap in view. He crouched down as h•
moved, scrambling on all fours when th•
slope was too steep for him to run
watching the man and ready to fall flat t•
the ground if he showed any sign o•
looking behind him, in just the way that •
stalker would freeze motionless if a sta•
looked in his direction. When there wer•
no more than 200 yards between them, h•
slowed down. Meantime the man ha•
gradually changed direction, veering to th•
left now, as though he intended to roun•
the summit of the mountain on its southen•
slopes.

Damn fool, MacDonald thought, if h•
keeps going in that direction he'll cut righ•
between the stalkers and the deer. Serve•
him right if he gets shot.

Without warning the man stopped, half-
turned and then sat down. His movements
were leisurely and unhurried, as though he
wished simply to relax and admire the
scenery. Presently he leant back against

the slope behind him until all MacDonald could see was the green and orange cap, sticking up above the heather.

MacDonald stopped also, glad of the rest, for scrambling up a heather-covered mountain was more strenuous than one might have expected. Turning, he looked down towards the valley and the village, curious to know what the man further up the mountain might be watching. The clouds had almost all moved slowly away to the south and the island was bathed in sunlight that was remarkably bright for autumn and free of either the haze or the mist which one might have found on the mainland on a similar day.

No one was moving on the slopes below nor in the valley nor on the track that ran through the peat moss. He found himself wondering whether Fiona had understood the directions he had given her. The French had been simple enough but he had used the word "tourbière" and she might not have known that it meant a peat moss. The ferry was well out at sea by this time, heading for the distant, blue hills that were Kilgona. Two women whom MacDonald could not recognize were walking slowly along the street at Carrabus gossiping as they went, and another had just come out of Mrs. Buie's post office. Life, it seemed, was meandering along in Alsaig at its usual peaceful pace, unaware of or unconcerned by the dramas that were being acted out on its hills.

As he gazed down on the scene he saw the Renault belonging to Matheson come out of the trees at the end of the drive from Tigh Geal. Once on the road it turned left, heading for Carrabus, looking from that height like a small red ladybird crawling along. Suddenly as it approached the distillery the car disappeared, enveloped in a pear-shaped ball of orange flame. Horrified, MacDonald watched as a pillar of black smoke rose slowly from the flames. Seconds later the roar of the explosion reached him.

Stunned and appalled though he was, MacDonald realized at once what he had been watching. A car bomb was the new weapon of assassination—easy to fix, given time and opportunity, and almost infallible. The man hired to kill Matheson must have attached the bomb to the

Renault as it stood in the garage at Tigh Geal only a few minutes before MacDonald had seen him coming from the direction of the house. He understood now why the man had seemed so carefree and relaxed and why he had immediately abandoned his rifle. Now he was up on the side of Beinn Laimsdearg, watching the results of his handiwork and waiting for the afternoon ferry to take him off the island back into the anonymity of whatever concrete jungle he had come from.

In his imagination MacDonald could see the bomb explode within the car, feel the searing heat of the flames, share the agony of the victim, smell the charred flesh. He felt sick and as the nausea slowly retreated it was replaced by rage. He began to swear to relieve his anger, cursing not only the man who had placed the bomb, but his own naïve credulity in believing that he still had time to save Matheson.

His immediate assumption was that it must have been Matheson driving the Renault, for Fiona, surely, would have used the sports car, but as he thought about it a tiny doubt began to nag at him. Was it possible that the Datsun had failed to start and that this was the reason for Fiona's delay in coming out to meet him? If so she might, in desperation, have jumped into the Renault. On the other hand, he reasoned, if it had been Fiona driving surely she would not have turned left on leaving Tigh Geal but right, making for the track up to the peat moss.

Abruptly, with an effort of will, he put speculation out of his mind. There was only one thing to be done now. He must track down the killer, grab him and hold him by force till retribution in the form of the police arrived. If in doing this he were compelled to use enough force to make the man suffer, to break his arm perhaps or cripple him with a kick to the groin, so much the better.

Feeding his anger with hatred for the man and for those who had hired him, he began crawling through the heather. His quarry had stood up again and was moving, still towards the west side of the mountain and still climbing, drawing nearer to another group of deer which could be seen only a few hundred yards away. MacDonald looked up the slope. If any stalkers were after a stag or stags in at particular group, they would have worked their way round to get above the deer, for he knew stalkers preferred if possible to approach their quarry from above for the final shot. But as far as he could see the slopes were bare and there was not a soul who might help him.

After a few minutes the hired killer dropped to the ground once more. That might well be as far as he intended to go, thinking perhaps that he was now safe, out of view of people in the village and unlikely to be seen by any stalkers if he remained lying down.

Cautiously MacDonald moved forward, edging crabwise up the mountain, for he too wished to be above his quarry when he jumped him, partly because he supposed that the man was more likely to be looking down towards the village than up a bare mountain and partly because it would be easier and quicker to attack from above. Crouched down as he was, sometimes on all fours, sometimes crawling, he could not actually see the man himself, but enough of the green and orange cap was visible above the heather to give him a target for which to aim. Conscious of the rustling noise he was making as he moved through the dry heather, and wishing that the wind were strong enough to drown it, he went forward only a yard or two at a time. Once when he accidentally dislodged a few small stones which tumbled noisily into shallow trench, he flattened himself into the heather, holding his breath, certain that the man would have heard.

Finally he was no more than 20 yards from the green and orange cap. This, he felt sure was as close as he could get without alerting the owner of the cap and surrendering the advantage of surprise. Now he must spring up, rush at the man overpower him and if necessary knock him unconscious.

For a while he lay where he was, planning the assault, trying to imagine how the man might try to defend himself and what measures he might need to improvise as a counter. Then, when he knew he was mentally and physically prepared he rose quickly to his feet.

At almost exactly that moment he heard a click from behind him. Twisting round he saw the man standing a few yards away. He was holding a hand gun, squat and gly which, for that reason looked far more lethal than any revolver. The gun was pointing at MacDonald.

In his surprise he could not stop himself looking over his shoulder at where he had thought the man was lying, wondering absurdly whether there might be two of him. All he saw was the green and orange cap, placed on a clump of heather at exactly the right angle to give the impression that it was being worn by a reclining man.

"What were you going to do, Yank? Eh? Rush me?" The man spoke with the accent of Clydeside, the ugliest of Scottish accents, with its heavy, dragged-out vowels, its consonants swallowed and never articulated, its coarse Irish undertones.

"You've caused me a lot of bother," the man continued. "Maybe I should have killed you last night while you were sleeping."

MacDonald realized then that the man had known all along he was being followed. More than that, he had left his rifle where it would be found to trap MacDonald into stalking him. In that way he had drawn him further up the moun tain, out of sight of the village, where h could kill him with impunity.

"Still, maybe this is for the best. Whe they find your body they'll be thinking yo were shot by one of the stalkers and befor they know the truth I'll be away." Ther was no satisfaction, no emotion in th statement. It was as though the man wer merely thinking aloud. He raised the gu slowly and precisely until the muzzle wa pointing at MacDonald's heart.

"You're mad! A mad animal!"

If MacDonald had been afraid, he woul not have abused the man, provoking hir perhaps into squeezing the trigger mor quickly than he otherwise might hav done. He was not afraid but strangel calm, thinking only of the futility of life i his were to be extinguished abruptly or a lonely Scottish mountain before he ha achieved anything, experienced any worth while emotion, formed any worthwhil relationships.

"Words!" The man with the gur sneered. "One bullet and that's an end t all your poxy words."

The man was mad. One could see in hi

eyes not the wild hysteria of an unbalanced mind but the cold madness of a man to whom another person's life meant less than nothing, who could kill without pleasure or excitement or emotion. He had been holding the gun in his left hand and now he added his right hand to steady his grip.

"Good-bye Yank."

The report of the gun was not as loud as MacDonald had expected. Instinctively he flinched, shutting his eyes, waiting for the bullet and for the sharp, unendurable agony before his mind would drift into oblivion. No bullet came. Incredulously he thought, the man's missed.

Opening his eyes he saw his astonishment mirrored on the hit man's face. The expression became frozen in a grimace, eyes staring. Simultaneously the man's body jerked convulsively and he fell, face forwards so that MacDonald could see the small, neatly drilled hole below his left ear.

Fifty yards down the slope Fiona was standing. Slowly she lowered the rifle from her shoulder till it hung loosely, held in both hands. MacDonald ran to her. Her face was white and shocked and she began to tremble so violently that he put his hands on her shoulders to steady her. She leant against him, still trembling.

"Oh, Mike, I was so afraid!"

"Afraid?" His question was a meaningless croak.

"I was so afraid I would miss."

22

BY mid-afternoon the few remaining clouds in the sky had vanished. From just below the summit of Beinn Laimsdearg, more than 2,000 feet up, the visibility in bright sunshine and clear air was almost unbelievable. To MacDonald it seemed that they could see almost all the outer Hebrides—Barra, South Uist, Benbecula, North Uist, Harris and distantly even the fringes of Lewis— stretching from north to south in a long archipelago, a broken chain of islands which ranged in colour from green to purple to parched brown, dotted with clusters of houses, tiny harbours, deserted beaches, all set in that astonishingly deep blue sea that is to be found only off the west coast of Scotland. To the east was the mainland itself, its mountains and hills differing shades of blue, indigo shading off to rich cobalt.

Fiona and he had climbed the slopes to the summit of the mountain together, not for any reason openly expressed, but because they had both wished to. Later, in retrospect, MacDonald would see it as a symbolic wish, a need to climb up beyond not only the distasteful aftermath of violence but the tainted memories of their own separate pasts.

Down below them in Carrabus the police were tidying up the debris of crimes that had solved themselves. Fiona, MacDonald and Matheson had all been questioned and had made statements. A helicopter was flying over to Alsaig from the mainland, bringing an explosives expert who would examine the wreckage of the burnt-out Renault to determine what kind of bomb had been used and from where it had been obtained. The same helicopter would take the bodies of Paul Stokes and the unidentified hit man over to the mainland for autopsies. Later there would be more questions and more statements and in due course inquests at which they would have to give evidence, but in the meantime Fiona and MacDonald had been free to climb Beinn Laimsdearg and find a flat rock near the summit where they could sit in the sun.

"Poor Sheena!" Fiona said. "Why should she have had to die? It all seems so pointless."

"She was murdered simply so that when your father was shot, everyone would assume that it was Hamish Grant who had killed him."

"It's monstrous! Unbelievable!"

"And Hamish behaved even more stupidly than the murderers could have hoped; rushing around in a frenzy of rage, swearing he would kill your father."

"Do you think he meant to?"

"One can't say. I always thought he was no more than a braggart; mere noise and wind."

"But he did go up on to the hills with his guns that night."

"Not willingly," MacDonald replied. "The hit man gave him a bottle of whisky which must have been doped. After Hamish had drunk it he was unconscious for hours. It would have been easy enough then to take him up on to the peat moss in his Land-Rover and leave him there to be found the morning after your father had been shot."

"But he'd have been able to prove he

didn't kill Daddy. For one thing his gun hadn't been fired."

"That wouldn't have mattered. By the time he had proved he did not fire the shot, the hit man would have left Alsaig and no one would have even known he had ever been here."

"Except the person who hired him."

"Right."

For a time neither of them spoke. MacDonald guessed there was a question which Fiona had to ask but that she was reluctant to ask it because she did not wish to hear the answer. Although they had known each other for only a few days, he was beginning to recognize intuitively her moods and to understand the feelings which lay hidden behind her natural reticence.

Finally she steeled herself to ask the question. "I suppose it was Paul who engineered the whole plan?"

"I guess so. He brought the man over here and had arranged to take him back the same way this afternoon. Your Volvo was parked opposite the ferry ramp, backed on to the fields, so the guy could have easily climbed in and hidden beneath the tarpaulin."

"No doubt the truth will all come out. Paul admitted to debts of £60,000 and probably owed much more and God knows what kind of people he had been borrowing from."

"Yes. He must have been desperate."

"The £10,000 he borrowed the other day must have been the contract price. My father wouldn't tell me what Thomson was offering for the distillery but it must have been upwards of a million," Fiona said, and then added without bitterness, "Paul would think of it as a bet. The odds were too good to resist."

When he had been stalking the hit man on the mountain, MacDonald had realized that it could have been no one but Stokes who had put out the contract for Matheson to be eliminated. The plan could only have been conceived by someone who both knew the island and knew of the relationship between Hamish Grant and Sheena Campbell, but also had reason to believe that Matheson too had some kind of relationship with the girl, which had aroused Grant's jealousy and hatred. It was only Stokes who fitted this description and also had a motive for wanting Matheson dead.

"Paul must have told the gunman that you were coming to dine that night," Fiona said, as though she were aware of the direction in which MacDonald's thoughts were working. "But what would have happened if my father had not gone out to see you leave?"

"They would have had an alternative plan, I guess. The gunman would have bedded down somewhere for the night and picked your dad off when he left the house in the morning to walk down to the distillery. Hamish would still have been there as the fall guy. He was still unconscious when they found him on the peat moss much later."

Far below them they could see Carrabus. A car travelling along the one street was passed by another, the police car, going in the opposite direction. A small group of people was standing outside MacNab's store and others were leaving the hotel. Soon the helicopter would be coming in to land and the afternoon ferry would be leaving for Kilgona with the first of several unusual loads it would be carrying for the next day or two. Activity on such a scale was rare on Alsaig and years might well pass before the placid life of the island was so rudely interrupted again.

Looking down on the scene, MacDonald wondered what effect the events of the past few days would have on the people of Alsaig. They had seen three savage murders, the cruel, calculated violence of man, greed for material possession, lust for power, all so foreign to their experience that they might well have been imported from another century, a different civilization. And yet he knew, instinctively, that life on Alsaig would not change, that the degradation which had engulfed it would quickly drain away like a flood tide, leaving no mark on an island and a people who for centuries had been resilient enough to survive the worst disasters that nature could inflict.

"The car bomb was meant to kill my father, was it not?" Fiona asked him.

"It sure as hell wasn't meant for Paul," MacDonald replied. "I'll bet he didn't even know the hit man had brought bombs with him. Those characters will accept a contract, but they won't specify how the victim will be rubbed out. My guess is that Paul told him your dad would be lunching with Mrs. Colville, expecting that he would shoot him on the way there or on the way back. The lonely road to Bally-mony would be a grand place for an ambush. But the hit man decided a car bomb would be easier and more reliable. What bugs me is why Paul went out in the Renault at all."

"I think I can answer that. My father overheard my phone conversation with you. He told Paul you knew there was a hit man on the island and that I was taking a rifle to you. Paul must have gone out to warn his murderous friend."

"That figures. I guess they would have had some means of communicating in an emergency."

To their right and level with them a golden eagle was circling slowly, its attention concentrated on something it could see on the heather far below. It may have been a dead stag and the eagle was specu-lating on whether the carcass would be left on the mountain for it to devour, an unlikely outcome of a stalk except on the rare occasions when a wounded beast escaped its trackers and limped away to fall and die alone.

Fiona was looking at the bird but she did not see it. The vision of her mind was concentrated, like the eagle's on death, on the body of a girl that had lain, bruised and savaged, in wet heather not far from the sea. Glancing sideways at her, MacDonald knew from her slight frown and troubled expression that she still had one question which had to be answered.

But she did not ask it as a question. Instead she remarked seemingly casually, "I wonder why Sheena was so excited about a date with a scruffy, unkempt character from Glasgow."

"Was she excited?"

"Her grandfather says so."

"Who knows?" MacDonald's shrug of the shoulders was as studied and as casual as his voice.

Fiona smiled wistfully and placed her hand in his. "You don't have to protect me, Mike."

"Protect you?"

"I'd sooner hear the truth. It was Paul

who arranged to meet Sheena that night, who lured her to the copse near our house where the hit man was waiting, was it not?"

"One will never know."

"But you believe so, do you not?"

Reluctantly MacDonald nodded. Paul had to be the rich boy-friend who had dated Sheena. The hit man was a contract killer, a real professional. He had taken pains to slip into Alsaig unnoticed, moved around the island watching and waiting, released Hamish from the hotel cellar so he would be at large when a second attempt was made to kill Matheson and then killed him just in case he might have remembered and indentifed him from his drunken stupor. He had done all this undetected by anyone, unheard, unseen. Such a man would never have risked giving his presence on the island away and destroying his whole plan by talking to a frivolous, talkative young girl. Paul, on the other hand, could easily have persuaded Sheena to meet him and to keep their assignation a secret.

"I don't need protecting," Fiona repeated. "Not from the past at least."

MacDonald understood what she meant. Years previously an elderly schoolmaster had told him that one could only face the future if one looked back squarely at the past. What he had dismissed as an empty aphorism was now a living truth. Fiona had married Paul and shared his way of life and for that reason had condoned his amorality, his readiness to live on other people's money, his selfishness. She must accept then that she was in some measure responsible for Sheena Campbell's death and for the depravity with which it had been contrived. To turn away or shelter behind excuses would be to acknowledge that she did not possess the will to escape from the hopelessness which had held her prisoner so long.

All this MacDonald understood because he was facing a parallel situation in his own life. He recognized now his share of blame for the destruction of his marriage and the sense of inadequacy which had made him turn to drink for support. Like Fiona he would never need that crutch again, of that he was certain.

"What of my protective instincts?" he asked her lightly. Her hand lay on his arm and he took it and held it between his own two. "Is my male ego to be frustrated?"

"None of your instincts will be frustrated, my darling," she said softly, smiling. "I promise you that."

He knew then the significance of the kiss she had given him unexpectedly in the cottage the previous evening. She had kissed him with her lips apart, not inviting, not offering, but promising; promising that she would bring him not only devotion and affection and companionship, but all the pleasures that her slim, athletic body had to offer, all the sensuality that lay hidden behind her façade of Presbyterian chasteness.

"Mind you," she added, frowning thoughtfully, "I'm not sure I would take kindly to an American campus."

"Why should you? I never did."

"And I'm worried about my father."

"Why is that?"

"He's stubborn and he's lonely. His stubbornness makes him resist all changes; even those that are inevitable."

"At the distillery, you mean?"

"Yes. Many of the new techniques which he scorns give a better control over the quality of the whisky and a greater consistency of flavour. That's why the leading brands of Scotch are of a finer quality today than they ever have been. And on Alsaig the new techniques could be introduced without sacrificing jobs. A younger man would see that."

"And his loneliness?" MacDonald asked, smiling.

"I'm rather hopeful that he and Bessie Colville might get together. They're obviously fond of each other and perfectly suited. For both of them this island is their life."

Although she was speaking of the future, Fiona was not trying to plan or make suggestions or even hints, but merely thinking aloud. Like prisoners unexpectedly reprieved from a life sentence, they would both explore their new freedom cannily, savour it gradually, one day at a time. Later there would be time enough for plans.

In early evening, as they walked home down to Tigh Geal, they saw the helicopter, which had come and landed and taken off, disappearing towards Kilgona. Finally the intrusive, interfering buzz of its engine dwindled away leaving the slopes of Beinn Laimsdearg silent.

"At last!" Fiona exclaimed. "We have our island to ourselves."

"Apart from a few incomers like me," he teased.

"You? An incomer?" She looked at him quite seriously. "We don't think of you as an incomer, Mike. Not any more. To us you've just come home."

THE END